I0614082

Sea Glass and Fireflies

by

Kate Ellington

This is a work of fiction. Names, characters, places, and incidents are either the product of the author's imagination or are used fictitiously, and any resemblance to actual persons living or dead, business establishments, events, or locales, is entirely coincidental.

Sea Glass and Fireflies

COPYRIGHT © 2023 by Kate Ellington

All rights reserved. No part of this book may be used or reproduced in any manner whatsoever without written permission of the author or The Wild Rose Press, Inc. except in the case of brief quotations embodied in critical articles or reviews.
Contact Information: info@thewildrosepress.com

Cover Art by *Jennifer Greeff*

The Wild Rose Press, Inc.
PO Box 708
Adams Basin, NY 14410-0708
Visit us at www.thewildrosepress.com

Publishing History
First Edition, 2023
Trade Paperback ISBN 978-1-5092-4880-3
Digital ISBN 978-1-5092-4881-0

Published in the United States of America

The sky was softening to the faintest hint of dusk. Elsie wished it was morning so they could begin their day together all over again. They continued down the trail and turned onto a narrow path that came out behind Max's stables, then walked up the lawn to the front of the house. An unfamiliar motorcar was parked in the drive.

"Who's here, Mr. Anderson?" Elsie asked when he opened the front door.

"An associate of Mr. Lambert's."

Charles's fingers slipped out of hers as they stepped inside. Elsie removed her hat and dropped it on the table beside the soda bottles and the bag from McGoldrick's.

"Let's go see who it is," she said to Charles, tugging on his jacket sleeve.

From the dining room came the sound of laughter: two gravelly chortles and one tinkling, delicate giggle.

Charles stopped in his tracks. Elsie looked up at him. The color had drained from his face. She opened her mouth to ask what was wrong, but Max called out: "Don't hang about in the doorway, you two. Come see what the cat dragged in."

Praise for Kate Ellington

"Kate Ellington takes readers on a journey of redemption, second chances, and love through this delightful historical romance. Readers will adore her characters and celebrate how one woman not only finds love, but finds herself along the way."

~*Christina Yother, Your Beta Reader*

Acknowledgements

This book couldn't have been written without the support of my friends and family.

I have to first and especially thank my wonderful husband, Tom, who listened to me talk about my characters and plot lines for hours on end and read every version. His encouragement meant the world.

Thank you to my kids, who were supportive, helpful, fun and patient during the whole process.

My incredible sisters, Peggy, Laura, and Pammy, support me in everything I do, this being no exception.

I want to thank my parents, who posted on the wall the first poem I ever wrote, and my grandmother, who shared her love of romance novels with me.

My niece Maria provided much needed hope that my story would one day be published.

My dear friend Brian gave me helpful feedback on various tidbits in my story and always makes me laugh.

I'm grateful to Ann Beattie, the Star Island historian, for information about the hotel in 1911.

Thank you to everyone who gave me unique name ideas for boats and characters. You know who you are.

I'd like to thank my beta readers for taking time to read the story and share their thoughts: Anna, Cat, Christina, Joann, Nancy, Pammy, Patricia, and Tom.

A special thanks must go to my cat, Luna. She sat with me while I wrote and was the inspiration for the sweet kitten in the story.

I must particularly thank my fantastic, lifelong friend Nancy, who couldn't have been more supportive.

Lastly, I am grateful to Nan Swanson and the team at The Wild Rose Press for helping me bring *Sea Glass And Fireflies* to life.

Chapter One

Elsie Hayward cried through most of her wedding day. Or what should have been her wedding day. Her betrothed, Gabriel, had been lost at sea five months before. So instead of a white gown, she wore a traveling cloak, and in place of the wedding march, she was listening to her mother trying to talk her out of her impending journey.

Elsie had assumed that no more need be said about it, but her mother had other ideas. She waylaid Elsie in the drawing room while she waited for her father to take her to the train station.

"I don't understand why you are so determined to leave." Mrs. Hayward stopped pacing and sat beside Elsie on the sofa.

"Uncle Max says I can stay with him for as long as I want to. I'll be better off away from all this." Elsie waved her hand to indicate the sofa, the drawing room, and the entire town of Holderness.

"But how can you be better off in Sherwood Bay?" Her mother was not able to suppress a shudder.

"I like Sherwood Bay. I haven't been there in two years."

The solitude of Uncle Max's home on the New Hampshire seacoast was exactly what she needed right now.

"You won't forget Gabriel there," Mrs. Hayward

said. She crossed her ankles and smoothed the imagined wrinkles in her skirt.

"I am not trying to forget Gabriel, though I know you wish I would. And furthermore, I know you're pleased he did not become your son-in-law today."

"Elsie!" Mrs. Hayward's hand flew to her chest as she gave a little gasp. "It's not as if I am glad that he died." She picked up her teacup from the mahogany side table and took a fortifying sip.

Elsie slumped down into the sofa cushions. "I know you aren't. But you didn't want me to marry him, either."

Her mother took her time gathering her answer. "I won't speak ill of the dead. I will only say—" She brought a hand to her lips and stopped speaking. It looked like holding her words in was costing her dearly. Her teacup rattled in its saucer as she placed it back on the table.

"I know," Elsie recited, for she'd heard it over and over during her engagement. "He was only a seaman. We would not have had an easy life." Her hand felt bare without Gabriel's engagement ring. There was still a pale mark where he'd slipped it onto her finger less than a year ago. She'd returned it to his mother yesterday.

"He could not have supported you. It would have been more difficult than you can imagine."

"Be that as it may, Mother, I was supposed to marry him today. If his ship had not been lost, we would be leaving *together* on the train this afternoon. He would be sitting beside me right now." She wiped her eyes with a handkerchief. "I can't stay here; it's too difficult. I'm going to Uncle Max's."

Her mother folded her hands in her lap and shook her head. "You'll be bored silly there."

"I'd like to be bored silly for a change."

After Gabriel's death, Elsie's life had become a series of heartbreaking days—the funeral, condolence callers, somber meetings with her parents and Gabriel's mother, solitary walks on the beach, countless hours weeping in her bedroom. In a matter of days, Elsie had unraveled all the plans she'd made over the few months of her engagement. Since then, she had fallen into a listless haze.

When Uncle Max wrote and suggested she come stay with him, she accepted his invitation at once. Her father and sister had agreed that it was a splendid idea.

Her mother had not.

"You are much better off here"—she took Elsie's hand—"where I can look after you."

Several loud thumps came from the direction of the staircase. That would be Elsie's trunks being taken out to the carriage.

"I need this time, Mother. I think of him whenever I pass by the docks and when I look out my window to the sea." Her eyes brimmed with tears. "He's around every corner here."

"I thought you were feeling better. You seem happier of late."

"The last month or so I've had days where I felt almost content. But the wedding day has brought it all back. The pain is just as fresh now as when I first heard he was gone."

"The problem is that you have not let go of your grief, Elsie. You hold on to it too tightly. It's time to think of your future. But I see that you are set on going to Max's." She frowned and said under her breath, "I only wish it wasn't quite so far."

This was the closest she would get to her mother's blessing, so she did not point out that staying home would drive her to distraction. Elsie stood and crossed the room to the window that overlooked the back garden, where purple anemones were just beginning to bloom.

"Ready to leave, Elsie?" her father asked as he came into the room, buttoning up his overcoat.

"Yes," Elsie said at the same time her mother said, "No."

"We're having a chat," Mrs. Hayward said. "You don't need to leave this moment, do you?"

"If we want to make that train, we do," her husband replied.

"I think we've said all we need to, Mother. Thank you for understanding."

"I don't know that I understand, but I know that you are going regardless of what I say." Mrs. Hayward stood and held out her arms to Elsie, who allowed herself to be enfolded in her mother's rose-scented embrace. When Mrs. Hayward pulled away, she straightened Elsie's black velvet collar. "Write to me, won't you?"

"I will."

"And do try to have a bit of decorum," her mother said, inspecting Elsie from head to foot with the kind of glance she used to give her every day before school.

"Decorum!"

"Max does let you run a bit wild, dear." She settled herself on the sofa and reached for her teacup.

"Oh, Mother, it's not as if I'll be meeting the president's wife in Sherwood Bay."

"You can't have that attitude, not if you want to find another beau."

Elsie just stared at her, unable to form a response.

Mr. Hayward, standing in the doorway, held up his pocket watch. "We really must go."

Elsie kissed her mother on the cheek and picked up her beaded bag off the sofa.

She followed her father outside, stepped into the carriage, and tossed her bag onto the seat next to her. Elsie crossed her ankles and glanced out the window facing the harbor.

When her father got in, she turned to him. "You'd think Mother would have a bit more faith in her brother to keep me respectable. She acts as if I am three years old."

Mr. Hayward signaled to the coachman, and they were off. Gravel crunched under the carriage wheels as they crept away from the house, gathering speed as the horses trotted through the streets.

"She knows Max is a bit of a free spirit." He smiled and looked at her with greenish-blue eyes that mirrored her own. "And so are you."

"Has it occurred to her that that's why we get along so well?"

"I imagine it has."

"She needn't bother about my decorum. I'm not going to Sherwood Bay to pay social calls." All she wanted there was peace and quiet, and above all to escape the oppressive atmosphere at home. Since Gabriel's death, Mrs. Hayward had alternated between consoling Elsie with kind words and disparaging Gabriel whenever a chance presented itself.

"I wish you'd allow me to accompany you," Mr. Hayward said as they trundled along. For the last three days, he'd been pressing to be her chaperone.

"I'll be fine on the train. You'll escort me into my

coach, and Uncle Max will meet me at the station in Portsmouth."

"Not a little girl anymore, I suppose."

"No. I was to be married today." She wiped her eyes and pushed aside thoughts of what she would have been doing right now if Gabriel hadn't died.

"You'll have your day." He gave her knee a little pat.

"I hope so. I'm getting rather old."

"Fiddlesticks. You'll find the right man when you least expect it."

"I thought I already had."

Her father didn't reply but took her hand. She leaned her head on his shoulder until the carriage pulled into the station.

Once her trunks had been stowed, Mr. Hayward escorted her to her private coach. Uncle Max had arranged it, for which she was grateful. It wouldn't do to cry in front of her fellow travelers.

"Goodbye, Elsie. And please, do write."

"I will, once I get settled."

She kissed him on the cheek and climbed into the coach. He closed the door after her and touched the glass with his gloved hand.

Then he was gone.

Now she really was alone, for the first time in she knew not how long. She kicked her shoes off and tucked her feet up on the seat. Tears obscured her view out the window. Her eyes appeared gray in the dull glass pane, and her light brown hair took on a muddy hue. A cluster of freckles, just on the crest of her right cheekbone, was not even visible in this light.

Memories chased each other through her mind as a

whistle sounded and the train pulled out of the station. Growing up in a coastal town not far from Boston, Elsie had found the beach a constant source of amusement and adventure. Her usual companion was her best friend, Charles. While she combed the sand for treasure, he dug deeper in search of shipwrecks. Sea glass turned up almost every day, but the shipwreck didn't appear until they were twelve years old, the same day she met Gabriel.

The masts were exposed after three days of driving rain and relentless wind. The next morning, the parks were empty; every child in town was on the beach exploring the ancient wreck at low tide. Elsie and Charles were making up stories about where the ship had come from when Gabriel sauntered over and introduced himself. That was ten years ago, and he'd been their friend ever since.

Gabriel was unlike any of the boys Elsie had grown up with in Holderness. Though only two years older than she and Charles, he carried himself like a man. And yet his face had a cherubic quality, especially when he smiled and showed his dimples. He had black, wavy hair, and eyes that called to mind the green perfume bottles on her mother's vanity. Gabriel's life ambition was to be a captain, like his father. He hadn't attended school with Elsie and Charles, spending most of his time on the docks or at sea. He worked as a deckhand on his father's ship, the *Scalloper*. When he joined Elsie and Charles in town, he amused them with tales about the places he'd lived up and down the eastern seaboard. Charles had often said his stories sounded too fantastic to be true.

When they were eighteen, Charles moved to San Francisco. Life for Elsie would have been lonely indeed if it hadn't been for Gabriel.

Elsie arrived in Portsmouth shortly after nightfall. She hurried off the train, eager to leave the cramped space behind. The train's shrill whistle signaled its next departure as she walked aimlessly around the platform, looking for any sign of her uncle. She sighed. He'd forgotten she was arriving tonight.

"Miss Elsie!" a voice called.

She turned to find her uncle's coachman jogging toward her.

"Tom," she said, the slight tension in her shoulders disappearing.

"Oh, you've grown since I saw you last, miss."

Tom still had the same wide grin and long black frock coat flapping around his knees.

"How long has it been? Two years?" Elsie asked.

"Yes, nineteen-nine was the last time you were here. And now you look quite the lady."

She smiled for the first time in hours. Tom probably still saw her as an eight-year-old girl scampering around the stables.

"I'll see about your trunks." He hurried toward a mountain of luggage stacked beside the train tracks.

Elsie took a deep breath of fresh, salty air as she went in search of the carriage. The clear spring evening held just a hint of coolness. Stars twinkled overhead, and crickets chirped in some hidden pocket nearby. As a child, every summer visit to New Hampshire had started here, at the Portsmouth station.

With its back windows and rust-colored trim, Uncle Max's brougham stood out among the buggies and motorcars. Elsie opened the door and peeked inside, hoping to find him lounging on the velvet bench, but it was empty.

After Tom returned and stowed her trunk, she joined him on the driver's seat—she'd had enough of enclosed carriages for one day.

Soon they were on their way to Sherwood Bay, a bustling port town a few miles outside Portsmouth. The road wound through a lush forest, white birch trees bright among the maples, firs, ashes, and elms. At the crest of a hill, the dense canopy gave way to open sky. Far below, the beach glistened in the moonlight. Elsie removed her hat and held it in her lap, relishing the evening breeze in her hair.

They trotted along the coast road to Birch Street, and soon Uncle Max's home came into view. Perched on a slightly raised bluff, the twilight-blue house with white trim and green porch railings was far enough away from stormy waves but close enough to afford views of the ocean from almost every window. Elsie had thoroughly explored its many snug nooks as a child. A narrow staircase at the end of the third-floor hallway led outside to a fenced balcony, where, looking up, one could see the round tower room. Many an evening had been spent on the balcony, waiting for stars to appear.

Tom dropped Elsie off at the front porch, and she mounted the steps. Before she had time to knock, the dark green front door swung open.

"Elsie!" said the housekeeper. "I trust you had a pleasant journey. Your room's all ready—it hasn't changed a bit since you were a little girl, but you certainly have. I think you've grown even taller since the last time I saw you." She opened the door wider. "Come in, dear, come in."

"Hello, Mrs. Holt," Elsie said, smiling.

Mrs. Holt had worked there for as long as Elsie could remember. She kept the house running smoothly and did so alongside Mr. Anderson, who had several responsibilities around the estate. Perhaps *estate* was too grand a word for it, but Uncle Max employed a number of people to maintain his sprawling, secluded property.

Elsie stepped inside, welcoming the heat and light. The house smelled just as she remembered, like summer grass and winter sunshine, fresh-tilled earth, and cozy fires.

Mrs. Holt took Elsie's cloak and hung it inside the closet beside the front door before turning back to Elsie, her eyes moist.

"I was so sorry to hear about your—the ship, the wedding…that is…your Gabriel."

"Thank you, Mrs. Holt." Elsie's eyes pricked with tears.

"You let me know if there's anything I can do for you. Anything at all." She softly patted Elsie's arm.

"I will." Mrs. Holt kept looking at her, but Elsie wasn't sure what else to say on the matter. "Is my uncle awake?" She peeked into the library, where he was often found in the evenings, reading or dozing in a chair beside the hearth.

"Yes, but where he is I couldn't say." Mrs. Holt put her hands on her hips. "He went out with that assistant of his hours ago, and they've yet to return. I thought, with you arriving, he'd have stayed at home."

"I'll see him in the morning. I'm hardly fit for one of his lectures tonight." Elsie barely stifled a yawn as she crossed the entryway to the oak staircase.

Mrs. Holt followed along and touched Elsie's shoulder lightly before she reached the stairs.

"Are you hungry? Would you like supper?"

"I would love some of your spice cake, if you have any on hand."

Mrs. Holt beamed. "I did find time to bake one this morning, knowing your fondness for it."

Though the cook could make any dish under the sun, Mrs. Holt insisted on being the only one in the house to prepare her special spice cake recipe.

"I'll have that, then, and some milk, please," Elsie said, her hand on the banister.

"A drop of brandy in it to ward off the chill?" Mrs. Holt gave her a tiny wink.

"That would be welcome."

"I'll have Daisy bring it up to your room." She dashed off to the kitchen.

Elsie made her way up the stairs, completely forgetting to skip the creaky eighth step. Her bedroom overlooked the back gardens and commanded a spectacular view of the beach during the day. Not only were the curtains blue—a stunning royal hue—but the quilt was a patchwork of it, from cobalt to robin's egg. Even the porcelain ewer and basin at the washstand were decorated with tiny blue roses. A mahogany vanity and chair were set up beside a matching wardrobe, and a pile of old favorite books still sat on the nightstand. She pulled the pins out of her hair, placed her hat on the vanity, and shook her hair loose with the aid of her fingers.

She crossed the room to the deep window seat and opened the windows, welcoming the cool breeze. The Mason jar full of sea glass she'd been collecting since childhood sat in its customary place on the sill. Sinking into the velvet cushions, Elsie closed her eyes and listened to the distant waves.

After a few minutes there was a knock on the door.

"Come in," she called, and Daisy came in with a tray.

"Thank you, Daisy."

Daisy put the tray on the nightstand, then left the room. Elsie took a few bites of the spice cake and drank half of the brandy-laden milk. It was more than just a touch, she noticed with a grin. She lay down on her bed fully clothed and closed her eyes. Before she had time to remove her shoes, the sea lulled her into peaceful sleep.

Chapter Two

Elsie woke up shivering in the morning. A cold mist had drifted in through the open windows. She wrapped herself in a blanket from the bed and went to look outside. The ocean was a steely gray, the horizon hidden by a heavy marine layer. Seagull cries pierced the air, and in the distance a foghorn blew. She closed the windows and settled herself in the soft seat.

This should have been the first day of her married life. She and Gabriel had planned to move into his mother's house right after the wedding. She would have awoken beside him but instead she was alone, waiting for this drab morning to brighten. Elsie rested her head against the window frame and recalled the day she had agreed to marry him.

"Did you enjoy the show?" Gabriel had asked, walking her home from the nickelodeon.

"Yes, very much. Did you?"

"It was hard to focus on." His eyes took on that soft look they sometimes did.

"And why is that? Something on your mind?"

"You." He leaned in to kiss her cheek.

Her heart pattered in her chest. "And what were you thinking?"

"That I've the prettiest girl in town. And the smartest. Though I'm glad you're home from college for good now." He slipped an arm through hers.

"I'm glad I'm home, too. And I'm with the sweetest man. Thank you for the bracelet." She held up her wrist, two silver heart charms swinging from a knotted chain.

"It's like us, isn't it? Two hearts on the same line."

"This talk of lines makes it sound as though we're fishing," she said.

"That fits when you're talking about me."

Now first mate on a schooner, he was closer to achieving his dream of captain. Some years earlier, his father and brothers had been lost at sea; now it was up to Gabriel to support his mother.

They walked in silence for a time until they reached the park near her house. He led her into a copse of trees.

"What are we doing here?" Elsie asked. "You know my parents will be expecting me." She glanced at the sky, now tinged with purple. She'd been given strict instructions not to stay out with Gabriel after nightfall, though she had no qualms about disobeying that order.

He wrapped his arms around her and pulled her close.

"Gabriel…" she said, "Not here. Everyone can see us."

"It's only you and me here."

She tried to step back, but he held her fast.

"Anyone could come upon us at any moment." She scanned the empty park.

"You're right. But I find it hard to keep my hands to myself when you're so near." He bent down and kissed her cheek.

"I feel the same way."

"As it happens," he said, "There's something special I'd like to say to you tonight."

He led her over to the wooden bench they'd shared

14

so many times before. He sat down, legs stretched out in front of him, and she settled in beside him, admiring his profile in the failing light.

"I think you know what I want to say," he said.

"I might…but I want you to say it first."

"About us? Getting married?" He shifted in his seat to face her.

She had, in fact, suspected this all day. Gabriel was always attentive, but he'd been especially affectionate today. He'd more than once alluded to the future they might share. And, truth be told, this was not the first time he'd asked. But it was the first time she'd been sure of her answer.

"What do you say?" he prompted, taking her hands in his.

She was surprised to hear a slight tremor in his voice and this timidity only endeared him to her.

The warm, secure feel of her hands in his spread through her. "I say…yes."

Gabriel let out a whoop of triumph. "Our life will be one long adventure."

"Your life already is an adventure."

"It will be all the better when you are my wife. Think of it—this time next year we'll be married."

"Sooner than that, I hope! A year is far too long."

"Oh, it will fly by. I'll make you happy, I promise." The look in his eyes left no doubt of his sincerity.

They sat in the park far past sunset, dreaming of their future.

The wedding took weeks of preparation. Elsie, her sister Margaret, and Mrs. Hayward took the quest for a perfect gown to heart and found one within a matter of days. They then busied themselves at the bakery to taste cakes, descended upon the local florist to find the perfect blooms for the bridal bouquet, and at last went to Boston to shop for Elsie's trousseau. After that, Elsie sat with Margaret on many an afternoon to pepper her with questions about married life.

But it had all been for naught.

The *Kraken* had never come home. Neither had its first mate.

Elsie wiped the tears from her eyes and glanced at the clock. The servants would be up, if not her uncle. She gave the bell pull a tug. Soon there was a soft knock on the door, and Becky, the upper housemaid, stepped in.

"Good morning," Elsie said. "I'd like some hot water, please.

"Right away, miss." She returned quickly, placed a full pitcher on the washstand, and left the room.

After a light wash, Elsie changed into a peach-and-white-striped day dress and pulled her thick, wavy hair back from her face in a loose chignon. She added some extra pins, as her hair insisted on escaping from any bun she tried to ensnare it in.

She went downstairs and into the library, trailing her fingers on the bindings as she walked along the three floor-to-ceiling bookcases. Brown damask chairs and a moss-colored sofa faced French doors leading to the patio. Over the years, she'd spent countless hours lying on that sofa, lost in a story. Uncle Max's favorite burgundy leather armchairs flanked the tall brick fireplace. Elsie smiled softly when she saw the pillows she and Margaret had embroidered in their youth. Uncle Max was showing his sentimental side by keeping them, as they in no way resembled the farmyard scenes they were meant to. Elsie was quite certain that what looked like a cat on the one she'd made was supposed to be a horse.

She stepped through the French doors to the outside, where a fresh ocean breeze greeted her. Lilac bushes crowded around the flagstone patio overlooking the beach. She could hardly wait for May, when their vibrant purple blossoms would be coming to life. Around the corner to her left was the garden.

Blueberry bushes and wild shrubs covered the hill down to the beach. If there hadn't been such a tangle of plants, she could have walked to the beach from there. As it was, she needed to go through the house to reach the garden path that led to the shore. She was tempted to do so now, but the savory aroma of a hot breakfast compelled her to cross the hall to the dining room.

The table was set, and several dishes waited in warming pans on the ornate maple sideboard. After serving herself poached eggs on toast and sliced melon, she sat at the table facing the curved bow windows overlooking the beach and front lawn.

She hadn't been there long when Uncle Max came in, yawning and raking his fingers through his hair. From the disheveled look of his clothes, he'd been up all night again. It was a comfort to see he was the same as ever, from his easy grin to the pencils crammed into the front pocket of his jacket. She'd never thought to ask why he carried so many around with him all the time.

"Elsie, so you've arrived at last," he said and held his arms out wide.

"Good morning, Uncle Max."

She stood and was caught up in a tight embrace that smelled of sweet pipe tobacco. He held her at arm's length and looked at her face for a long moment.

He answered her unspoken question. "It's still there," he said, tilting his head.

"What's still there?"

"That shadow. Never mind, it will pass." He patted her shoulder, then sat at the table and poured himself a cup of coffee.

"Shadow?" she asked, the grin sliding off her face as she took her seat.

"The shadow of grief," he said, as though it was the most obvious thing in the world.

"It has only been a few months since Gabriel—since I heard he wasn't coming home."

"You can't keep looking to the past. You need to move forward." He picked up a scone and liberally buttered it.

Elsie let out an exasperated groan. Why must everyone—her sister, her mother, now Uncle Max—tell her she had to let Gabriel go? Did they expect her to cast aside her grief as if it were a coat she had buttoned up that morning?

"But I'm not—"

"I know it will take time," he interrupted. "That's why I invited you here. There's plenty for you to distract yourself, or you can sit on the beach all day if you wish. Before you know it, this time in your life will all be just a sad memory."

"I don't want Gabriel to be only a memory." She leaned her elbow on the table and rested her chin in her hand.

"I know," he said kindly. "We'll do all we can for you here. The run of the beach and all the spice cake you can put away."

Their eyes met, both well aware that good food and

sunshine wouldn't cure what ailed her. But she loved him all the more for his efforts.

"Thank you, Uncle Max."

He cleared his throat gruffly and reached across the table for the strawberry-rhubarb jam. "Now, what do you plan to do while you're here? I can give you a list as long as your arm if you want to keep busy. But if you don't, this is your home and you are under no obligations. You may come and go as you please as far as I'm concerned."

He slathered his scone with jam and took a bite, his eyes on Elsie all the while.

"Once I'm settled, I thought I might help you with your work." She sliced her eggs and toast into triangles and scooped a bit up with her fork.

Uncle Max nodded. "Last night I accepted a delivery of silks. You could look it over today, tell me what you think. And if any strike your fancy, put them aside. I'll get Joan up to the house to make you some dresses," he said, referring to the local seamstress. He finished his scone in three bites and wiped his fingers on the tablecloth.

"Perhaps next week. I've only just arrived. At the moment what I'd dearly like to do is…nothing." She exhaled slowly and allowed her shoulders to relax just a touch.

"Oh, yes, on your own time. As I said, you are under no obligation. I'll see you at supper then? I'm glad you're here." He took a gulp of coffee and stood.

"I am too. Coming here is exactly what I need, as I'm sure you know."

He nodded once and left the room, shouting for Mrs. Holt as he went. He reminded her to take a breakfast tray to the guest upstairs. Elsie would be sure to get outside before whoever it was came down. It was much too early in the day to form a new acquaintance.

The cuckoo clock on the wall behind her struck seven. She'd always loved that clock. As a child she would sit under the table and count down the minutes until the little blue bird popped out again. She leaned back in her chair and finished her breakfast. It was a relief to have some time to herself.

After eating, Elsie strolled along the wraparound porch to the back of the house, where a staircase led to the garden. It was like stumbling into an enchanted, secret copse overrun with flowers. The leafy canopy kept the garden cool while letting small patches of morning sunshine in, and the dewy grass was as soft as any carpet. Daffodils, tulips, and grape hyacinths abounded, along with a myriad of colorful blossoms she couldn't name. Too many scents mingled together to choose the sweetest one. Combined with the salty ocean breeze, it was nothing short of magical.

A wooden bench encircled the trunk of the biggest apple tree, perfect for idle afternoons. The initials she and Margaret had carved into the bench had barely faded since her last visit. As children, the sisters had guessed they would last for one hundred years. Thus far, they'd lasted about fifteen. She meandered through the early blooming flowers, hoping to find some tiny wild strawberries. She'd have to keep waiting for those, as well as the lilacs.

Elsie pushed through the back gate to the well-worn path to the beach—empty as far as the eye could see, as usual. Uncle Max's house was far enough from town that other people wandered down only once in a blue moon.

When she reached the sand, she took her shoes off

and left them on a pile of smooth gray stones, then removed her stockings and tucked them into the toes of her shoes. So much for decorum. Her bare feet sank into the cold sand as she ran down to the shore. At water's edge she stood with hands on hips, welcoming the salty breeze on her face. The haze had burned off, revealing the gentle swell of the ocean. Waves washed over her feet, wetting the hem of her dress.

A glint of blue in the sand caught her eye, and after a moment of digging, she found a beautiful piece of cobalt sea glass, its edges worn smooth. It would join the others in the Mason jar on her windowsill.

She strolled along the beach, now and then spying another piece of glass and slipping it into her pocket. After wandering for some time, she sat on a boulder beside the tidal pools and watched the scurrying crabs and darting fish. Wind made ripples across the water, mimicking the waves just out of reach. The pools had always fascinated her and she'd often wondered if the creatures felt safe or trapped when the tide cut them off from the rest of the ocean. She glanced at the watch pinned to her blouse and was surprised to see that it was almost lunchtime.

As she turned toward home, a tiny gasp escaped her lips. The last man she would have dreamed of seeing here was walking in her direction, his eyes on the sand. It was too extraordinary. Could that really be him? Just then he looked up. Even from here she could see his smile. Elsie took a deep breath and tried to still her racing heart while she waited for him to reach her.

Chapter Three

He lifted a hand to wave, then broke into a jog. Elsie waved back, but Charles was still too far away to speak to.

Her thoughts rushed back to the last time they were alone on a beach together, over three years ago, long before she and Gabriel were betrothed.

The night before Charles left for California, he made it clear—or so she thought at the time—that he wanted to be much more than her best friend. She was so sure he was going to kiss her, she went so far as to shut her eyes and lean in close. But then Gabriel and his dog came running down the beach, breaking up their little interlude. He hadn't seen it, or at least he never mentioned it. At any rate, that was months before Gabriel showed interest in her as anything more than a friend. Charles said goodbye to her, with a promise to write every week. The next day he left for San Francisco.

For the first year or so, he kept to his promise of writing once a week. But the letter she hoped for never came—the one explaining what was in his heart that night, perhaps even a declaration. After a while his letters arrived less and less frequently, finally ceasing altogether.

For a long time, she regretted that interruption on the beach. Not only had he made her aware of his feelings, he made her aware of her own, as if something as obvious as the sun had just been pointed out to her. What could be more natural than for her and Charles to be together? But he never mentioned that night, even after she alluded to it in one of her own letters. Perhaps it had been a mere moment of whimsy for him. Over the years, Elsie pushed it to the back of her mind. Once Gabriel began courting her in earnest, she'd succeeded in erasing it entirely. Until this moment, when she was alone with Charles on a beach once more.

"Elsie," he said when he reached her and swept her up in a tight embrace. He stepped back and gave her that special smile that had always been just for her.

She couldn't help being glad to see him. When they parted three years ago, he was still a boy.

Now he was a man.

The teenaged softness of his face had given way to a square jaw and his mother's high cheekbones. Elsie had been about his height, yet now she came to just above his shoulder. He was wearing a linen sack suit but had forgone a hat, as she had. His hair, quite fair when they were children, now hovered between blond and brown.

"Charles, what are you doing here?"

"Not sorry to see me, I hope," he said, nudging her arm with his.

"Of course not." In truth she was sorry to see anyone at the moment. Her seclusion was certainly at an end with Charles in town. "But what brings you to Sherwood Bay?"

"Didn't your uncle tell you?" He was looking at her as though memorizing her face. Or perhaps he was noticing the changes in her, as she had in him.

"Tell me what?" She brushed an errant lock of hair out of her eyes.

"I'm working with him now. I arrived three days ago."

"No, he didn't tell me. But you know Uncle Max. One thing drives another out of his head."

But forgetting something *quite* so important as her closest childhood friend being upstairs while she ate breakfast was unprecedented even for her uncle.

"Yes, well, he's hired me as a sort of apprentice."

"So you're the guest I hurried out of the house to avoid," she said with a laugh.

They started walking up the beach, just out of reach of the waves breaking on the shore.

"If I'd known you were arriving today, I would have come downstairs much earlier," he said, turning to look at her. She'd forgotten how blue his eyes were. They'd always reminded her of a summer sky just before dawn.

"I arrived last night. Don't tell me he didn't tell you I was coming!"

"Something along the lines of 'Elsie will be here some time or other,' " Charles said in a fair imitation of Uncle Max's voice. "He could have meant this week or next June."

"I must say, I'm shocked to see you. I had tea with your mother last week, and she didn't mention that you'd left San Francisco." Their mothers were best friends since their own childhoods, and Mrs. Rockingham was like an aunt to Elsie.

"She didn't know it herself until we arrived in Boston. It was to be a surprise. My parents met us there for a visit."

"We?"

"Oh, James tagged along with me on the train. It's been so long since either of us was home."

"Jim's back too? How marvelous! Where is he?"

Though she'd been closest to Charles, she'd spent a fair amount of time with James when they were children. Their elder sister, Harriet, rarely tolerated their antics.

"He traveled to Providence to see some old school chums." Charles pointed south, though many miles lay between themselves and Rhode Island.

"I hope I'll have the chance to see him before he goes back to California." Elsie put her hands into her pockets, forgetting they were full of sand and sea glass.

"I'm not sure when he plans to return, but he's going to Holderness next week." Charles stooped to pick up a rock and tossed it into the waves.

"Why didn't you go to Holderness yourself?"

Charles shrugged, that slight tilt of his right shoulder she'd seen him do more times than she could count. She wondered how long it would be until he unconsciously swept his bangs out of his eyes.

"I wanted to get settled in here." The would-be casual tone of his voice made it obvious that he wasn't being entirely truthful. He put his hands in his own pockets.

"I see."

He gave her a sidelong glance and let out a slow breath. "Honestly, I knew it was close to the wedding date. I didn't want to bother you. Oh, Elsie, it's terrible about Gabriel."

"It's hard to believe, even now, that he's really gone." Her spirits began to sink.

"Not the three of us anymore." Charles's attention shifted to the space between them, as if acknowledging where Gabriel would have stood.

"No, not anymore." Elsie pressed her lips together

and looked toward the horizon.

"I'm sorry I didn't make it to the funeral. I couldn't get home in time."

"I know you would have been there if you could." She didn't add that she had expected him home months ago, as soon as he'd heard of Gabriel's death, and had felt his absence more keenly than at any other time since he'd gone away. "I appreciated your condolence letter. I apologize for not replying. For a long time after he died, I was so distraught it was difficult to rouse myself to anything, even correspondence."

He placed a warm hand on her shoulder. "Think nothing of it, Elsie. I wouldn't have expected a reply at such a time."

"Thank you for understanding. I knew you would."

"And you were to be married," he said softly, looking at her with eyes so tender she wanted to weep. His expression held something beyond pity. He truly understood her pain and loss better than anyone else. Gabriel was his friend too.

"Yesterday." Her voice caught in her throat. She simply couldn't talk about Gabriel anymore. She changed direction, heading home. "So, Charles, whatever gave you the idea that you'd be bothering me if you visited?"

"It's been so long since we've seen each other. And my mother said you've been having a difficult time."

"I see our mothers have been gossiping again." She should have been annoyed, but expecting them not to gossip about their children was like expecting a duck not to quack.

"Have you? Been having a difficult time?" His voice took on the tone of one visiting a sick friend. Perhaps she was. Sick at heart.

"I'm doing fine." She took her hands out of her pockets and rubbed them together to brush off the sand.

Charles turned to her with one brow slightly raised. Elsie didn't give him a chance to question her further. "How did you end up working with Uncle Max?"

"Your mother told him about a fossil I found in California, and he wrote to me about it. We've been in correspondence ever since."

"Ah, yes, his collection."

"I've sent him some things to add to it. When I told him I'd be coming home, he offered me a job."

"What of your uncle's store in San Francisco?"

The sun was fully out now. Thin white clouds stretched across the horizon.

"Uncle Richard's doing a brisk business. James and I helped him set up shop and worked there for a few months."

"Was he disappointed you didn't stay on longer?"

"No, he always knew it would be temporary. He was helpful when I decided to finish college in California instead of coming home. There's something to be said for living in a place without our snowy winters. I did miss Holderness, though," he said, briefly meeting her eyes.

"I didn't expect you to stay there for so long. I assumed you'd come home after a year, at the most."

He looked away, his forehead creased. After a moment he answered. "My studies kept me very busy, and crossing the country isn't the easiest journey."

"No, I suppose not."

"After graduation, I traveled around the state. The landscapes are breathtaking, and there are places where you can pluck fossils off the ground like sea glass."

"So you moved on to adventuring. Like Gabriel."

"Yes, like Gabriel. No sea life for me, though," he said, and looked out at the ocean.

"It was a hard life, but he loved it. He was away often, even before that last voyage." She stared blankly at the waves. A lump was forming in her throat. "Mrs. Holt will be wondering where I am."

On the way back to the house, Charles described some of the fantastic places he'd explored out west. Elsie could almost see the vast canyons and feel the desert heat as he spoke. When they reached the path up to the garden, Elsie stopped to put her shoes on and surreptitiously slipped her stockings into her pocket.

They walked through the garden and stepped onto the porch.

"Wait a moment, Elsie," he said, just before they reached the door.

He held out a closed hand.

"What's this?" Elsie asked.

"Open your hand." He dropped a few pieces of sea glass into her palm. "For your Mason jar."

She grinned and followed him into the house.

A week later, Elsie was curled up on her window seat, looking outside yet not seeing the view. A forgotten book lay open in her lap. As usual, her mind had drifted to Gabriel. The morning he left for that fateful voyage, she had gone to the dock to say goodbye. He assured her he would return soon, and she stayed until she couldn't see the *Kraken* anymore.

Their life together had not even started when he was taken from her. She missed the ways Gabriel had made her feel cherished. She'd teased him about the care he took with her, the way he acted as if she were breakable. He refused to take her out on his boat or go ambling over the rocks with her the way Charles did. The older she got, the more he said she should be treated like a lady.

They'd been friends for so long she barely noticed when it slipped into something else. The first time that new spark kindled, they were talking on a park bench, and he tentatively reached for her hand, as though it might not be allowed. She had allowed it. They both looked down at their hands as they entwined their fingers, then locked eyes. That had been the beginning.

She was about to get up when she spotted Charles on the beach. He stopped and tried to skip rocks on the waves, but the surf was too choppy and they sank with a splash. He put his hands in his pockets and continued on. She guessed he was heading into town again. He was kept so busy at Uncle Max's office they hadn't spoken much since that first day. For the most part, being with Charles was the same as always. Even so, a certain intimacy was lacking. She supposed she couldn't expect them to have that same easy camaraderie they'd had before he left for California—something was lost when the only communication for three years was irregular mail. At first Charles's letters had been animated; she'd almost been able to hear his voice coming off the page. But after a while, they grew stilted.

He'd confided in Gabriel, not her, about the heartbreak he'd suffered in California. For the first time, Charles had kept a secret from her. Gabriel told her that Charles had met a woman in San Francisco and proposed to her. This was before she and Gabriel had become betrothed, and he had joked that if Elsie said yes, they could have a double wedding. Later, after Elsie accepted, he told her Charles's relationship had turned sour. The engagement was broken, and Charles was depressed. Around this time there was a marked difference in his letters.

Elsie stood, leaving her book on the window seat. It was early; she had the whole day ahead. After initially telling her he had so much for her to do, Uncle Max had decided she needed to, as he said, "convalesce." The first week or so she'd welcomed the cosseting under his firm direction. But by now she was tired of being treated as though she should be wrapped in cotton wool and kept away from loud conversations and strong breezes.

Whenever she tried to knit, or read, or do anything quiet, Gabriel would come to mind and destroy any serenity she had managed to gain. She had so many happy memories with him. But then there were the others, the black linings of silver clouds. She paced around the room, lest the feelings she had been ignoring burst out of her.

She hastened down to her uncle's study and entered without knocking. He was at his rolltop desk in the back of the room. She stood in front of him, waiting in vain for him to look up. After a few minutes, she spoke. "Uncle Max?"

"Mm?" He looked up from the papers he'd been reading. His eyes had that distant look she knew so well, as if he saw numbers and itemized lists rolling across her face.

"Uncle Max?" She moved behind the desk and put a hand on his shoulder.

"Yes, yes, what is it?" he said, blinking up at her.

"Come with me." She sat on the floral settee under the window and patted the seat next to her. He settled into it and looked at Elsie like he wanted to put a hand to her forehead, the way her mother did when she suspected she might be ill.

"Uncle," she said, taking his hand, "I can take no more of this convalescing you've prescribed for me."

"That didn't take nearly as long as I thought it would," he said and chortled.

"What do you mean?" She drew her head back and narrowed her eyes.

"I knew you'd grow tired of it eventually," he said, his eyes sparkling.

"You were trying to see how long it would take until I was driven mad with boredom?"

"No, of course not. I only wanted you to have the chance to come out of your sullens on your own."

"Sullens? Have I been acting morose?"

"You're good at hiding it, but don't forget I've known you since the day you were born. I commend your efforts, but it's not good to get so lost in your mourning."

"Look, Uncle Max, if you think I will suddenly stop grieving Gabriel because I spend some time knitting…" She started to rise.

He gently grasped her wrist to stop her.

"I'm not saying you should stop grieving. Heaven knows you'll most likely grieve him for the rest of your life. Just don't forget yourself."

"Of course I won't." She had to restrain herself from rolling her eyes.

"You haven't been yourself, Elsie. You're usually so curious, so vivacious. You haven't paid any calls since you arrived, and haven't even mentioned leaving the house, except for the beach."

"You've practically had me under lock and key,"

Elsie said, a lilt returning to her voice.

"Consider yourself released from convalescing! Oh, and one more thing. Now that you've reached the grand age of twenty-one, I think you can dispense with calling me Uncle."

"What on earth for?"

"Truth be told, it makes me sound rather old." He rubbed a hand across his stubbly chin.

"Oh, Uncle Max." She lightly squeezed his arm.

He looked at her, eyebrows raised.

"All right then. Max!"

He pulled out his pipe, then patted all his pockets until he found a box of matches. "What do you plan to do now that you've been released?"

"I thought I might go to the library. Isn't there a poetry reading on Thursdays?"

"I haven't the foggiest. Mrs. Holt would know, I'd wager." He struck a match and touched it to his pipe, then disappeared behind a cloud of smoke.

"I'll go over and see for myself." Elsie waved her hand to fan the smoke out of her face. "If there's no reading today, I'll check out some new books."

"You might do that. Or you might go over to the office and see Charles. He's working on a rather special project for me."

"I don't want to see Charles," she said, avoiding his eyes.

"But why not? He's your best friend."

"He *was* my best friend. I'm not sure what he is now. He reminds me too much of Gabriel. Or rather, the absence of Gabriel."

"You said yourself you don't want to forget him."

"I don't. But as *you* said, being lost in mourning is

wearisome." She reached behind them and opened the window. The wisps of smoke rushed out.

"You need a distraction. You've been cooped up here too long. Go along and see Charles." He started to rise, his eyes on the door.

She remained firmly in her seat. "Things aren't the same as before he went away."

"It's only because you've been apart for so long. You'll warm up to each other again." He leaned back against the cushions when she made no move to stand.

"He hardly ever wrote to me from California. Perhaps he's outgrown our friendship." She put her arm on the back of the settee and ran her fingers over the tassels of the cushions.

"I doubt that. Not everyone is good at correspondence, so don't let that convince you of anything. Look at me. If I wrote every time you crossed my mind, you could paper your bedroom with my letters."

"If you installed a telephone, we could talk to each other every week and there would be no need for letters." She couldn't help needling him a little. She'd been encouraging him to get one for the past two years—through her letters, of course.

Max waved a hand dismissively. "I'll get to it one of these days. So, you'll go see Charles?"

Elsie rose and stretched. "I suppose it couldn't hurt. What's he working on? More silks?"

"No, this is a more personal acquisition," he said, his face lighting up.

"Not more of your bones?" A smile came to her lips, and she raised a brow.

"Charles found them in California and arranged a

shipment. They only just arrived." He stood up and followed her out of the study.

"I'm surprised you aren't down there yourself right now."

"I've seen them. Charles and I went to the office before breakfast," he said, snuffing his pipe out.

"What are they like?"

"You'll see that for yourself when you go to the office."

"It seems there's not a moment to lose." She went to the closet to fetch her coat.

Chapter Four

The trip into town was welcome after going no farther than the beach for the past week. Elsie crossed the lawn to the front gate, which opened onto Birch Street. It was an easy half hour walk to Bennington Square, the town center. Various shops and restaurants lined the square, and most of the shipping offices were within a block or two. Elsie followed a side street to a short, steep hill that came out on the same level as the docks.

Max had forgone a warehouse in favor of a tall, narrow brick building with plenty of rooms to store his goods. It was a few streets away from the wharf but not far enough to escape the bustle of a busy port.

A bell jangled over the door when she entered. Charles wasn't in the front room, so she walked down the hall, peeking into open doors until she found him.

Sunlight filtered through the dusty windows of the smallest storeroom. Elsie crinkled her nose at the dank, musty smell. Charles was hunched over a desk, examining a spiral-shaped rock with rough edges.

"May I open a window?" she asked in lieu of a greeting.

Charles didn't look up. "They don't open. I've tried."

Elsie crossed the room and fiddled with a latch, but it wouldn't budge. She gripped the handles and pulled with all her might, then took a step back, rubbing her red palms. After trying two more windows with no success, she put her hands on her hips and scowled up at them.

"I told you they don't open. They're painted shut."

"You'd think that even Max would take the time to fix his windows. It's stifling in here." She wiped the dust off her hands and walked over to the desk to peek over his shoulder. "What is it?"

"An ammonite," he said, standing up.

"It reminds me of a seashell."

"Not surprising. Ammonites were sea creatures that lived millions of years ago." He took a step back so she could get a closer look.

"Fascinating," she said, picking it up.

"This is a rather special one. I haven't found many in such good condition."

"What will you do with it?"

"Clean it and put it with the rest." Charles pointed at the table, where straw and crumpled bits of paper were overflowing from a wooden crate.

"More ammonites?" She put the fossil down and perched on the edge of the desk, swinging her ankles.

"Some. But there are at least twenty other pieces I haven't unpacked yet. All sea creatures, I believe. Max was down here pawing through the package this morning." He drew out a handkerchief and wiped his brow. "I was about to get some air. Will you join me?"

"That would be welcome," she said, casting a peevish glance up at the stubborn windows.

Charles donned his jacket and hat, and they left the office. Elsie appreciated the sunshine and cool breeze coming off the ocean the moment they stepped outside. Charles took her elbow and, after waiting for several carriages to pass, they crossed the street to a shop with a pink-and-white awning. *Finkelstein's Ice Cream Parlor* was etched on the glass window. A waft of vanilla drifted over to them outside.

"Wait here," Charles said, and pulled a chair out for her at a round table. He went inside and spoke to the man at the counter, gesturing to where she sat. After paying, he came back and settled into the chair across from Elsie.

"What did you order?" she asked.

"You'll see. It's Mr. Finkelstein's specialty."

Before long Mr. Finkelstein brought out two glass dishes, each filled to the brim with chocolate, vanilla, and strawberry ice cream topped with a mountain of whipped cream and cherries. He gave them a friendly wave on his way back into the shop.

"I knew you'd want to try Finkelstein's since it wasn't here the last time you visited Sherwood Bay. Max told me this place just opened last summer." Charles bit a cherry off its stem.

"How did you know I haven't been here?"

"My mother hasn't written about your summer trips here for a couple of years. I always asked after you in my letters." He dipped his spoon into the chocolate ice cream.

Elsie's stomach twisted. Charles had apparently kept up his correspondence with everyone he knew in Holderness *but* her. Naturally he'd write to his mother. But Gabriel? He'd had time to write to Gabriel, but not her, his oldest friend. Elsie pecked at her sundae, unable to enjoy it with this unanswered question swirling around in her mind. She put the spoon down.

Charles looked up. "Don't you like it? Would you like me to get you something else?"

"I'm not upset about the ice cream, Charles. I

haven't heard from you for almost a year. Why didn't you answer my letters?" She'd spoken much louder than she'd intended, and several people on the street looked at her in alarm.

"I did answer your letters. The few I received." He took a bite of strawberry ice cream and leaned back in his chair as if the matter was of no consequence, but she knew him better than that. There was a tightness around his eyes.

"I wrote to you two or three times a month," she said, pushing her ice cream aside.

"And I wrote to you at least as often. But I haven't heard from you regularly for some time. I assumed you were so absorbed in Gabriel you didn't have time to write." There was something in his voice she didn't like. Had *anyone* approved of her betrothal to Gabriel?

"I did write." She leaned toward him across the table.

"I was often in the desert. The post isn't regular there, Elsie."

She found his tone far more condescending than necessary.

"Letters certainly could have reached me in a year," she insisted.

"I could say the same of yours," he said, pointing his spoon at her. "I didn't get answers to half the letters I wrote you." He paused, his brow furrowed. "Did you receive the letters I sent the first few months after I left?"

"Yes, and I replied to every letter I received."

He closed his eyes and let out a long breath. "Every one?"

"Yes. But you didn't reply to all of mine. You wrote to your family and to Gabriel but not to me." Her voice had taken on a petulant tone. She cleared her throat.

"I think we've established that some of our letters must have been lost," Charles said. "Or perhaps you didn't write as often as you think you did." The vibration of his tapping foot rattled the spoon in his dish.

"I know exactly how often I wrote to you."

"Does it matter now who wrote more? We're not children in a competition." He dabbed the corners of his mouth with a napkin and surveyed her coolly.

All this time she'd thought he was ignoring her, and he'd been thinking the same about her. It had a certain ironic humor to it. Almost. It still didn't explain how his family had received letters from him and she hadn't. But she wouldn't bring that up right now.

Elsie kept her voice light as she said, "It seems the post office needs to make some improvements." She offered him a smile and was relieved when he reciprocated.

"No doubt about that. From now on, we needn't bother with letters. Anyway, I'd much rather speak to you in person." Charles rested his hands close to hers on the table.

"Out of curiosity, do you remember the last letter you received from me?" she asked.

"Yes, it must have been close to a year ago. You were asking if I'd made any headway with my fossil research, and when I would be coming home."

So he hadn't received *that* letter. The one where she'd shared her doubts about Gabriel and asked for his advice.

"Are you certain that's the last one you received?"

"I think so. Why? Have I missed some of your news?"

Elsie deliberated about how much to tell him. Gabriel was gone, so the problem no longer existed. How could she confess to anyone, let alone Charles? It was better that he hadn't gotten the letter, that she alone should carry the burden of her doubts.

"Elsie?" Charles was leaning forward in his chair, watching her.

"Oh, no, it was nothing important. Just telling you about my silly trifles." She picked up her spoon. "We should finish our ice cream before it melts."

Charles followed suit, but she found his eyes upon her often while they ate.

****

Before Elsie knew it, she'd been in Sherwood Bay for a month. There was much more freedom here than at home—she did whatever struck her fancy on any given day. She visited the beach daily, seeking treasures for her Mason jar. It sat on her windowsill, casting dazzling colors on the wall when the sun struck it just so. She'd been to Max's study numerous times to delve into his fossil collection. Elsie's favorite was a large tooth that Charles said came from a shark the size of a whale. She touched its rough edges and pictured the ancient creature gliding through the sea.

Elsie found, upon reflection, that she had reached a contentment she wouldn't have thought possible so soon after losing Gabriel. It reaffirmed her decision to come to Max's instead of wallowing in Holderness.

In mid-May, the scent she'd been awaiting since winter drifted in through the library windows. She put her book aside and followed it outside.

The garden was ablaze with lilacs. She drifted from bloom to bloom, breathing in the sweet scent. Under the fragrant canopy of the largest tree, she made herself a bed, paying no mind to the dew clinging to her dress or the grass tickling her ankles. The spring sun warmed her skin, and a gentle breeze carried hints of the ocean.

A cloud moved across the sun, cooling her by a few degrees. She opened her eyes.

It wasn't a cloud.

"You remind me of the fairy in that painting in the old playroom back home," Charles said.

"I feel like her," Elsie said with a dreamy sigh.

She scooted over to make room for him. He sat down, his outstretched legs surpassing Elsie's by several inches. The long hours lolling about the garden together when they were children came to mind. Gabriel had always been one for chase games like tag or, if he could persuade James to join them, capture the flag. Charles had shared Elsie's delight in doing absolutely nothing.

"How long have you been out here?" he asked, plucking a blade of grass and twirling it between his fingers.

"I'm not sure. Not long enough," she said, sitting up.

"You have flower petals in your hair." He brushed the back of her head, sending petals fluttering.

"I don't mind." She brought a lilac to her nose and inhaled deeply.

"What are you doing today?" He leaned back on his elbows and squinted at the sun through the leaves.

"Dawdling under the lilacs until the fireflies come out?"

"You'll be waiting a long time," he said with a grin.

"They will be worth the wait."

"I recall many an evening when we walked into the woods to find them, but not many days that we started looking at…" He paused and looked at his watch. "Ten o'clock in the morning."

"I suppose it is a trifle early. Back then we didn't even need to look very hard. You knew all their favorite hiding places."

"You found just as many. More than one summer we were out past dark every single night watching them."

"Under the big oak tree," she said and grinned.

"Yes, and the birch wood, and your rose garden, and my backyard. More places than I can count. But they won't emerge for hours." He peered around the garden as if planning where he would search tonight.

"You're right about that. I've been meaning to go to Bennington Square. Perhaps this is a good day for it." She could do with a visit to the milliner's, and her stationery supply was low. McGoldrick's Candy Shop carried her favorite maple-sugar candy and delectable, creamy chocolates.

"I'm about to go into the office to check on a shipment that's come in. Why don't we go together?" Charles said, getting to his feet.

"Yes, let's. But in a few minutes." She flopped back into the grass. Her light giggle mingled with his deep laugh.

"Up you get, Elsie," he said, giving her a hand.

She went into the house with only one regretful look back at her purple oasis.

As they walked down Birch Street, she had a chance to broach a subject that had been on her mind for some days. "Charles, do you ever miss Gabriel?"

"Sometimes. But I was away so long I'd grown accustomed to not seeing him. Do you?" He shook his head and glanced down at her with a red face. "What am

I saying? Of course you do."

She met his eyes with a wistful expression. "Do you remember when we were young, how much fun we had with him?"

Charles grinned. "He was always up for adventures, and never ran out of amusing stories."

"At the time, you accused him of telling tall tales."

"I still don't believe half of them, but they *were* amusing."

"As I recall, there were other occasions when you doubted his honesty." Elsie slowed her pace, and Charles adjusted his steps to hers.

"I did." He shrugged. "But we were children."

They'd always disagreed about that aspect of Gabriel's character. Elsie thought it was harmless—he was stretching the truth a bit to impress them—but Charles seemed to take every white lie as a personal affront.

She was silent for a few moments, looking at the beach on their left. Birch Street was lined with only a few tall oak trees, none of which obstructed her view of the ocean.

"He would be up for games whenever he had time," she said.

"He was so good at marbles. I think I lost all my favorite poppers to him. I'm still not convinced there wasn't some sleight of hand going on."

"That's why I never played for keeps with him," she said lightheartedly.

"He also taught us that special way to build card houses. Do you remember?" Charles looked off into the distance, perhaps picturing the impressive structures he and Gabriel had built.

"I remember he *tried*. Mine always collapsed," Elsie said. "He was a good friend."

Charles nodded. "And he was good to you after I left. I'll always be grateful to him for that."

"Yes," was all she could say. He had been good to her, but not all the time. There was no need to mention that now.

"Were there any fossils in the latest shipment?" she asked as they approached town.

"No, not this time." She couldn't help noticing the relieved note in his voice.

"Only things for the shops?"

They entered Bennington Square.

"Yes, in fact—" Charles was interrupted by a voice calling, "Elsie!"

She scanned the crowd and spotted Lucy Hunter, an old friend from her summers in Sherwood Bay. Tendrils of auburn hair escaped Lucy's hat as she bounced on her heels, waving from across the square. She loved nothing more than a nice long chat, though Elsie had learned years ago not to tell her anything she wished to keep private.

Elsie and Charles changed direction to meet Lucy in front of Cantwell's Tea House.

"I hadn't heard you were in town!" Lucy said when they reached her.

"I've been here since April but not making any calls."

Lucy was staring at Charles.

"Oh," Elsie said at once, "may I introduce Mr. Rockingham." She turned to Charles. "This is my friend, Miss Hunter."

"It's a pleasure to meet you," he said, inclining his

head.

"Oh, the pleasure is all mine," Lucy twittered.

"Do you have time for a chat, or perhaps we could go to Griffith's for lunch?" Elsie asked.

"I'm on my way to the library for the poetry reading and tea," Lucy said. "Why don't you join me?"

"I'd be happy to come," Elsie said. She turned to Charles. "My trip to McGoldrick's will have to wait for another day. I'll see you at supper?"

"Most likely. Enjoy your afternoon, ladies." He tipped his hat to them and strode toward the wharf.

Lucy took Elsie's arm and steered her through the square. "I did hear you were to be married. Is that your fiancé? He's quite handsome."

A cloud descended on Elsie. "Mr. Rockingham is a childhood friend. My betrothed was Mr. Reed, but he was lost at sea."

Lucy furrowed her brow in sympathy. "Oh, I do apologize. How clumsy of me."

"You couldn't have known," she said as they turned onto Middle Street. The massive brick library was at the end of the block.

"Was he in the Navy?"

"No, he's—was—first mate on a schooner." Elsie swallowed, keeping her tears at bay.

"When did it happen?" Lucy seemed undeterred by Elsie's discomfort.

"Not seven months ago." She picked up her pace— the sooner they were inside, the sooner Lucy would stop pressing her for details.

"How brave you are, and how sad you must be." Lucy leaned in close, bringing with her a cloud of gardenia perfume.

"I'd rather not discuss it now," Elsie said, pulling away.

"Of course. Another time."

Elsie just nodded and made a mental note to avoid the topic at all costs in future.

When they arrived at the library, Lucy led Elsie to a parlor off the main chamber. A woman stood reading aloud, while a group of women and men sat in chairs facing her. Elsie settled herself beside Lucy but couldn't focus on the poetry. She thought of Gabriel and how he'd detested reading, calling it a waste of time. She smiled to herself, remembering the day she tried to convince him otherwise. In hindsight it may have been the very beginning of their courtship, though she hadn't recognized it at the time.

She'd been sitting on the front porch of her house, reading an adventure novel that Charles had sent her. Based on the earmarked pages, he'd read it himself first. He had left six months prior, and she was especially lonely, still waiting for a reply to her last letter.

Her house, on the crest of a hill, was only a few streets away from the sea, offering a clear view of the harbor. When she glanced up for a moment, she saw Gabriel approaching.

"Good afternoon, Elsie," he said with a wave.

She waved back and looked over her shoulder to the windows. It seemed her mother hadn't seen him arrive, which was just as well, as she'd made no secret of her dislike of Gabriel.

Elsie marked the page in her book and set it on the table beside her.

"Don't see why you bother with such nonsense," he said, dashing up the stairs. "You could be living life, not reading about it."

"I doubt I'll ever have the opportunity to visit Egypt, or fly in a hot-air balloon," she said and grinned.

He looked to the spot beside her on the bench.

"Oh, would you like to sit down?" she asked, making room for him.

He took off his cap, sat down, and loosely crossed his legs. "You should be a sailor. Then you'd see Egypt and more," he joked. He scratched his dark, wavy hair.

"I cannot imagine my mother allowing that."

"That she wouldn't, and I doubt you've the sea legs for it."

"I have been sailing, as you well know. Charles and I took our boat out often."

"Oh, I remember that tiny thing." Gabriel smiled and his dimples appeared.

"Speaking of Charles, have you been to the post office? Have any letters come?"

He drew a folded envelope from his pocket. Her heart leapt, and she tried to take it from him.

Gabriel held it above his head. "You're so keen for my call to end?"

"Don't be silly, Gabriel. I hope you'll stay as long as you want to."

Mollified, he handed her the letter. It felt much too thin, perhaps only one or two pages. She slipped it inside her book to read later when she was alone.

"That will give you something to read besides your stories," he said.

"You should take a novel with you when you're out on the ship. It would help you pass the time." She looked beyond, to where the ships were moored.

"I watch the sky or the waves. Not much slack time

on a ship," he said, following her eyes to the harbor.

"I imagine not. Would you like to stay for tea?"

He managed to turn his chuckle into a cough. "Tea?" He glanced down at his grubby clothes. "No, I'm wanted at the docks. But I knew you'd want your letter. Any to send out?"

"Not yet, but most likely tomorrow." She didn't want to leave Charles waiting for her reply.

"Then I'll be back tomorrow." He got to his feet and looked down at her, his cap in his hands.

"If you have time, we could go to the park."

"I'd like that."

"I'll leave you to your book, then."

The next day he did come back, carrying a book of his own.

****

When the poet finished, the audience applauded and stood up. Elsie rose a moment later than everyone else, still in her memories. The chatter of voices intensified as people filed into the tearoom. On her way through the hall, she paused at a table with pamphlets displayed. One about a women's photography class in town caught her eye. She slipped it into her purse and headed for the tearoom.

At each seat was a three-tiered tray filled with pastries, fruit, and finger sandwiches. She poured herself a cup of Earl Grey from the silver teapot, then ate a cucumber sandwich and a lemon tart. Before long, Lucy arrived with her friends. Elsie recognized both of them from her summers in town.

The two women looked at Elsie with that pitying expression she had grown to know so well in these last months. Lucy must have told them everything she knew about Elsie's tragedy.

"Elsie, I'm sure you remember Miss Maynes and Miss Gates." Lucy motioned to each woman in turn.

Miss Gates was petite and elegantly dressed. Her eyes met Elsie's with a kind smile. "You must call me Nancy, as when we were children."

"How nice to see you," said Elsie, standing up. "I recall spending time with you at Lucy's when we were young."

"Of course. We would have such fun." Nancy took her seat at the table.

Miss Maynes, standing stiffly beside Lucy, said, "Though we are hardly children anymore, you may still call me Grace."

"It's lovely to see you again," said Elsie, tempted to take a step back from the chill in her voice.

"So we're all old friends," Lucy said, clasping her hands together.

Grace swept her eyes from Elsie's hat to her shoes, as if observing something unpleasant she'd stepped in, and narrowed her gaze infinitesimally. "Miss Hayward—Elsie—I believe you have something on your cheek." She put a hand to her mouth, not quite hiding a smirk.

"They're freckles."

"How unfortunate." Grace turned away from her and sat down.

Elsie's mother would have been proud of her decorum, as she simply returned to her seat, fortunately as far as possible from Grace.

The women settled themselves at the table, their attention evenly divided between Elsie and their tea trays.

"What brings you to Portsmouth?" Nancy asked.

"I'm staying with my uncle, Mr. Lambert." She bit into a mini Victoria sponge cake.

"Oh, Mr. Lambert. He's a trifle eccentric, isn't he?" Grace said.

"I wouldn't say so," Elsie said coolly.

"Doesn't he collect bones?" Lucy asked with an exaggerated shiver that nearly knocked her hat off.

"Of a sort," Elsie said. "He collects fossils."

"How interesting," Nancy said.

"It really is. In fact, just the other day, Charles—that is, Mr. Rockingham—showed me a fossilized sea creature that is millions of years old."

"You say Mr. Rockingham is your childhood friend?" Lucy asked, eyes alight with interest.

"Yes," Elsie said, sipping her tea.

"How long have you known him?" Nancy asked.

"Since we were babies; our mothers are best friends. Our birthdays are four days apart."

"How sweet!" Lucy said, stirring sugar into her tea.

Grace parted her lips slightly but said nothing.

"Will he be in town long?" Nancy asked.

"I don't know what his plans are." It wasn't the first time in her life Elsie had been plied for information concerning Charles, and always by ladies.

"Is it true that Mr. Rockingham is also staying with Mr. Lambert?" Grace asked, blinking her eyes like a doe. "Without your mother on the premises? I assume you *do* have a chaperone."

Lucy coughed into her teacup. Nancy's eyes, widening as big as lemons, suddenly focused on her petit four.

Elsie paled at the insinuation and immediately rose

from the table. "It really is time for me to be getting home. I thank you for your company and hope we meet again soon."

"Yes, indeed," said Nancy enthusiastically.

Grace flashed a tight smile that was gone in an instant.

Walking Elsie to the front of the library, Lucy said, "I'm so happy I ran into you."

"I am too. We have so much to catch up on, and there was hardly time today."

"I'm sorry about Grace," Lucy said, placing a hand on Elsie's arm.

"Did I offend her in some way?"

"No." Lucy came closer and whispered, "She's out of sorts because of an issue with her beau. I can't say any more without breaking her confidence." Her lip trembled from the effort of not divulging the secret.

"I see. Perhaps I'll see her on another day when she's feeling better."

"I'm sure of it. We'll get together again soon," Lucy promised, and went back inside.

Elsie wasn't ready to return home yet; she had merely wanted to escape the probing questions.

She walked down Birch Street, mulling over her day. She couldn't remember the exact year she'd met Lucy, only that she was as much a part of summers in Sherwood Bay as flying kites and building sandcastles. Nancy, the daughter of Max's business associate, had been happy to play with dolls and eat ice cream with them occasionally in the evenings. Grace, on the other hand... She had moved here from Boston when they were fourteen. Elsie had seen her only a handful of times. She'd turned her nose up at much of the pastimes of the other young women and only deigned to spend time with them because she was—as she called herself—"Lucy's *winter* best friend."

It was such a warm and sunny day that Elsie took her hat off to let the sea breeze ruffle through her hair. In the distance, a group of children played in the sand. In her mind's eye it was her, Charles, James, and Margaret laughing on the shore. They'd spent endless summer days frolicking in the waves. A fishing boat, the *Mo Annette*, was now pulling into the dock as Elsie passed by.

She couldn't help thinking of her many friends and neighbors in Holderness who had made their livelihood on the sea. Gabriel's father and three older brothers were all fishermen, and when the time came for him to choose his path, Gabriel had gone the same way. *The wrong way*, she thought. She'd tried to persuade him to go to college, but he'd been against it. How different her life would be if she'd been able to convince him. Elsie's insides churned as she thought again of Gabriel and her doubts. She wiped a hand over her face, trying to forget. But how could she forget, here of all places?

As she approached home, she saw Max sitting in one of the chairs at the side of the house, facing the sea. Pipe smoke billowed around as if he was sitting in a cloud. She went over and sat in the chair next to him.

"How was your outing?" Max asked.

"Very nice. I ran into Lucy Hunter in Bennington Square, and we went to the poetry reading." Elsie stretched her legs out in front of her and put her hat in her lap.

"Did you enjoy it?" He drew on his pipe.

"I couldn't pay attention. She'd been asking me

about Gabriel."

"What did you tell her?"

"Only the shortest version of the story I could. Two of her friends had tea with us. They were all agog to hear about Charles."

"So they're interested in your Charles?" he said with a snicker.

"Not *my* Charles, but yes."

"He's a handsome young fellow, isn't he?"

"You could say that. I haven't noticed," Elsie said with a shrug.

"No, you wouldn't," Max muttered. "Perhaps you've grown blind to him, knowing him for so long."

"I don't know about that," Elsie said. "He's changed so much since the last time I saw him."

"Yes, you've both changed." He attempted some smoke rings that dissolved in the air and vanished in an instant.

"I should think so. It's been over three years since he went to California. What have you been doing today?"

"Paperwork, mostly, and looking over that new ammonite Charles brought over. I'm in correspondence with a friend in California. He says he may be able to find me a triceratops skull." He puffed on his pipe, a satisfied gleam in his eyes.

"Speaking of your collection, I wonder if there's anything I could do to help with the fossils. I'd like to learn more about them." They were interesting enough to look at, but most of them were a complete mystery to her.

"You could help me organize the study. Heaven knows, it needs it, and I don't want to send Daisy in there." He tapped his pipe out on his shoe.

"That sounds like just the thing to get me started. Maybe I could get some books from the library to help identify them, or perhaps Charles could help."

"You won't need to know much for the type of work I have in mind. I'll lend you some books; no need to go to the library. Join me while I have my lunch, and then we'll look over what I have in the study."

Chapter Five

Elsie started her work for Max the following week. Even knowing his passion for fossils, she never dreamed there would be so much. Mr. Anderson had scoured the house for packages that Max had tucked away in various rooms. The long table in the middle of the study was covered in boxes. Some were open, their contents spread out on the table, and others were still sealed tight.

One wall of the study was made almost entirely of windows facing the backyard, woods, and stables. Elsie looked out and saw Daniel saddling a frisky black mare while Max stood by in his riding clothes, laughing over some joke with Tom and Mr. Anderson.

Warm oak cabinets went from floor to ceiling on the opposite wall. A deep counter divided small drawers from the bottom cabinets, which were large enough to hold a few sacks of flour. In the back corner of the room was Max's desk and two wooden chairs. A bay window behind the desk faced the ocean. The settee she had shared with Max was now covered in even more boxes to be sorted. Her uncle had left fossils willy-nilly all over the long worktable, his desk, and any horizontal space he could find.

Sunshine poured in through the open windows, while a crisp breeze stirred up little scraps of paper and packing materials on the floor. Elsie spent the morning putting the fossils into what she thought were the correct categories, based on illustrations from Max's books and her best guesses. Some were clearly marine fossils—ammonites, snails, sharks' teeth—and others looked like plants or fish embedded in stone. A multitude of fragments—impossible to identify—made up the rest. On the long table, she left Max's finest pieces, the ones she knew he would want to examine over and over.

She'd need Charles to identify some artifacts for her so she could write out an inventory. There was one piece in particular she was curious about. She turned it over in her hands several times, trying to decide what it was. At first she thought it was a tooth, but it looked too curved for that. Perhaps a horn or even some manmade tool?

Elsie glanced at the clock. Lunchtime had come and gone. There was still work to do, but the study was much tidier than when she'd started. Several groups of fossils were ready to be sorted upon her return. There were no more boxes, and she had picked up the papers and swept the floor.

Outside, white-capped waves skittered across the sea, and dark, dense clouds bore down on the horizon. The windowpanes shuddered against the gathering wind. She closed them tightly, then went to ask Judith about a late lunch.

After a quick meal she went back to the study to collect the mysterious fossil. She wrapped it in cloth and put it in a basket. There was just time to make it to the office and back before the rain came.

Halfway to town, cold, fast drops began to fall. The wind picked up and Elsie gripped her hat to keep it from blowing away. In Bennington Square, a number of people milled around one of the shipping offices. Some whispered urgently to each other, others ran to and fro along the pier. It was far too blustery to stay outside and find out what the commotion was about.

She let herself into Max's office and found Charles not at his desk but at the window.

"Good afternoon," she said brightly. "I've brought one of Max's pieces over to get your opinion. I have no idea what it could be."

"Oh…good afternoon." He turned around, his arms stiff at his sides.

Alarmed by his pale hue, she asked, "Charles, are you all right?"

He stood there as if trying to block something, and spoke gravely: "I thought you must have heard."

Elsie went and stood beside him. Down on the docks, men were deep in discussion, some holding women who wept openly.

And then she knew.

Had she not been one of those women months ago? Her breath deserted her, and she would have fallen to the floor if Charles hadn't caught her. She collapsed into the chair he half carried her to.

From what seemed like miles away came the sound of liquid being poured. A crystal glass was suddenly in her hand. She lifted it to her lips and molten liquor slid down her throat.

"Which ship?" she whispered.

"The *Seafarer*."

Elsie wanted to ask about survivors, but could not find her voice. She was back in Holderness when the black-bordered letter arrived from Gabriel's shipmate, Matthew Newkirk, who explained that they had tried everything to save the *Kraken*, but it had foundered, and Gabriel had gone down with it. Matthew was the only survivor.

She was so lost in the memory that it took her a moment to realize Charles was speaking to her. "Elsie, let me take you home," he said gently.

She downed the rest of her drink. He took her elbow and helped her to stand. She hardly noticed the driving rain and wind on the way home, conscious only of Charles's support when she stumbled on trembling legs.

And then Mr. Anderson was there, opening the front door, asking what was wrong.

"I…" Elsie began but couldn't think how to answer.

Charles helped her into the house, and she stood shivering in the entryway. He whispered something to Mr. Anderson, who disappeared and returned a moment later with Mrs. Holt in tow.

"Has she been hurt?" Mrs. Holt cried as soon as she saw Elsie.

"One of the fishing boats has been lost in the storm. Elsie just heard the news," Charles said before she could speak. Everyone clustered around her. All she wanted was to sit down.

Mr. Anderson and Mrs. Holt exchanged looks of understanding. Of all things, this is what summoned the tears to Elsie's eyes.

"How can I help?" Mr. Anderson asked, his typically clipped tone soft.

"I'd like to go to my room," she said in a flat voice. Her knees would not stop shaking. She reached out to Charles, who took her hand between his own and tried to rub some warmth into it.

"I'll tell Mr. Lambert what's happened and see that Becky doesn't go up to your room for the rest of the day," Mr. Anderson said and hastened down the hall.

"Come with me, love," Mrs. Holt said, putting an arm around Elsie's shoulder, and took her hand.

They were treating her like a child with a scraped knee, but instead of being irritated, she was grateful. She let Mrs. Holt lead her away, not even remembering to thank Charles or Mr. Anderson for their assistance.

Soon she was settled in bed with a dry nightgown, a warming pan, and a cup of strong tea close at hand. The fumes coming off it suggested Mrs. Holt had added her customary drop of brandy. Elsie lay in bed, her face buried in her hands. She understood only too well what those women on the dock were going through. When Gabriel died, she hadn't wanted to believe it at first. She'd held on to the slim hope that perhaps he had swum to shore, or was clinging to a piece of the wreckage, or had been picked up by another boat. But as the days— then weeks—passed, she knew her future was gone.

She tried to ignore the tight burning in her chest, but the tears came in a torrent. She cried until glorious, oblivious sleep claimed her. In the wee hours of the morning she awoke, her eyes puffy and sore. Sitting up in bed, she sipped her cold tea. The *Seafarer* was at the bottom of the ocean. In houses all over town, other women would be awake weeping over their missing men, their broken lives.

Sleep was impossible now. She threw back the covers and tiptoed across the room to the window seat. The windows swung open easily to reveal the dark, starless sky. The wind and rain had ceased, but thick gray clouds still obscured the moon.

Her mind conjured up an image of what might be left of the *Kraken* in the depths, then she closed her eyes tight to banish the vision. She wanted to remember it whole, with Gabriel smiling at her from the stern. Not Gabriel sinking into the depths, never to be seen again. He might never stop haunting her. But was it not her own guilt that haunted her most of all?

She hadn't spoken of it yet to anyone, but perhaps it was time. The first person she thought of was Charles, but she didn't think she could bear the look on his face. In the past he might have understood, but now? They weren't as close as they'd once been. If she told him, she might be relinquishing any chance of regaining the special friendship they'd once shared. Having him back in her life meant more to her than she would have imagined. Her childhood friend, she'd told Lucy. But he was much more than that. No, she couldn't tell Charles. That left only Margaret.

Merely the thought of her sister's face buoyed her.

She couldn't stay in Sherwood Bay after this tragic wreck. There would be long days of grief, recoveries, and funerals. Growing up on the seacoast, she was no stranger to disasters such as this. When ships were lost, the tragedy hung over the whole town like a black veil. She could not bear to watch as the widows and mothers stood on the beach or the dock, day after day, hoping for and yet dreading a sign of their lost men. Just thinking about it brought tears to her eyes. They'd never found Gabriel.

From outside came the sound of the foghorn. Touches of pink and orange were creeping into the sky. It would soon be daybreak. She fetched her suitcase from the wardrobe and started filling it with what she would need for her journey.

She then sat on the bed, waiting for the house to come to life. As soon as she heard movement downstairs, she rang the bell.

Daisy came up quickly but with a slightly puzzled look on her face. "Good morning, miss."

"Good morning, Daisy. I'll need Tom to take me to the station as soon as he can, and please ask Mr. Anderson to take my suitcase downstairs. I wish to go to the station for the seven o'clock train."

"Yes, miss," Daisy said and scurried down the hall.

Elsie went downstairs as soon as she had washed and dressed. At the dining room table, Max ate breakfast with his newspaper propped in front of him.

"You're up early," Elsie said, and sat beside him. She poured herself some coffee and took a warm slice of apple cake off the tray.

"I haven't been to bed," he said, scraping up the remains of his fried eggs.

"Why ever not?"

"I was lost in that study you organized. I found things I haven't seen in years. Although there were some items I couldn't find, and some pieces you grouped into the wrong place entirely."

"I thought I'd ask Charles for help with that when I return." She finished her cake and wiped her fingers with a napkin.

"When you return from where?"

"I need a break, Max. I'm going home."

"You've hardly been here a month. Am I working you too hard? Not providing enough entertainment?" A hint of worry broke through his jovial tone.

"No, not at all. It's this wreck, and what will come after."

He placed a hand over hers and looked into her face. "It's more than that, I can tell. What's eating you?"

"There are some things I need to deal with. Some things about Gabriel. And I can't do that here."

Until she said it out loud she hadn't realized how true this was. Perhaps going back to where it had happened could help her to come to terms with Gabriel's death and move on. She knew now that she didn't only *need* to get past it, she *wanted* to.

"Can I help? Anything you need, you only have to ask."

"No, it's something I need to deal with on my own. But thank you."

"Well, you'll be welcome back when you're sorted."

"I don't think I'll be gone very long." She looked fondly around the dining room, already looking forward to her return.

"If you're taking the seven o'clock, you'd better be on your way," Max said, glancing at the cuckoo clock.

"I'm glad I got to see you before I left."

"I am, too." He patted her hand. "You'll want to say goodbye to Charles. Shall I send for him?" He was already reaching for the bell to call Daisy.

"No, I really must go now if I want to make that train. Please tell him where I've gone, and that I'll see him soon."

"He won't like that."

"He'll understand." Elsie rose to her feet. "Goodbye."

"Goodbye," Max called after her.

She went out the front door, where Tom was waiting with the carriage. They made it to the station in plenty of time, and soon Elsie was right back where she'd started.

Her parents were just sitting down to lunch when she arrived home. They were surprised and delighted to see her. While they ate, she listened to her mother happily chatter about Harriet's confinement—she'd had a girl! And to hear news of Margaret and baby Brian—he could now sit up by himself! She also heard the welcome news that James was still in town.

Elsie spent a quiet day at home and retired early. When she reached her room, she went straight to the plum settee beside her vanity and removed her shoes, then dressed for bed. While she brushed her hair, she looked around her room at her old treasures. Sea glass lined the sills and sat in a Mason jar on her corner whatnot shelf, along with numerous shells. Over the years, she'd had to choose only her favorite pieces to display, lest they overrun the place. A jewelry box shaped like a treasure chest—a gift from Charles—still held a place of honor on her vanity. They must have been eleven or so when he'd won it for her at the fair.

A cozy alcove held her bed, wardrobe, and bookcase. She chose a tattered book of fables and climbed into bed, nestling into the patchwork quilt that Mrs. Rockingham had made for her years ago. There was a gabled window on each wall surrounding the bed. Looking to her left, she could just make out the tall chimney of Charles's house.

After reading for only a little while, she set her book aside and lay on her back, watching the clouds turn from white to purple as they glided across the sky. It was wonderful to be away from Sherwood Bay. She laughed at the irony. But it was different now. She was far better off here at the moment, away from the aftermath of the shipwreck. But she would only stay for a week or so. Max would want help with his project, and in truth she'd been sorry to say goodbye to Charles so soon after reuniting with him.

She turned over in bed, facing the harbor window. In the distance, ships were rolling on the tide and beyond that the ocean, a blackish blue in the fading light. She'd told Max that she needed to sort some things out. This was true. She wasn't sure how, but she had to come to terms with the doubts she'd had about Gabriel and put all that behind her. Perhaps here, where they had spent their years of courting, was the only place it was possible, if at all. After a time, Elsie switched off the lights. Despite being back in her old bed, she found sleep was evasive.

****

Elsie woke feeling as though she hadn't slept at all. She took her time getting dressed, choosing a teal dress that made her eyes look more green than blue. She went downstairs to the drawing room and stepped out onto the balcony overlooking the harbor. A sea breeze rushed up to greet her. In days gone by, she would stand here and keep an eye out for Gabriel's ship, sometimes using the bronze telescope attached to the railing. If he knew she would be looking, he would stand right on the prow of the ship so she could see him.

She turned her back on the harbor and went into the house, where she found her father reading the paper by the drawing room fire.

"Good morning," she said.

"Good morning."

"Where's Mother?"

"She's upstairs getting ready to go with you to Margaret's," he said, looking at her over the top of his newspaper.

Elsie groaned inwardly. It would be impossible to pour her heart out to Margaret with her mother listening.

"I'll have breakfast then, so I'm ready to go when she is."

As she was finishing her meal, Mrs. Hayward came into the dining room, with her coat on and a peacock feather perched jauntily in her wide-brimmed hat.

"Did you sleep well?" Mrs. Hayward asked, sitting next to Elsie at the table.

"Very well." Hopefully the restless night did not show on her face.

"You're home much sooner than I expected. I thought you were enjoying your time with Max. I *assumed* you were, since you hardly wrote to me."

She took a piece of Elsie's toast and nibbled it.

"I'm sorry, Mother. With one thing or another, I haven't had much time to write." She blew on her hot chocolate and took a sip.

"You must be busy indeed. What have you been doing?"

"I ran into Lucy Hunter and some other old friends from Sherwood Bay. I've also been helping Max organize his study." Elsie didn't mention that she had been busy with that project for only one day.

"He must appreciate the help. My brother never was one for keeping things organized." Her mother filled a cup to the brim with hot chocolate.

"I've been to Uncle Max's office a few times to see what Charles is working on."

Her mother let out a theatrical gasp. "Charles? Charles Rockingham?"

"What other Charles would I be talking about? Didn't you know he was staying with Uncle Max?"

"I knew he was going there some weeks ago, but Lily didn't mention that it would be such a long stay."

"How is Mrs. Rockingham?"

"Happy to have James home. And she's busy with her new granddaughter. As you know, Harriet only gave birth four days ago. That's probably why Charles didn't tell you about it. In fact, I don't know if he's gotten his mother's letter yet, and of course Lily can't telephone him at Max's. Perhaps you could give him the news when you go back."

"He will probably have heard by then."

"I'm so anxious to see the baby again. Lily told me they're not having visitors for several weeks but that I may come anytime I wish." Mrs. Hayward's chin jutted up a notch.

"When did you see her last?"

"The day of the birth. Lily did want me on hand, you know. I told her I'll wait for just a few days to come back. Harriet must be exhausted. Births are so tiring."

"Have you seen much of James?"

"Oh, that boy! He gets up to such skylarking sometimes, I'd think he was still a child." Mrs. Hayward tried to look stern but the gleam in her eyes gave her away.

"I'd like to see him while I'm home. Perhaps we could have him over for supper?"

"You may bank on that. Shall we go? I telephoned Margaret a half hour ago to tell her we were on our way."

Margaret's home was an easy walk from the Hayward house. On their way over, her mother filled Elsie in on the town gossip, but she was too distracted to pay much attention. Every street held a memory. The shop where she and Charles had gone to buy candy, the library, the beach where she had first met Gabriel, the tree under which he had first held her hand. She grinned when she saw the dock where she and Charles had moored their boat, the *Flying Catfish*.

Margaret was sitting in a rocking chair on her porch, holding Brian. Mrs. Hayward took the baby as soon as he was within arm's reach, and Margaret gave Elsie a tight hug. Somehow, even with all their differences, they still looked like sisters. Elsie's light brown hair was in stark contrast to Margaret's brunette locks. Elsie hadn't inherited the petite frame of their grandmother; she was taller than Margaret and curvier all around.

They went into the parlor, where a table was laid with a variety of pastries and a steaming pot of jasmine tea. A crystal vase on the hutch was overflowing with lilacs, and Elsie went over to smell them before sitting down.

While Mrs. Hayward poured the tea, Elsie was allowed to hold Brian, a chubby little boy with wisps of dark hair. Elsie wondered if one day he would inherit Margaret's velvety brown eyes. Brian grabbed at Elsie's collar and her dangling aquamarine earrings. She laughed, gently holding his hands.

"Would you like me to take him?" Mrs. Hayward asked, arms at the ready.

"No, I'll keep him. He's changed so much since I saw him last."

Mrs. Hayward looked disappointed but sat in a chair and gave her attention to her angel food cake and strawberries.

Elsie settled herself on the floor with Brian, who had not yet learned to crawl but had indeed mastered sitting up. He wobbled precariously, so Elsie kept a hand on his back to help him balance. He chewed on his hands, babbling.

"Tell us what you've been doing in Sherwood Bay, Elsie. How's Uncle Max? And have you given any more thought to finding a job?" Margaret asked.

"I haven't start—"

"A job!" their mother cut in. One of her hands flew to her mouth while the other barely kept her cake from sliding off her lap.

"Yes, Mother. Elsie would probably enjoy having a job," Margaret said, and took a sip of her tea.

"It seems Elsie has enough to do without seeking *employment*," Mrs. Hayward said, stiffening in her chair.

"She did go to college, if you remember."

"And came out of it without a husband. She could be married by now!" She fanned her face with a napkin. Cake crumbs flew into the air.

"I would be married by now," Elsie reminded her coldly, "if not for Gabriel's wreck. I came out of college with an education, Mother. That could prove much more useful than a husband, if things continue as they are."

"I'm sure someone else will propose to you," her mother insisted. "You are quite pretty, dear, and it's not as though you were jilted." She put her cake plate on the table and picked up her tea.

"That is the last thing on my mind," Elsie snapped.

Brian looked at her in alarm but was soothed when she handed him a wooden block. He began to gnaw on it at once.

"Don't wait too long until it is the *first* thing on your mind again. It has been months since…well, courting can take some time," her mother said. "You are still young."

"Almost twenty-two," Elsie said, tilting her head in her mother's direction. "Not so young."

"Soon you'll be finished with your mourning and

will be free to…" Her mother sipped her tea through tight lips.

"Free to what, Mother?" Elsie asked, her voice hard.

"As a matter of fact, I have some young gentlemen in mind to introduce you to while you're home." The words tripped out of Mrs. Hayward's mouth as though speed would make them more amenable to Elsie's ears.

Elsie moved her head slowly from side to side and closed her eyes.

Margaret immediately said, "Mother, I see it's time for Brian's nap. Should I call his nurse, or would you like to take him upstairs and put him in his crib?"

Their mother plucked Brian up off the floor. "I'll rock him. He always loves that."

They heard her talking to the boy in a high-pitched voice all the way up the stairs.

Margaret closed the parlor door and turned at once to her sister. "Elsie, tell me what's wrong."

"What do you mean?" Elsie looked away, blinking rapidly.

"You don't need to pretend with me. What's wrong?"

Elsie's head slumped forward as she let the tears have their way. Margaret helped her up off the floor, led her to the sofa, and put an arm around her shoulders.

"Is it mother's talk of getting married?"

"No, that's what I'd expect from her. It's Gabriel." Elsie sniffed and wiped her eyes on the back of her hand.

"It hasn't been that long. Give it time."

"Most days I could almost forget my sorrow. But then the memories flood back and it's like the first day I heard he was gone." She put her elbow on the arm of the sofa and rested her cheek in her hand.

"That makes perfect sense, Elsie. You were to be married. You loved him." Margaret handed her a handkerchief.

She dabbed her eyes. "I did love him. But…"

"But?" Margaret's eyes widened.

Elsie's stomach tensed as she turned to her. "Did you ever have doubts about Paul before you married him?"

Margaret's face took on a dreamy, glazed look, and Elsie knew before she spoke what the answer would be.

"Paul always felt so right for me. Almost as soon as we met, I knew I would marry him."

Elsie hoped the envy didn't show on her face. She would have cherished that kind of confidence in her relationship with Gabriel.

"Margaret, I feel guilty—"

"Don't feel guilty! You can't blame yourself for what you felt months ago."

"It isn't that, it's—"

"I'd guess that many brides have doubts before the wedding."

It sounded so much nobler than her true feelings that she didn't correct Margaret.

Margaret gave her hand a squeeze. "You must go forward from here. I know it's been so difficult for you, but Gabriel would never expect you to mourn him forever."

"You're right. He would want me to enjoy my life as much as I can." Elsie twisted the handkerchief in her lap until it resembled a piece of licorice.

"He would. And pay no attention to Mother and her marriage schemes. She doesn't want you employed, because she thinks it will cut into your husband-hunting time. Whenever she tries to discuss it, I'll tell her that Brian needs a nap."

"Thank you," Elsie said, and gave her sister a hug.

Margaret rang for fresh tea, and they settled into the sofa for a chat.

Over an hour later, Mrs. Hayward came back downstairs. "Brian is asleep. And now it's time Elsie and I were heading home," she said, reaching for her coat.

Margaret escorted them to the door. "You must come back tomorrow, and every day you are in town, Elsie."

"We'll need to plan Elsie's birthday party," Mrs. Hayward said. "It's in just a few days."

"Mother, I don't need a birthday party."

"Of course you do. And how perfect that you came home just in time for it," her mother said.

"It would be such fun, Elsie," said Margaret. "We'll invite the Rockinghams. Harriet won't be able to attend, of course, but James will. A pity Charles isn't in town. We could invite a few of your other friends, too."

"All right. As long as it's mainly family."

It would be Elsie's first real social event since Gabriel had died.

Margaret stayed on the porch and waved until they were out of sight.

"I'm going to take the long way home," Elsie said as soon as they turned off Margaret's street.

"I thought you might. But don't be out too late. I have a special supper planned, and your father will want to play chess with you this afternoon."

"I won't be long."

She smiled fondly after her mother as she bustled away. Her talk of marriage was vexing, but it was clear she had Elsie's best interests at heart.

The route home was one she'd walked so many times she could do it with her eyes closed. She passed many of her and Charles's old haunts—the meadow where they'd picked wildflowers, the pond they would skate on in wintertime, and the little wood that always had the most fireflies.

Elsie strolled through the park that she and Gabriel had often visited, holding hands and planning their future. Here was the bench where he'd proposed to her all those months ago. She sank into it and closed her eyes, trying to remember his voice. Little snippets of it floated into her mind, but it was growing fainter. When she'd sat here beside him, she couldn't have envisioned a future without him. But now that time was all she'd ever have. A twinge of something like shame stirred inside when she realized she would be all right; she could live without him. And in some ways, perhaps that was best. Her cheeks reddened even though she was alone. This was not the place to think of such things.

Caught up in memories, she saw the afternoon dwindle away. It was past time to go home. On her way down the promenade that fronted the beach, a man coming from the other direction briefly made eye contact as he passed her. She thought nothing of it until he addressed her.

"Miss Hayward?"

She stopped and turned around.

He took his cap off and held it in his hands.

It took Elsie some moments to place him. He was Gabriel's shipmate from the *Kraken*, the sole survivor. They had last met at the funeral. "Mr. Newkirk."

"Matthew," he said with a slight nod. "May I join

you?"

"Certainly. I'm just on my way home."

They fell into step together, he with a distinct limp.

"Someone said you went to New Hampshire?" Matthew said.

"Yes. I've been staying with my uncle. I'm only home for a visit."

"And how are you, since…since the accident?" He looked away toward two men on the beach repairing lobster traps, pipes clenched in their teeth.

"I would rather ask how you are, Matthew." There was no answer she could give him that would suffice.

"I'm getting by."

"Are you working?" She glanced at him from the corner of her eye. There was something about him that reminded her too much of Gabriel. Perhaps his sailor's cap and tanned, rugged face. His hair was black, but unlike Gabriel's wavy locks Matthew's was cropped short.

"Yes. But no longer on the sea," he said, with a tremulous glance at the waves heaving onto the shore.

"I'm glad to hear it. You like the work?"

He chuckled. "It's stable—that's what I can say about it."

Perhaps she could excuse herself now and get away. Only a few more minutes until they reached her house.

"I wanted to tell you, though you likely know…" Matthew paused, twisting his cap in his hands.

"Yes?"

"Gabriel was so pleased about your wedding. He'd been talking about it earlier that same day." He cleared his throat and said, "That day *Kraken* went down."

Elsie didn't really know how to answer.

"Gabriel said he would finally be accepted in town, marrying into a family like yours."

"A family like mine?"

"That is to say, a family that was more well-off than his. And your family having lived in Holderness for so long. Gabriel never felt he fit in, not moving here till he was ten, and growing up more or less on the docks. He thought your family was—how did he say it? More respectful. He said he could give up the sea after the wedding. He said he'd be a gentleman. He was that pleased about it!"

"Oh, I'm glad to hear it," she managed.

Matthew didn't seem to register the shock written all over her face. She'd had no idea Gabriel planned to relinquish his job. As a first mate, he would have made a reasonable salary, and she had already known they would need to economize to get by. She'd thought that any difficulties they faced would be easily overcome, as they would face them together.

Matthew continued speaking as they walked, not even noticing her momentary lapse of attentiveness. "Gabriel did say how things are done different in families like yours, and that matches could be, um…advantages?"

"Do you mean advantageous?" Elsie's insides went cold.

"That's it. He said life would be good after you settled, and he would be at leisure, or maybe work at the bank. He said he would be moving up in the world."

Matthew seemed to be under the impression that he was delivering news that would please her, so she just nodded and gave him a tight smile, unable to speak. Thankfully, they had reached her house.

"I do hope things go better for you from now on," he said.

"And you. Perhaps I will see you again when I am next in Holderness," she said, unsure if she ever wanted to see him again. What other tidbit of information could he have to unsettle her?

He gave her a courteous bow and left her standing by the door, awash in knowledge she did not want.

Chapter Six

Elsie couldn't face her parents just yet. She trudged up the porch steps, collapsed onto the bench, and looked out to sea. Had Gabriel only been marrying her for her family connections? Impossible! He had been kind to her from the time they met, and outright friendly once Charles had left Holderness. As children the three of them spent time together whenever they could. When they grew older, her mother said it was "unbecoming" for Elsie to gallivant around unchaperoned with two young men, but they'd found ways around her rules.

Then there were all the times she and Charles had been thrown together without Gabriel. With their mothers being so close, Elsie and Charles didn't go more than two days without seeing each other. But not Gabriel. Her mother wouldn't have intentionally excluded him because of his upbringing, would she? Would Gabriel have noticed being treated differently by her, or possibly by others in town? She pondered this, wondering if a sense of not belonging could drive him to marry only for status. No, she knew he'd cared about her. But was he as smitten as she'd believed, or was it more of a convenience for him? What a dreadful thought.

And yet.

When she considered what her own feelings had been about their union, it brought some relief. If only she could talk to him.

She stood up, on the verge of going after Matthew to question him further, but stopped herself. He had most likely told her all he knew, and it would be humiliating to try to pry information out of Gabriel's friend. No, she would have to let it lie for the time being.

When Elsie went into the house, she wasn't surprised to see Charles's mother in the drawing room, drinking tea with her mother. She was tempted to go straight upstairs without saying hello, as her mind was too full of Matthew's words to idly sit and chat. But it seemed only polite to at least pop in for a few minutes. She smoothed down the front of her dress and walked into the drawing room, exhaling slowly to erase the strain of the last hour from her face.

"Elsie!" said Mrs. Rockingham, who looked remarkably like her son. Or, Elsie supposed, Charles looked remarkably like his mother. She had the same deep blue eyes and dark blond hair.

"It's good to see you, Mrs. Rockingham." Elsie took a seat beside her on the sofa.

"When will you call me Lily, as I've asked?"

"It will be some time yet. Perhaps when I turn thirty."

Mrs. Rockingham laughed and Elsie joined in.

"Are you here for long? I know your mother loves to have both her daughters close by."

"No, I'm only here for a short visit."

"Too short!" Mrs. Hayward interjected from the rocking chair across from the sofa.

"And how is Harriet's baby?" Elsie asked, heading off her mother's complaints.

"Pamela—Pammy—hardly fusses at all and is the most beautiful baby girl you ever saw," Mrs.

Rockingham said, glowing.

"Babies are such darlings," Mrs. Hayward said.

The grandmothers started rhapsodizing about babies and the specific wonders of their own two grandchildren. Their chatter was a comforting reminder of Elsie's childhood days: the hours of instruction on how to sew or knit or embroider, or sometimes sitting close by and reading while they talked. When they were small, she and Charles were often reprimanded for scurrying around in the drawing room while their mothers were trying to share secrets. Try as they might, they never quite got the hang of listening at keyholes.

"And will we have important news from Charles anytime soon, Lily?" Mrs. Hayward asked.

Elsie was about to pour herself a cup of tea, but that could wait. "What kind of news?"

Mrs. Rockingham just smiled into her teacup.

"Has there been a new development?" Mrs. Hayward leaned forward in her chair. "An attachment?"

"I get the sense that things are moving in that direction," Mrs. Rockingham said, stirring her tea slowly.

"Did you ask him about it?" Mrs. Hayward asked.

"Naturally. But he won't tell me any more than he did in his last letter." Mrs. Rockingham gave a delicate version of Charles's shrug.

"Maybe not so settled as you would wish then." Mrs. Hayward eased herself back into the rocker.

"All I can say is that I know my son. He has his eye on someone."

"Are you saying that Charles is courting someone?" Elsie asked. Perhaps the woman he'd been engaged to in San Francisco had come back into his life. It was possible Charles had taken up with someone in Sherwood Bay but kept it secret from her.

"I won't say anything more about that today, dear. But you see him so frequently you may hear before I do." She placed her teacup in its saucer on the table.

After that Mrs. Hayward drew Charles's mother into a long discussion about baby clothes, much to Elsie's chagrin.

When Mrs. Rockingham left, Elsie cornered her mother in the parlor.

"Mother, what is all this about Charles courting someone? Who is the woman?" She sat beside her on the sofa.

"I have no idea." She barely glanced up from her embroidery hoop, her needle working as fast as always.

"Charles has mentioned nothing about it to me."

"Oh, Elsie, why *would* he mention it to you? He must know you're still upset over Gabriel. He probably doesn't want to talk to you about such things."

It would certainly be like Charles to try to spare her feelings. She took the pins out of her hair and let it cascade over her shoulders. Her mother spared a look from her work to frown at her.

"Do you know who the woman is?" Elsie asked again.

"Lily didn't say." Mrs. Hayward picked up her work to peer at it closely.

"Do let me know if you hear anything else about it."

"I will. Or you could ask Charles yourself," she said, recommencing her work.

"No, I don't want to pry." To be truthful, she did want to pry but felt it would be rude considering the delicate nature of the situation.

Elsie met her father in the library for two games of chess, and afterwards they each selected a book to read until suppertime.

She excused herself from dessert, choosing instead to go upstairs to her bedroom. She engaged in one activity after another, trying to keep her thoughts at bay. When the sun went down, she stood beside the window, waiting for fireflies to appear in the garden below. Over an hour later, she changed into her nightgown and climbed into bed, but too many memories of Gabriel were swimming in her mind for her to sleep.

Soon after Charles left for San Francisco, Gabriel had started calling on her more often. She'd thought nothing of it. It was Margaret who first gave her the idea that Gabriel might have something in mind besides friendship. Elsie had scoffed at the idea, but every time she came home from school for the holidays or for summer break, Gabriel was there—scrubbed clean and smartly dressed. He took her on walks, invited her to supper, sometimes even to the nickelodeon. Elsie began to suspect that Margaret was right about his intentions.

But in the back of her mind, there was always Charles. She couldn't forget their night on the beach before he went away. He'd almost kissed her, and that changed everything. It triggered something deep inside her and allowed her to think about him in a whole new way. She was certain that Charles would stay in touch with her, perhaps even begin courting her the next time he came home. But he hadn't come home.

And there was Gabriel. Attentive, thoughtful, amusing. She would never say that she had settled for Gabriel. She had cared about him, had even grown to love him. She'd had some hope of their future happiness together. True, Gabriel had some habits that she didn't like, but she chose to look past them. Like the drinking. He was never drunk in her presence but spent too many evenings with a bottle within reach. When she mentioned it to him, he told her he was only having fun and would stop once he had a wife. He would take her hand and gently touch her bare ring finger. At other times, he would be secretive, not talking to her when something was clearly troubling him.

And then there was that incident she tried hard to forget but still lingered like the scent of old perfume on her clothes.

She was going to the harbor to surprise Gabriel with a basket of oatmeal cookies she herself had baked, his favorite kind. It was a gloriously sunny day just weeks after they'd become engaged. That sharp, woodsy scent of dried leaves swirled in the air.

She wanted to talk to him about the wedding—if he took the spot on the *Kraken*, they'd have to delay it even longer.

Halfway down the steep street that led to the docks, she turned a corner and stopped cold. She saw Gabriel at the bottom of the hill. But he clearly did not see her. A pretty woman Elsie had never seen before was leaning against a brick building. Gabriel stood in front of her, holding her hands and shaking his head. The deep murmur of his voice reached Elsie, but she couldn't make out the words.

Elsie turned to go back up the hill but thought better of it. She continued on, slowly, her eyes never leaving them. A prickle of something icy ran up her spine.

Gabriel put an arm around the woman, and they started walking up the street, he whispering in her ear, she giggling. Suddenly Gabriel looked up, and his face drained of all color. He removed his arm from the woman and practically shoved her away from him. She furtively glanced at Elsie then disappeared down a side street.

Gabriel strode up the hill, his dimples back in place by the time he reached her. "Elsie," he said, taking her elbow. "Why didn't you tell me you were coming?"

"Who was that woman?" She yanked her arm out of his grip.

"Woman?" He ran a hand over the back of his head as he turned to look down the street. "Oh, that's just the widow of an old friend. You wouldn't know her."

"Which friend?" She crossed her arms, the cookie basket dangling off one hand.

"You don't believe me?" he asked, a pained look on his face.

"Should I? You were holding her hands." She kept her eyes on his. He didn't look away. Perhaps she was overreacting.

"Of course you should. You know me."

Elsie simply thrust the cookie basket at him and marched back up the street.

"Wait!" He easily caught up to her and jogged backward up the hill, not letting her pass. "Don't tell me you're going to be a jealous wife," he said, on the verge of laughing.

She came to a stop. "I'm not jealous."

"She needed my help. She's trying to track down the captain of her husband's ship to see if he has any back pay. That's all. I can't turn down a lady in distress, now, can I?"

He edged his way closer and put a hand on her waist.

She looked into his unguarded eyes. She didn't want him to think she would be jealous of every woman he talked to. And there would be many; he was that type of man. She hoped that once they were married, he would stop being so friendly with any woman who crossed his path. She ignored a squeamish feeling in her stomach. There was no sense worrying about the future when he was beside her right now.

Elsie lifted a shoulder, her eyes averted. "Of course you should help her."

"I'll likely never see her again. Now what did you come down for, besides the cookies?" He took the basket, and before she could speak, he added, "And no, there are no letters from Charles. He must be very busy with his fiancée to stop writing to you."

"I wasn't going to ask about letters. I wanted to talk to you about the *Kraken*. If you don't go, we can be married two months sooner."

He put his hand in his pocket.

"I told you—it's done. I can't go back on my word just because a certain young lady took her time in accepting my proposal." His voice was light, but his green eyes had a flinty core.

"But if they understood the circumstances…"

"No. I have my reputation to think of if I'm going to be captain someday. Besides, we can do with the money after the wedding."

"You're right. It's only that I don't want to wait any longer than necessary."

"I can hardly wait to call you mine. If it was up to me, the ship would not be going out so late in the year. I'd much rather stay home with you." Gabriel slung an arm around her and kissed her cheek.

"You may already call me yours, for that's what I am."

He stopped walking and pulled her into an embrace, right there on the street, and looked into her eyes. "I'll make you a good husband."

"I know you will."

He took her home, and she forgot about the incident until later, when she was overcome with doubt as she lay in bed that night.

He never mentioned the woman again but Elsie assumed she lived in the same neighborhood as Gabriel, because she would see her from time to time when she walked that way.

If they were to be married, there should be no secrets between them. She assumed that after the wedding he would open himself up to her more. That perhaps, in time, with love and understanding, Gabriel would change. Elsie guessed many women looked the other way when confronted with the unpleasant behavior of their fiancés, even husbands. No, life with Gabriel had been far from perfect. But she would never have expected him to be so mercenary as to marry her for anything other than love.

After a while, she drifted off to sleep. But the uneasiness since talking to Matthew never quite went away.

****

A week later, Elsie was sitting at the vanity in her bedroom, pinning up her hair. Tonight was her party. On her last birthday, Gabriel had taken her on a picnic and given her a necklace with a silver anchor on it. After what Matthew had told her, she wasn't sure she'd ever wear it again.

She crossed the room to the full-length mirror and ran her hands over the bodice of her new gown. The deep, square neckline was quite a bit lower than she remembered from the fittings. At least the color was perfect: peacock blue, with aqua beads stitched into the short sleeves and tiered skirt. Her bright eyes held a hint of the lustrous shades of the gown.

After a knock on the door, Margaret entered, looking like a little sun fairy in her yellow gown.

"Do you think I should add lace?" Elsie asked, turning from side to side in the mirror. "The seamstress appears to have forgotten an inch or two of silk." She tugged at the bodice.

Margaret came over for a closer look. "Absolutely not. You look beautiful and that gown is perfect on you."

Elsie tucked in a stray lock of hair that was already making a bid for escape, and they went downstairs.

"Happy Birthday!" her mother said when she reached the parlor.

In the middle of the room, a magnificent three-layer cake sat on a round table. Plates and forks were piled up next to it, as well as glasses full of champagne.

Elsie tried not to stare at the crowd packed into the room. Yes, crowd. Everyone was standing, all eyes on her. She'd been expecting an intimate family party. There were at least a dozen young men that Elsie knew only vaguely, if at all. She wondered where her mother had found them. A number of women from her grammar-school days were also in attendance. Mr. and Mrs. Rockingham and Elsie's parents stood beside the table.

From the back corner, James waved with a brilliant smile. Everyone joined in a rousing round of the birthday song and afterward enjoyed the vanilla cake. Someone handed her a glass, and her father made a toast. Elsie wandered through the room, chatting with people, growing more relaxed as the evening wore on. It was the most delightful time she'd had in months and she was glad her mother had insisted on the party.

When the band started to play, Mrs. Hayward had a parade of young men on hand to dance with Elsie for every song, but none of them made the impression her mother had been hoping for.

Late in the evening, Elsie retreated to the back garden, though she knew her mother wanted her to mingle more with the guests. The beach was tantalizingly close, only a few streets away, but it wouldn't do to desert her own birthday party. She went into the gazebo and looked up at the stars.

"May I join you?"

"Jim!" she exclaimed, a smile lighting up her face.

James was striding across the lawn, carrying two champagne glasses. He leapt up the three steps into the gazebo and licked his finger where a bit of the bubbly had spilled. There was no other word to describe him besides "polished." He was dressed in a finely cut black suit and had swapped out his bowler for a top hat, which he removed and set down on the railing after handing Elsie her champagne. His dark hair was slicked back from his face, and he wore an expression that made him look almost haughty. Nobody would expect him to be full of high jinks, unless they were his friend, and James considered everyone he met a friend.

"Happy Birthday," he said, clinking his glass to hers.

"Thank you." She took a sip of the golden drink.

"Are you enjoying yourself?" He leaned against the

railing and crossed his ankles.

"Very much. But it feels odd having a birthday party without Charles here."

"Yes, it does. I'd expect him to be in there with you, fighting over who was allowed to blow out the candles."

She let out a loud, merry laugh. "He hasn't done that for quite some time."

Elsie and Charles had shared many birthday parties, but she never minded. Having him with her only added to the fun. Except when he tried to blow out all the candles—and he had been known to take more than his fair share of cake.

"Speaking of Charles, I have a letter from him. He asked me to give you a birthday greeting." He gave her a kiss on each cheek.

"I will count that as a gift from both of you," she said, eyes shining.

James lifted his glass to her. It occurred to Elsie that he would be the perfect person to ask about Charles's courtship. After all, they'd spent all those years together in California.

She set her glass down and shifted a little closer to him. Her tone was light, as if asking about the weather. "James, do you know anything about Charles and a woman in California?"

"Do you mean Amelia?"

She knew he wouldn't let her down, but such a fast and forthright answer proved especially satisfying. "Who is Amelia?"

He almost choked on his champagne. "Didn't Charles tell you about her?" he asked, swiping at the droplets dripping down his tie.

"No. Your mother mentioned he's possibly courting

someone. But she couldn't—or wouldn't—tell me who."
She stood in front of James, who had the look of a
cornered animal.

"Amelia is a woman we met in California."

"And she's a friend of Charles's?" Something
tightened in her chest. But why should she be jealous?
He had a right to have a friend.

"They did see quite a bit of each other around the
excavation site." James drained his champagne glass.

"And you met her, too? What's she like?"

James looked to the sky for a long moment.
"Amelia's lovely. Very pretty. Smart."

A slight chill ran though her despite the warm
evening. Had this Amelia taken her place? Perhaps that
was why Charles had stopped writing to her—because
he'd found a new, "lovely" friend in California? Even
though Gabriel had said Charles was engaged, the
woman had been a nameless phantom. Now she had
taken form: Amelia. But was this the same woman?
Certainly if Charles had proposed to her, James would
have known about it.

"Were they very close?" Closer than she and
Charles had been before he went away?

A tinkling waltz could be heard coming from the
house.

James wrinkled his brow and waited a beat before
answering. "I thought so, at the time…" He trailed off.

"Close enough to be considered courting?"

"Well, he came home, didn't he? Amelia is still in
California. There's only so much courting he can do
through the post." A few tiny beads of sweat appeared
on his forehead.

"Oh, are they in correspondence?"

"Yes, as far as I know. But shouldn't we get back to the party?" He craned his neck to look at the house.

"Did he propose?"

James's eyes widened. "Not that I'm aware of."

"Do you think he might marry her?"

"I don't know, Elsie. I can't really give you all the details. Look, why don't we go inside and dance. It's your birthday, and we haven't had a turn on the floor yet."

He offered her his arm and she took it, but she would rather have had his answer. They walked across the lawn to the house. Dusk was falling, and tiny fireflies flickered among the bushes at the edge of the garden. She wished Charles was here to see them.

The crowd inside had thinned considerably. James, always an excellent dancer, led her onto the floor.

"How long will you be in town?" she asked him as they moved through the steps.

"I only intended to stay for a week or so, but I've already stayed longer than I planned. There's something about Holderness that anchors me." His face took on a happy glow as he spotted his parents on the other side of the room.

"I'm sure your mother loves having you home." Mrs. Rockingham's gaze was following them around the dance floor.

"She has Harriet to dote on—she hardly needs me around as well. And, of course, baby Pammy."

"It's funny, none of my friends' mothers take such an interest in their grandchildren. Earlier today my mother gave me a detailed account of Brian's miraculous sleeping habits."

"It must be peculiar to our mothers, then, because

my mother can't get enough of Pammy." James whirled her around the dance floor until she was dizzy.

"Oh, Jim, do stop!" she said, laughing so much she could barely stay on two feet.

He pulled her to a standstill, keeping her in his arms until she'd regained her composure.

Before long the party broke up.

After wishing her parents good night, Elsie slowly climbed the stairs to her bedroom, shoes in her hands. It had been a surprisingly pleasurable evening.

****

For the next two weeks, Elsie's mother swept her along on social calls, shopping expeditions, visits to Margaret, and tea parties with Mrs. Rockingham. One damper was the near daily announcement by her mother that some young man or another "just happened to pop by" for supper. Elsie smiled at, talked with, and listened to each one all evening, so adept at feigning interest that even her mother could not fault her decorum.

The only bright spots were when James actually *did* come for supper, though Elsie strongly suspected her father had a hand in those invitations. Her mother would have to be delusional to think of a match with him. Elsie loved him, of course, but as the older brother she'd never had.

Sitting in her parents' garden one morning, Elsie knew it was time to leave. She'd lingered in Holderness far longer than she'd intended. Coming here had done nothing to assuage her grief. If anything, it had added to it. The revelations from Matthew were shocking. Elsie hadn't spoken to Margaret about Gabriel again, but he was ever present in her mind. It was obvious now that he had not been all that he seemed. What she had *thought* she knew about him was slipping away, and it felt like losing him a second time.

More than anything, she wanted to see Charles. Here in the garden, where they had whiled away so many days as children, she felt his absence more than anywhere else. She hadn't even written to him since she left Sherwood Bay.

She walked into town and sent Max a telegram, letting him know she would arrive tomorrow evening. Then she went home to tell her parents. Her mother was alone in the library.

"But you've only just arrived!" Mrs. Hayward said, putting her book down and giving Elsie a doleful look.

"I've been here for over a month." Elsie sat next to her on the sofa and pulled her feet up onto the cushions, resting her chin on her knees.

"But that's not long. Perhaps you should stay through the summer."

"I really must get back."

Her mother gently pushed her feet to the floor without a word. "But why? There's so much more to do here. I have a supper party planned for next week."

Elsie wondered what men in town she had not been introduced to already. Or perhaps her mother was starting over with the list of men Elsie had met on her birthday.

"I told Max I'd be back weeks ago."

"But wasn't going to Max's just to get away for a short time?"

"I like Sherwood Bay, and I want to help Max with his fossil research. And there's too much here to remind me of Gabriel." Even their home reminded her of him. He'd come to call so often there wasn't a room in the house he hadn't been in—except her bedroom.

"Elsie, it has been almost six months. That's more than sufficient time for mourning a fiancé. It's time you started taking an interest in your future." She crossed her arms over her chest, like a wall against Elsie's reply.

Elsie took a moment to compose herself. It wouldn't do to argue with her mother the night before she left. She kept her voice calm as she spoke.

"I've only recently come to terms with my past. I have ample time to think about my future. It's true I'm not grieving as I was months ago, but that does not mean the pain is gone, nor Gabriel's memory. I have no intention of courting anyone right now, let alone getting engaged."

"But I've introduced you to so many nice young men. There must be one of them that caught your fancy," her mother implored.

"No, there isn't. And I would appreciate it if you would stop trying to foist potential husbands on me. If I ever love again"—Mrs. Hayward reached for her smelling salts—"it will be a man of my own choosing. Fate brought Gabriel to me. Perhaps destiny will bring someone new into my life. But I doubt I will meet him at one of your supper parties."

Her mother leaned back against the cushions, fanning her face with her hand.

"You might at least give them a chance. Some of them are quite charming."

"Mother..."

"I suppose there's nothing I can do to change your mind?"

"Not a thing."

Mrs. Hayward clicked her tongue. "You are so

stubborn."

Elsie met her mother's eyes but did not utter the words on the tip of her own tongue. Based on the glare her mother was giving her, there was no need to say them out loud.

After a few moments, her mother spoke again, defeated. "Well, I do hope you'll let Father travel with you to Sherwood Bay this time."

"Oh, you're going back?" her father asked as he walked into the room.

"Yes. And I'm perfectly capable of traveling by myself. Women today don't need chaperones for every little thing."

"Traveling all the way to Sherwood Bay is not a little thing," Mrs. Hayward said.

"I've done it twice by myself. You don't need to worry."

"I do worry. And it would do no harm to postpone leaving for a week. I've already sent out the party invitations."

Elsie was about to remind her of the conversation they'd had not five minutes ago, but her father spoke.

"She knows her own mind, Laura. Elsie can travel by herself, she's not a little girl anymore." He gave Elsie a smile before sinking into his arm chair.

"Well, Nicholas, you said just the other day how much you like having Elsie home."

"I do, but she's enjoying her time at Max's. Let her have her fun," he said and picked up his paper.

Mrs. Hayward deflated into her seat and turned back to Elsie. "I hope you won't stay away so long this time."

"I'll most likely stay through the summer."

Her mother didn't reply but crossed the room and

settled herself at a table, where she took up her embroidery and jabbed it.

After supper Elsie and her father played backgammon while Mrs. Hayward sat beside them, extolling the many virtues of Timothy Boisvert, the young man Elsie would have met at the party. Close to ten o'clock she finally went upstairs to pack, then went straight to bed.

Chapter Seven

Elsie arrived in Portsmouth just as stars were emerging from the indigo darkness. Charles appeared the moment she stepped off the train.

"Good evening, Elsie." His hair was windswept as if he had been outside for a long time. The sight of him chased the chilly dampness away. It had only been a month since she'd seen him, but it felt like much longer. She wanted to wrap her arms around him the way she'd done when they were young, but she just beamed and placed a hand on his arm.

"Charles," she said, her fatigue disappearing at once. "What brings you here? Was Tom busy?"

"No, Max told me you'd be arriving tonight, and I wanted to meet you." He was looking at her as though they'd been apart for a year.

"That was sweet. Thank you."

"Do you have a trunk?" He peeked into the coach she'd just exited.

"No, only my suitcase. I checked it with the porter."

"I'll find it and meet you at the buggy." He put his hands in his pockets and strolled into the station.

Elsie climbed into the front seat of Max's Concord buggy, and before long Charles came over with her suitcase and secured it to the back.

When he took the seat next to her, she said, "Happy Birthday!" and handed him a box wrapped in brown paper, along with a bundle of slightly wilted lilacs.

Charles laughed and brought the flowers to his nose. "They smell like home."

He *sounded* like home. Some tiny place inside her felt calm for the first time in weeks.

"Open your present." She already knew he'd love it.

He looked at her and grinned, then unwrapped the package. Inside was a box of saltwater taffy from the candy store they'd frequented as children.

"My favorites. I haven't had them since I went to California. Thank you, Elsie."

He opened the box right away, put a taffy in his mouth, and closed his eyes, chewing slowly. He gave her a blissful smile and offered her the box. She took one and ate it as he started driving.

"Have I missed much while I was away?" she asked. A strong wind rustled the leaves overhead.

"We've taken a few shipments, but nothing of interest." He faced forward, loosely holding the reins.

"Have you called on anyone, or been to any balls?" she asked, trying to see his profile in the semidarkness.

"Balls! You know I avoid such things when I can."

"I've always wondered about that. You're a very good dancer."

"Not as good as James."

"I'd argue the point, but I just danced with him at my birthday party. He also came over for supper a few times." Elsie removed her hat and held it in her lap, enjoying the evening breeze in her hair.

"I almost wish I'd gone with you," Charles said wistfully. "Although it sounds like you had a full social calendar for such a spontaneous visit."

"I did. My mother's trying to marry me off," she

said with a mirthless laugh. She knew she sounded ungrateful—indeed she didn't like being paraded like a horse at the fair—but there was really no other way to explain it.

"Already?" he asked with a disapproving note in his voice. "But what about Gabriel?"

He slowed the horse to a walk as they started up the hill.

"My mother never liked Gabriel as my groom. She must have introduced me to twenty different men while I was home. I don't know where she found them all. I suppose she's eager to replace him with someone of her choosing."

After a moment he cleared his throat and asked, "Did anyone catch your eye?"

"No. Even if someone had, I'm not ready to begin a new relationship."

Charles nodded, and they continued in silence for a while. The only sounds were the whistling wind in the trees, the horse's creaking harness, and the hooves on the road. He came to a stop at the top of the hill. Far below, the ocean stretched out in its infinite vastness. Moonlight peeked out from heavy gray clouds high above the trees.

"I always love this view," he said, his voice full of smooth contentment.

"I do, too. It's beautiful, and it means that home is just around the corner." She leaned back in her seat, taking a moment to appreciate it.

"Look," Charles said, touching her arm and pointing to the forest. "The fireflies are coming out."

Twinkling lights flittered among the trees that lined the road.

"Not as many as we've seen some nights," she said,

watching them weave in and out of sight.

"It's early yet."

After a few minutes, he clucked to the horse, who set off at a walk.

"Did you see my mother when you were in Holderness?" he asked.

"Yes, she and my mother get together as regularly as they ever did."

"Every Tuesday and Thursday," Charles said.

"And Sunday," they said together, looking at each other and breaking into laughter.

Before long they arrived at Max's. Charles dropped Elsie at the front of the house and drove to the stables. She mounted the steps, wrapped in that cozy feeling only a homecoming can bring. A welcoming light flickered to life in the window beside the door.

Mr. Anderson greeted her at the top of the porch stairs. "Good evening," he said with what could almost be considered a smile.

She stepped inside, and he closed the door after her, then took her coat.

"Good evening," she said, giving him a genuine smile in return. "Is my uncle home?"

"He's in the parlor, I believe." He hung her coat in the closet and went on down the hall.

Just then Max came out of the parlor and leaned on the banister. "A good journey? Productive?"

"Yes, but I'm glad to be back." She dropped her hat on the table beside the door.

"How did you find my sister?"

"Pleased as punch over her grandson," she said, joining him at the foot of the stairs. He smelled of pipe tobacco and whiskey. Or was it rum?

"She would be," he said with a grin. "Will you eat something?"

"No, Mother sent me on the train with a picnic lunch that would have served four hungry men."

"Then I'll say good night." Max turned to go up the stairs.

"Good night."

Elsie started to follow him but changed her mind when thunder rumbled in the far distance. If she hurried, she could get to the beach and back before the storm broke. She grabbed a light coat from the hook beside the back door on her way out. Invigorated by the stirring wind, she ran through the garden to the beach. It was her favorite kind of weather.

When her feet touched the sand she let out a happy sigh. After walking for a few minutes, she reached a driftwood log as big as a tree, its roots and branches removed or washed away years ago. With the tide as high as it was now, the log was close to the shoreline. She sat down in the sand and rested her back against the cold wood, facing the sea. The full moon reflected on the dark, undulating waves.

In the distance, the foghorn sounded. It was mournful yet held the sound of safety for those ships out on the water. She closed her eyes and listened to the gathering wind. Soon there came a new sound: rocks crunching under light steps. She didn't have to turn to know it was Charles.

He sat on the log, his knee almost touching her shoulder. "What are you doing out here, Elsie? A storm is coming."

"This has always been my favorite time on the beach," she said, craning her neck to look up at him.

"I know, and I've told you since we were children it isn't safe."

"We'll go in before the storm really hits." She turned her face into the wind.

"Are you ready to talk now about why you ran away?" Charles sounded like he was awaiting a confession.

She traced patterns in the sand with her fingers. "I wasn't running away."

"I know you, Elsie. Was it the wreck?"

"That was part of it," she said and looked out to sea.

"But not all?"

She turned to look at him. "It's nothing, really."

The wind picked up, bringing with it the first stinging drops of rain.

Charles swept the bangs off his face and met her eyes. "Like I said before, I know you."

Her stomach tightened.

He did know her.

She held his gaze. No matter how many years had gone by, he was still her best friend and she could trust him. She scrambled to her feet.

"I saw Matthew Newkirk in Holderness. He was on the *Kraken* with Gabriel." She cleared her throat, which was suddenly bone dry.

"Is that why you went there? To see him?"

"No, I bumped into him on the street. He told me something."

"About the day the ship sank?"

"Not about the ship, but about Gabriel. About Gabriel and me." She stood before him, wringing her hands.

"What did he say?"

"He said Gabriel only wanted to marry me for my money and my family's name," she blurted out, close to tears. Her hands flew to her mouth.

Charles stood up so fast he nearly tripped backward over the log. "I can't believe that of Gabriel!"

She wrapped her arms around herself, staring at the ground.

"Tell me exactly what this Matthew said. Perhaps you misunderstood."

Elsie recounted the whole conversation.

"Why would he say such a thing?" Charles asked, raising his voice to be heard over the wind.

"Because that's what Gabriel told him!" she said and threw her hands up.

"And you believe what Matthew told you?"

"I don't know what to believe. Maybe I never knew Gabriel," she said, rubbing her forehead.

"Of course you knew him. He was our friend for years," Charles insisted.

"But it was different after you left. *He* was different." She started walking back and forth along the beach.

"Different how?" He shadowed her steps and looked at first like he was going to put an arm around her, but instead he let it fall to his side.

"It was so subtle I doubt anyone else would have noticed it besides you and me. You weren't here; you can't understand what it was like. You were gone for so long, Charles. Around a year after you left, he started courting me. He came to my house almost every day to take me out. He was romantic, so kind and attentive." The wind tugged at her hair, loose tendrils swirled around her face.

"And you loved him enough to say yes when he proposed."

"I—well, I did say yes. But I shouldn't have."

Charles barely kept up with her frantic pacing.

"Why not? Why shouldn't you have?"

The thing that had been weighing down on her for months was finally coming through the surface, and she didn't have the strength to hold it back anymore.

"Because I wasn't in love with him!" Her tears started in earnest at the same time the clouds finally burst.

"What? Of course you loved him."

"Not enough, not the right sort of love! He was everything a fiance` should be. But there was something—I can't say what. Something wasn't right. That's what I meant when I said he changed after you left. He became someone else. He tried to be exactly the man he guessed I wanted. But it wasn't the real Gabriel. And there were other things amiss, too. The secrets, the company he kept. Even before he died, I thought the marriage might be a mistake, but I couldn't possibly call it off!"

"Elsie—"

"And now I find out that he didn't love me, that he didn't even want me. I was a means to an end to him." She let out a strangled cry of despair, hot tears mingled with the icy rain on her face.

"We don't know any of this for certain. It's only what Matthew told you."

"If I had loved him better, or stronger, or sooner, he wouldn't have died. He would never have been on that ship if I'd married him earlier, like he wanted." White, frothing waves came higher up the shore, swirling around their feet.

"You said yourself it may have been a mistake," he reasoned.

"But his staying alive would have been preferable!" she wailed.

Their eyes held for a long moment before he pulled her into his arms.

"It's all right, Elsie," he said, rubbing her back. "I'm here. I'm here."

She clung to him as she would to a raft in a churning sea. Encircled in his arms, she released the tears she had suppressed for so long. As he stroked her hair, her knees quivered, and the tension in her shoulders melted away. The strain of keeping her secret flowed out with her tears. When they finally ceased, she took a deep, shuddering breath and wiped her eyes on her rain-sodden sleeve. A peace she hadn't known for months enveloped her.

Water seeped into her collar and dripped down her back, finding its way through every article of clothing she had on. Her hair hung limp around her face. She looked at the sand and seriously considered lying down to sleep there.

"Let's get you home," Charles said.

Her teeth were chattering too much to attempt a reply, so she simply nodded.

The house was quiet, heat from the smoldering library fire beckoned. Elsie turned that way, but Charles reached for her hand.

"We need to change first," he said.

"I suppose you're right." A tiny river ran from her feet to the back door.

Charles kept an arm around her as they climbed the

stairs, then followed her into her bedroom, which was dark but for the hurricane lamp on her nightstand.

She stood in the middle of the room, dripping all over the floor. "Mrs. Holt will have my head when she sees this mess."

"It will dry by morning." He reached forward and undid the top button of her coat.

"Really, Charles," she tutted, and pushed his hand away. She unfastened the rest of the buttons and let him remove the coat from her shoulders. She stood there, soaked, in her dress, stockings, and shoes. A thunderclap boomed, and a flash of lightning lit up the sky.

"If I sit beside the fire downstairs, it will all dry on its own," she said, pulling at her soggy bodice.

"And you will catch cold to boot."

"You're just as wet as I am."

Charles's hair was plastered to his face. His beige trousers were now a muddy brown, and his waterlogged jacket hung loosely off his shoulders. "I'm going to my room to change. I'll be right back."

"You don't need to do that. Once I'm out of these wet things, I'm going to sleep." Her bed had never looked so welcoming.

"We need to talk, Elsie," he said and walked out the door.

Elsie paced around her room. What else need be said? Would Charles chastise her?

She sank into the chair in front of her vanity and turned on the lamp. A bunch of lilacs bound with green ribbon stood in a vase next to a pile of sea glass. A note in Charles's handwriting read, *Happy Birthday, Elsie.* Smiling, she leaned close to smell the lilacs before undressing and peeling off the cold, sandy stockings. It was doubtful they would ever be restored to their proper shape again. After toweling off, she slipped into the warmest nightgown she could find, then wrapped herself in a pale pink dressing gown. There was a knock on the door just as she finished braiding her damp hair. Charles entered, wearing a green dressing gown over his brown striped pajamas.

"Come downstairs with me," he said.

She silently followed him into the library, wondering what was coming. As rain lashed against the rattling patio doors, Elsie turned on lamps while Charles added logs to the fire. She sat on the edge of the sofa and stared at the flames.

He poured two glasses of sherry and retrieved a tin of ginger snaps from the sideboard before joining her. After taking a few cookies for himself, he handed the tin to Elsie. She ate one and sipped her sherry.

As they basked in the warmth of the crackling fire, it was Charles who broke the silence. "You can't seriously blame yourself for what happened to Gabriel."

She took a sip of sherry to ease the last bite of cookie past the lump that formed in her throat, then put her glass and the cookie tin on the floor. "If we'd been married, he never would have been on that ship." She looked at him with an expression that brooked no argument.

"Elsie—"

She held up her hand. "I should have accepted his proposal sooner. But I hesitated because, the whole time, I think, deep down, I knew."

"Knew?"

"That we weren't right for each other." She let out a long sigh and sank back into the cushions.

"Then why did you say yes?" He draped an arm over

the back of the sofa, angling toward her, and slid closer.

"I thought—at least hoped—that I was wrong, and we'd be happy. You know Gabriel. He was always so positive. When I was with him, it wasn't hard to imagine that we could make a go of it. I was swept away by how much he wanted the marriage. But now I see why." She cast her eyes down to her hands folded in her lap. "He was using me to escape the sea."

"Gabriel cared about you."

Elsie brushed away a tear. "I'm certain he did, but not as a husband should love a wife. I see that now. He cared about the opportunities he thought I could provide."

"Perhaps it would have changed."

"Perhaps. But now I'll never know. He would still be here if I'd said yes the first time he asked."

"You don't know what would have happened if you'd said yes earlier," he said, and she detected a hint of impatience creeping into his voice.

"No matter how much I tell myself it's not my fault, it feels like it is."

"It is *not* your fault! It could also be the fault of the man who captained the voyage, or the people who buy fish at the market, or the fault of the wind that day. You are not to blame, and you must stop trying to make yourself responsible for what happened." Her alarm at his vehement reaction must have shown on her face, because he took a moment to calm himself. "This is in the past. Gabriel is in the past. You must move on without him. And the only way to do that is to leave your perceived guilt behind as well."

"I've been trying to. These last months have been so difficult. Hearing that he died was devastating. And believing it was my fault has been a terrible burden. And…" She paused, barely holding back the sobs waiting to overtake her.

Charles took her hand and held it. "What?" he asked gently.

She looked at him through eyes brimming with tears. "Everyone believes I'm grieving because of how deeply I loved him. I feel I don't deserve their pity. I did love him, but not in that desperate way most women seem to love their betrothed. There's a hole here where he used to be," she said, pressing a hand to her heart. "And where our plans and dreams were. I have mourned him, and I still miss him, but knowing I had doubts about the marriage has tainted it all. I feel that I've betrayed him, and in order to make up for that, I should never let him go. But I want to. I have to."

"You didn't betray Gabriel by having doubts. You were going to marry him. You were going to keep your word. If he had lived, you would be married to him right now. So you needn't feel guilty about that." He paused for a moment. "And grief is not so simple. You're not mourning only your fiancé but your childhood friend."

Elsie nodded and wiped her eyes. "I know you're right. I wish you'd been here to talk to when it happened. It was such a lonely time. I haven't told anyone about my doubts, and the fear of it being my fault. I've only told you." She gripped his hand tightly and lifted her eyes to his. "You've always been my dearest friend. I only hope you will not think ill of me from now on."

"Nothing could make me think ill of you," he said, and she believed him.

They sat quietly together and listened to the storm. Thunder and lightning had given way to a steady rain and howling wind. Gradually the sky shifted from coal black to smoky gray. They had been up for most of the night.

Sleep was encroaching, but Elsie was too comfortable to move. She leaned her head against Charles's shoulder. "You were gone a long time."

"Yes, for too long. I regret so much that I wasn't here during those years." He put an arm around her. "But I'm home now."

****

It was still dark outside when Elsie woke up. The fire had grown cold. She and Charles had fallen asleep with his arm around her shoulders. She sat up at once, rubbing her eyes, and sighed happily. The weight she'd been carrying around for months was gone, and it was all due to Charles. He'd listened, understood, and supported her last night. Knowing she could still trust him with her innermost feelings was a balm to her soul.

"Good morning," Charles said sleepily, running a hand through his disheveled hair.

"Good morning. Can you believe we stayed here almost all night?"

"It wouldn't be the first time. Remember when we camped out in the fort we built but neglected to tell our parents? They were none too pleased."

"My mother had me inside mending curtains for a week after that," Elsie said with a grimace. She brought her feet up onto the sofa and hugged her knees to her chest.

Charles stood up and stretched his arms, then crossed the room to the French doors and swung them open. A taste of ocean rushed in with the cold predawn air. She went to stand beside him and heard enormous waves crashing onto the beach.

"A walk?" he asked, offering his arm.

"A fine sight we would be, traipsing along the beach in our dressing gowns. Besides, it would be prudent to return to our own rooms before the servants are awake." According to the mantel clock, it wouldn't be long now.

"Perhaps you're right."

They went upstairs together, but when he turned to go into his room, she took his hand.

"Thank you for being there for me last night," she said.

"I always will be." He squeezed her hand before going into his room and closing the door.

Elsie crossed the hall to her own room, feeling lighter than she had in months. She'd had no idea how heavy the burden of her secret had been. Her bed beckoned, but it was doubtful she could fall asleep even if she climbed under the soft covers. She rumpled the blankets; it wouldn't do to have Becky think she spent the night elsewhere.

She shrugged out of her dressing gown and sat in front of her round vanity mirror, brushing her hair. There was a castle's worth of sand in it. A bath was too tempting an idea to ignore. Her hair needed to be lathered and rinsed twice before it was free of sand. By the time she finished, the bottom of the bathtub had turned into her own private beach.

The scent of lilacs greeted her when she returned to her room. A fresh vase full of the delicate blossoms sat on her nightstand. Beside them was a note:

These may be the last of the summer.
—Charles

In the dining room, food was waiting on the sideboard. She chose a blueberry muffin, fried eggs, and strawberries, then sat at the table.

It was her first day of really breaking free of the past. Gabriel's death had brought her to a standstill, but now she had the chance to start over. The question was, what would she like to do? Today she was going to the photography club she'd read about at the library, but every day after was open to any possibility. Ideas were flitting through her mind when Max came in.

"Good morning," he said.

"Good morning."

"Why, Elsie!" he exclaimed, looking at her closely. "That shadow—it's gone!"

Elsie shook her head at him. "You have such fancies, Max."

At the sideboard, he heaped his plate with eggs, toast, and sausages.

"Whatever has helped your shadow to pass, I'm glad of it."

"Some things have become clear to me." She deemed it unnecessary to go into all the details of Gabriel's subterfuge.

"It shows. Now that that's taken care of, what will you do with yourself?"

"I was just pondering that. I wonder where I could find employment opportunities in town. Perhaps I could advertise in the newspaper."

"Aren't you assisting me with my collection?" he asked, sitting down beside her and buttering his toast.

"That won't take long. I've organized the lion's share already."

"It must be catalogued. Charles could help you."

Elsie considered this. It would be as good a way as any to fill her time, and she could seek other employment afterward if she wanted to.

"I have plans this morning, but I'll ask Charles about it when he comes down for breakfast."

"Oh, he's come and gone. Off to the office."

"I'll ask him later, then," she said, sorry to have missed him.

"Yes, do that," Max said, beginning his breakfast in earnest.

Right after her meal, Elsie walked into town. As she entered Bennington Square, she took the pamphlet out of her bag to read the address. The camera shop was tucked into a side street close to Max's office. *Wright's Cameras and Developing* was stenciled on a wooden sign above the window.

A bell jingled over the door when she stepped in.

"Good morning," a woman said. Her gray hair was swept into a tight bun, and she wore a gingham dress. A pair of oval spectacles sat on her nose.

"Good morning," Elsie said. "I'm here for the photography class."

The woman's face lit up. "I'm Mrs. Wright. I'll be your teacher."

"My name is Miss Hayward. It's nice to meet you. Do you own the shop?" From where she stood, Elsie surveyed the glass cases full of cameras and other items she'd never seen before.

"I run it with my husband," Mrs. Wright said, gesturing to a white-haired man sitting at a desk, fiddling with a camera.

Just then, the door opened, and Lucy and her friends came in, all carrying cameras.

"Hello, Elsie!" Lucy said. She and Nancy hurried to Elsie's side.

Grace merely offered a curt nod and went through a door to their right.

"I had no idea you were a photographer," Lucy said.

"I'm not. This is my very first class. Have you been attending for a long time?"

"Oh, yes. It must be over a year by now."

"We'd be happy to help you in any way we can," Nancy said. "There's so much to learn."

"Thank you," Elsie said.

Elsie followed Nancy and Lucy into the back room. It was furnished with sofas, chairs, and mismatched wooden side tables. The walls were covered with photographs. When the class began, Elsie sat with Nancy, Grace, and Lucy on one of the couches, choosing the seat farthest from Grace.

"Welcome, everyone," Mrs. Wright said, standing in front of them. "I trust you all had a good week. As you can see, your latest photographs have been developed and are on display. Today we will be walking into town to look for subjects. Are there any questions?"

Elsie had a hundred but didn't raise her hand. Nearly everyone else had questions about the composition of their subjects, or about technical things Elsie didn't understand.

When the group got up to look at their photos, Mrs. Wright sought Elsie out. "Would you like to try using the camera today, or wait until next week's class?"

"Today, please. What do I need to start?"

"I'll fetch one our spare cameras. Just a moment."

Mrs. Wright left the room and before long returned with a camera. She handed it to Elsie and pointed out the viewfinder and the shutter button. "It isn't so hard," she said kindly.

"No, it looks quite simple." Elsie examined the camera, which was not as fragile as she'd expected.

Mrs. Wright spent half an hour with Elsie, teaching her the basics of how to use it. She then gathered the class, and they went out the back door of the shop. For the most part, the group stayed together, but periodically someone would wander away if something caught her eye.

After taking instruction from Mrs. Wright for the first half of the outing, Elsie went in search of Lucy. She found her in a park with Grace and Nancy.

"Have you taken any photos yet?" Lucy asked.

"Yes, Mrs. Wright showed me how."

"Do you have any film left?" Nancy asked.

"Yes. Is it difficult to photograph moving objects? I thought I might try a boat."

"The first time I tried taking a picture of my dog Sam, he looked like a gray blur," Lucy said.

Nancy showed Elsie how to hold the camera steady. "Why not try stationary subjects first?"

Elsie noticed a burst of purple behind a wrought iron bench—lilacs. She took her time to focus the camera, then tentatively pushed the button.

They spent the next couple of hours wandering around town. It was a whole new way to see Sherwood Bay. Unexpected visions appeared when she looked through the lens: the scrolled ironwork under the baker's sign, angels on the library cornices, and the way Plainfield Street wound up and around the corner like a vine. In the end she did take some photos of moored ships, the *Puffer Fish* and the *Leviathan*.

After making their way back to the shop, her friends filed into the motorcar Nancy's father had sent for her.

Elsie bought a camera right away. Mrs. Wright helped her choose one appropriate for a beginner and taught her how to load film into it.

She left the shop and stopped at Griffith's Cafe for lunch, then spent the afternoon roaming into neighborhoods she hadn't visited in years, snapping photos of towering gas lamps, stained glass windows, and hourglass porch spindles.

Late in the day, she turned toward home. On impulse, she stopped by Max's office. Charles was locking the door, his back to the street. She focused her camera on him, hoping she was doing it correctly. When she pressed the button, the camera clicked, and Charles turned around.

His face lit up. "What's that you've got there?"

"My new camera. I went to a photography class today. It was such fun. Afterward I bought this." She held it up for him to see.

"That's an excellent thing to learn. I sat for a photographer when I was in San Francisco."

"I didn't know that."

"We haven't had very much time for long talks, have we?" Charles asked as they crossed Bennington Square, which was nearly empty. One carriage and a motorcar rolled by.

Most of the tables outside Griffith's and Cantwell's were vacant. Three children speeding past on bicycles were the only people who seemed to be in a hurry. Elsie guessed they were heading to McGoldrick's candy shop, which closed in ten minutes. High above the rooftops, mountains of puffy golden clouds floated across the endless blue sky.

"No, but I'd like to hear more about your time out

west."

"What do you want to know?"

Elsie put her hands behind her back like she was reciting a poem at school. Her camera swayed on the strap around her neck. "What did you like best, and what did you miss about home? How did you like living there?"

Charles tilted his head, apparently gathering his thoughts. "It was interesting to see another part of the country. The deserts are beautiful, and the mountains are much bigger than anything we have here. But I missed our quiet coastline. There were many things I missed about home."

"How did you become interested in fossils?"

"I took a paleontology class at school. The professor was a friend of my uncle Richard's. It was he who took me to my first excavation site, and I went on my own a few times after that."

"Did you make any new friends in San Francisco?" Her voice went up an octave. She cleared her throat.

"A few. I spent most of my time with Uncle Richard and his family. James and I shared an apartment above his shop."

As they walked along, she debated about whether to ask or not.

She probably shouldn't.

But she had to know.

"Charles, I've been hearing some things about you."

"Such as?" he asked, glancing at her with a grin.

"About you and someone named Amelia," she said, watching his face closely.

He tripped over a rock—or his own two feet—and skidded to a halt.

"Who told you about Amelia?"

"James."

"What did he say?" Charles shifted his shoulders as though trying to loosen his jacket.

"He said you knew her from the excavation site, and that she was your friend. A rather special one."

Charles set off again. "You should know by now not to believe everything James tells you," he said over his shoulder.

Elsie quickened her step to keep up with him. "Was he right about Amelia being a special friend?"

"Amelia is… We've been writing to each other since I came home."

"Corresponding? Is that all? James seemed to think…" Her voice trailed off as soon as she saw his shoulders square. They continued for a few moments in silence. His clenched jaw should have made her reconsider her next question.

"Are you courting her? Amelia?"

He looked at her with brows raised so high they nearly disappeared under his hat. "Courting her? Elsie, who planted these ideas in your head? Is it James, or are you coming up with them all on your own?" He sounded irritated, angry, and embarrassed. It was hard to tell which emotion was winning out.

"I overheard our mothers talking when I was in Holderness," she admitted sheepishly, scrunching up her face.

"It's really nobody's business. Why is everyone talking about me?"

"*Everyone* isn't."

"My mother shouldn't be telling anyone that I'm courting. I never told her that I was."

An unexpected wave of relief rushed through Elsie. But she didn't stop there.

"So…so you're only friends?"

"Elsie, must we delve into this?" he asked, turning to scowl at her.

"No," she said, "not if it's private."

"Yes, it is," he snapped.

"I understand." She pressed her lips together. She understood much more than he realized.

After a silent ten minutes, they reached the house.

"It smells like we're in time for supper," he said and mounted the porch steps without her.

Chapter Eight

Elsie mulled over Charles's reaction as she went upstairs to change. He'd given her some indication that James was right about Amelia, even if Charles wouldn't admit it. If he wasn't romantically attached to her, why wouldn't he confirm that they were only friends instead of evading her questions?

The sound of the cuckoo clock chiming reminded Elsie it was time for supper. After washing her face and tidying her hair, she changed into a rose-colored dress. She considered bringing her camera downstairs but ultimately left it on the window seat. If Max saw it, he wouldn't want to discuss anything else, or more likely he would want to dismantle it to figure out how it worked.

Elsie's stomach rumbled loudly when she entered the dining room. Judith had outdone herself in the kitchen. She'd prepared lobster for the main course tonight, with corn on the cob, green beans, biscuits, and apple jelly. Bowls of lemon slices and melted butter sat beside each plate. Max, Elsie, and Charles served themselves off the heaping platters. For dessert they had coffee and sweet, creamy bread pudding still warm from the oven. The food was delicious but so rich Elsie had to recline in her seat after eating.

After supper they went into the library, where Max sat in his favorite chair beside the hearth and lit his pipe. The earthy smell of tobacco filled the room as Charles and Elsie went to the sofa. She kicked her shoes off and tucked her feet under her. When she smiled at Charles, he looked away. His eyes suggested he was far from their little corner of the world.

"What did you do with yourself today, Elsie?" Max asked, puffing away.

She told him about the photography class and her new camera.

"Would you be willing to photograph my fossils?" His eyes lit up at the prospect.

"I'd be happy to." Fortunately, fossils couldn't move.

"In fact," Max said, pointing his pipe at her, "perhaps a photographic record of my collection to go along with the inventory you made. I could pay you. Then you'd have no need to find a job."

"Really, Max," Elsie said. "I don't need to be paid. It will be good practice with my camera."

"Excellent. Could we persuade you to help, Charles?" Max asked. "Charles?"

Charles looked up at Max, his brow furrowed as though trying to recall the last sentence he'd heard.

"Oh, yes. I'll be happy to help," he said at last.

"All settled then." Max stood up abruptly. "Well, I'm off. I have papers waiting for me on my desk. Charles, be sure to tell Elsie about that Star Island idea." And with that, he left the room.

Charles was biting his thumbnail, his eyes unfocused. She couldn't believe he still did that when he was perturbed.

Since he showed no sign of speaking, she said, "I'm sorry I pestered you earlier about your friend in California. It's really none of my business. In the past, we told each other everything. I forgot for a moment that we're not children anymore. I'll keep my questions to a minimum in future."

Charles raised his head, an amused yet incredulous look on his face. "I think we both know you'll still have questions. But I may not have answers."

She could live with that. She'd rather not hear any more about Amelia. "So I remain overly curious, and you answer only what you deem necessary?"

"Yes," he said and laughed. She was glad to see the worry lines disappear.

"What's the Star Island idea Max mentioned?"

"Star Island is off the coast of Portsmouth. It has a hotel and beautiful grounds. Max and I went out the day after I moved here. I think you'd enjoy seeing it." He turned on the sofa so that one of his knees was almost touching her foot.

"It sounds interesting. Yes, let's go there sometime."

"There's a large ferry that takes hotel guests out. I think it's daily. I'll look into it."

"Wonderful," Elsie said, always eager for a new place to explore. "Perhaps I could bring my camera." She shivered at the thought of going out on a ship—she hadn't been to sea since Gabriel died—but she couldn't avoid sailing for the rest of her life.

"You could photograph the chapel and the birds. There's an enormous population of seagulls."

The clock chimed ten o'clock, and Elsie yawned. "I'd better be off to bed," she said, lacing up her shoes.

"You must be tired after last night," Charles said.

"I'd guess that you are, too."

"Yes, I think I'll turn in myself."

They walked upstairs together, parting when they reached Charles's door.

****

As soon as Elsie's eyes fluttered open, she knew it wasn't morning. She burrowed her face into the lavender-scented pillow, hoping to fall asleep again at once. Snuggled under the blankets and on the verge of sleep, she heard a soft cry. Soft moonlight illuminated her room as she lit the hurricane lamp beside her bed and looked around. There was nothing out of the ordinary. Whatever the sound was, it was not coming from inside her room. She couldn't go back to sleep without knowing what it was.

She hopped out of bed and put on her slippers, not bothering with a dressing gown. Her lamp cast dancing shadows upon the walls as she crept down the hall, failing to avoid the creaky step on the way downstairs.

In the entryway, she stopped for a moment to listen. The sound came from the direction of the library.

Lights were still glowing there, and a low fire burned behind the grate. Max must have only recently gone to bed. She began to search, looking into corners and under furniture, wondering if it had only been the wind whistling through the trees.

Then she heard it once more—outside.

She crossed the room and opened the French doors, her lamp held high. Nothing on the flagstone patio, but just outside the ring of light—a movement in the bushes. Inching closer, she dropped to her knees to peer under a lilac bush.

A short gasp escaped her as something edged its way out: a kitten!

Elsie immediately picked it up and held it close as it

shivered from fear or from fright. There was no sign of any other cats under the bush. How had it ended up alone in the lilacs? She cuddled it close and went straight to the fireplace, set her lamp on the mantel, and settled herself on the thick hearth rug. The kitten was still mewing, but it had stopped shivering.

Charles appeared in the doorway in his pajamas and dressing gown. "Elsie?"

She jumped and almost dropped the kitten. "Charles! What are you doing awake?"

"You're still not very good at being stealthy, Elsie." He laughed quietly.

She rolled her eyes. "Perhaps not. But I, too, was drawn downstairs by a noise."

"What have you got there?" He moved closer to get a better look at what she held in her lap: a gray tabby with white chest and legs.

"It was all alone in the garden. I could hear it crying from upstairs."

She handed him the kitten, which looked tiny in his large hands, and got up to stand beside him as he stroked the small bundle of fur.

"It must have come from the stables," he said. "There are so many cats down there."

She felt a strong desire to keep the kitten with her. It mewed again.

"I think it's hungry," she said.

"I'll go get some milk from the kitchen." He handed the kitten back to her.

"Be sure to warm it. And perhaps bring back a spoon. It may not know how to drink from a dish." She scratched under its chin.

"I will," he said with an indulgent smile.

"Don't make a mess in there. Judith will notice if anything is amiss when she gets up to make breakfast."

"I'll be tidy, don't worry."

Elsie took the kitten back to the fireplace and held it in her lap as it batted the strings of her nightgown. It looked around three months old. One quick peek and Elsie deduced it was female.

Before too long, Charles returned. Sitting beside Elsie on the rug, he placed the dish on the floor. The kitten took one precautionary sniff and started lapping up the milk.

"Oh, she likes it!" Elsie said.

"It's a girl?"

"I checked while you were gone."

"You're keeping her, aren't you?" He smiled, meeting her eyes.

"Yes, I'm keeping her. And I already know what I'll name her: Luna, because the moon is so big and bright tonight."

"Luna," Charles said, picking her up. "Yes, she looks like Luna."

He handed her back to Elsie, who held her close. Milk clung to Luna's nose and whiskers.

"I suppose I should get back to bed," she said.

"So should I. It's getting late. Or rather, early." He turned the light off on their way out and followed Elsie upstairs to her bedroom.

"Where will Luna sleep?" he asked, surveying the room.

"She will sleep with me in my bed."

"I'm sure she could not ask for a more comfortable spot."

"Thank you for your help tonight. You always seem

to appear when I need you."

"It's my pleasure. Good night, Elsie. And good night, little Luna," he said, giving the kitten a pat.

Elsie closed the door after him and crawled into bed with the kitten. Luna snuggled close and they both slept.

When Elsie woke up the next morning, Luna was resting in the crook of her neck. She picked her up and brought her close to her face, where she noticed her bright green eyes and very short whiskers. She put Luna on the floor, and the kitten tottered around the room, sniffing at things. Elsie dressed, then picked her up and brought her downstairs to the dining room.

Max and Charles were already eating a breakfast of orange omelets, fruit, and toast.

She sat down across from Max, who asked, "What have you got there, Elsie?" He folded his newspaper and placed it on the chair next to him. Freshly shaven, he looked debonair dressed in one of his best suits.

"I found her last night in the garden. Isn't she darling? Her name is Luna."

Luna squirmed out of Elsie's hand and crawled across the table to sniff at the butter. Elsie brought her back and poured some milk into her tea saucer. She lapped it up right away.

"So what will you do with the little mongrel?" Max asked.

"She can sleep in my room and play outside during the day." She buttered her toast, then applied liberal amounts of marmalade, keeping her eyes on Luna.

"I think she'll miss the company of the other cats down at the stables," Max said.

"Isn't she young to leave her litter?" Charles asked.

"I've had kittens her age before. She's definitely old

enough to be away from her mother, and she drinks well enough from a dish."

Luna was splashing milk everywhere while she drank from the saucer.

"In that case, let her spend the day at the stables and bring her up to the house to sleep some nights," Max said.

"That's a splendid idea."

"Let's take her down there now," Charles said.

"Not yet," Elsie said, picking Luna up and holding her while she cleaned a paw.

Mr. Anderson appeared in the dining room, holding a silver tray. "The post has arrived," he said to Max, "and the carriage is ready to leave at your convenience."

Max nodded and took the mail off the tray. "Thank you, and tell Tom I'll be out momentarily."

Mr. Anderson gave a bow and left the room.

Charles sat up straight, his eyes on the letters as Max rifled through the mail.

Each time Max pursed his lips, Elsie guessed he was reading a bill. Then his face brightened, and he broke into a grin.

"Here's one for you, Elsie, from your mother." He handed it to her.

Just getting started on her omelet, Elsie set it down next to her plate to read after breakfast.

Max scrutinized the address of another envelope. His eyes widened, and he looked at Charles.

"And one for you, from—"

Charles instantly reached across the table and grabbed it out of Max's hand. "I'll take it," he said, and crammed it into his pocket. He took a gulp of coffee that sloshed down his shirt. He dabbed at it with a napkin but

125

only managed to spread the stain. Muttering something to himself, he pierced his omelet with a fork.

Elsie and Max exchanged a curious look across the table. She had a good idea where that letter had come from, but after apologizing for prying last night, she kept her questions to herself.

"Charles," Max said, "I hoped you'd help Elsie with identifying some of my specimens today. She made a bit of a mess of it." He threw her a look that was half-apologetic, half-amused.

"A mess?" she asked.

"Only because you don't know what you're sorting, my dear."

"Today would be a good day to start," Charles said as he rose from the table. "The *Sea Tiger*'s been delayed again, so I'll have some spare time on my hands."

"I'll get a basket for Luna and meet you in the study after I've finished my breakfast," she told him. Luna was curled up in the crook of Elsie's arm, which was adorable but made it impossible to finish eating.

"And don't forget to take photographs," Max said.

"We won't," Elsie said. "What are you doing today, Max?"

"I have some business in town. I'll be out for most of the day." With that he got up, leaving his napkin in a heap alongside a pile of crumbs.

Charles sat on the edge of the table and took Luna from Elsie. He put her right into his coat pocket. She fit perfectly and didn't even stir.

"I'll take her to the study," he said. "You stay here and finish your breakfast." He walked away, keeping one hand in Luna's pocket.

The letter was sticking out of his other pocket. The

envelope was covered in neat, flowery script. Elsie suspected it also smelled flowery.

Chapter Nine

After breakfast Elsie sipped her coffee in front of the window. A fishing boat was just visible on the horizon. It brought Gabriel to mind, of course. She hardly knew what to think of him anymore. He was clearly not the besotted, lovestruck man he had pretended to be. Yet she could not so easily drive him from her thoughts. Whatever had happened when they were adults, he'd been her friend for years before that.

The grief still lingered but felt lighter somehow. She didn't blame herself for his death anymore, and that made all the difference. Perhaps letting go of her guilt would allow her to, over time, let go of him. Gabriel himself had told her to always look forward, not back.

She went back to the table and opened her mother's letter.

Dear Elsie,

I hope this letter finds you well. Would you be able to get away for a few days? I'm hosting a party next week. David Doane will be coming and I think you would enjoy his company. His father owns that lumber yard just outside of town. Do write and tell me if you will be able to attend. Margaret will be here. I will invite James also. Please do write.

—Mother

David Doane? Elsie hadn't seen him since grammar school. Her mother was truly grasping at straws. She'd be sure to pen a note informing her that she couldn't possibly get away. Perhaps she should also send notes to Margaret and James apologizing for her mother using them as bait to lure her back to Holderness.

She went upstairs to her bedroom to get her camera. It was on the window seat where she had left it the night before. In the wardrobe she found her knitting basket—just the right size to make a bed for Luna. After removing the needles and yarn, she went to meet Charles.

On her way down the stairs, she heard him talking to someone in the study. Max had apparently returned early from town. But as she got closer, she heard the words. She peeked into the room from the hallway.

"This is a tooth, and this looks like part of a femur. No, don't chew on it."

He was talking to Luna, who was crawling around the table, sniffing hopefully at the bones. He picked her up and put her on the table in front of him. She leaned forward to paw at his chin. Elsie put the basket down quietly and took her camera out, then found Charles and Luna in the viewfinder.

The click of the button made him look up. "I thought you were photographing the specimens," he said and smiled.

She pressed the button again.

"Yes, but I'd rather take photographs of more interesting subjects." She placed Luna in the basket on the floor, where she immediately curled up and went to sleep.

"You find me interesting?" He tilted his head and gave her a playfully roguish grin.

Elsie giggled. "More interesting than a box of old ammonites. Where do we start?" She leaned against the table, her eyes on Charles.

He rubbed his chin with his thumb and forefinger, looking around at all the fossils.

"Some of it has been sorted already," Elsie reminded him.

"Yes, you did give us a head start." He put his hands on his hips.

"But it's all wrong?"

"Well, not *all* wrong."

"I think the first thing to do is bring everything out again."

Charles agreed and they set to work. There were bones as long as her arm and some the size of her little toe. Certain items couldn't be anything other than teeth, and others were obviously claws.

More often than not, they looked like bits of rock to her.

"Can you identify the animals?" she asked, looking at the artifacts.

"No, not all of them. I have a smattering of knowledge from my time in California, but I can't tell what many of these things are."

"I wonder why Max keeps them all." Elsie poked at a hunk of black rock—or it could have been a fossilized armadillo, for all she knew.

"He must have plans for them."

"You never know with Max. He started collecting them on a whim, when he found the old shark tooth on the beach. That's what made him curious about what else he could collect. I suspect, at some point, he'll tire of it and use them to line his flower beds."

They spread the objects over every available surface in the study, including some of the floor. From there they tried to see if they could fit anything together. Like the day Elsie had worked alone, they found a number of sea creatures. Prehistoric clams, snails, sand dollars, and fish skeletons embedded in pieces of rock. Elsie set these aside to photograph. Some items were utterly foreign to Elsie, like bits of dinosaur bone and bird fossils. Charles pointed out some plant fossils that were remarkably similar to the ferns in Max's garden.

By midmorning they opened the windows to the let fresh air in. Dust spiraled in the shafts of sunlight. Listening to the distant cry of sea gulls and the pounding ocean surf, Elsie found herself truly enjoying what could have been a tedious task. The main difference from the last time she'd worked on it was having Charles with her.

As they sat on the floor examining artifacts, Elsie heard more about his time in California.

"You've had so many adventures! It's a wonder you wanted to come home at all." She held a snail shell and was sifting through the other piles to find a similarly shaped one. She couldn't help thinking of needles and haystacks.

"I did enjoy it, but I missed being here." His hands wandered deftly from pile to pile.

"Would you ever go back?" She placed her piece in with the other odd, mismatched ones.

"To California? I doubt it. Unless I was going back there permanently."

"Is that a possibility?"

"I suppose anything is possible," he said with a lift of his shoulder, still looking down at his pile.

She didn't want to think about saying goodbye to him a second—perhaps final—time. If he went back to California, someone would be waiting for him there.

Now that he was home, it was difficult to comprehend how she had lived without him for so long.

They worked in silence for a while, but then Elsie stood up and stretched. "How am I going to choose what to photograph? It will all be a jumble of bones! It would look macabre once developed."

"You can start with what we've already identified, like these enormous shark teeth. I know how much you like them."

"That's a good idea. But not now. I need lunch, and so does Luna."

Luna had woken up an hour before and was a constant source of distraction as Elsie tried to keep her out of the cupboards, the window, and their sorted piles.

"Yes, lunch is in order," he said.

"It must be a picnic. The ocean has been calling to me all morning, and I simply must get down to the beach," Elsie said. "I propose that we take Luna back to the stables. She'll like to see her mother, and I don't fancy trying to keep her out of the water at the beach. Then we'll pick up lunch."

"An excellent idea." He stood up and stretched his arms above his head. He seemed to take up the whole room.

Elsie rang the bell, and before long Daisy appeared.

"Daisy, Charles and I fancy lunch on the beach. Could you ask Judith to get a picnic ready for us?"

"A perfect day for it. I'll leave it on the porch. It shouldn't be more than a quarter of an hour." She said and left the room.

"That will give us time to find Luna's mother," Charles said, and picked up the kitten. With one hand he held her to his chest, and with the other he grabbed the inventory of which fossils he had identified—a short list—and placed it in the desk.

It was easy enough to find the cats in the stable yard. Elsie put Luna on the ground, and within seconds she ran to a dark gray tabby, who purred loudly at the sight of her. Five other kittens scampered over and snuggled up to Luna. Soon they were all playing in the dirt and chasing after each other.

"Do you remember that old black cat Gabriel had?" Charles asked.

Her stomach jerked at the sudden mention of his name. "Yes. She tried to follow him into the house sometimes when he called." Her mother approved of the cat even less than she did of Gabriel.

"She was perpetually having litters of kittens. Gabriel would take them to the docks and leave them on the corner in a crate."

Elsie frowned. "I always told him he shouldn't do that. I could have found homes for them. Who knows what could have happened to the tiny things." She shuddered at the thought of her Luna unceremoniously dumped at the pier with nobody to look after her.

"I recall a few such instances, and not only the way he treated his cat. I'm afraid he wasn't always the kindest person." Charles's expression was difficult to read, though he sounded apologetic, or perhaps he was regretful.

"No," she muttered, "not always."

****

Once they were engaged, Gabriel had given up trying to impress her.

The month before he was due to leave on the *Kraken*, Elsie called at his house. She had just knocked when she heard shouting from within. She turned to go, but the door opened. There stood Gabriel's mother with red cheeks and troubled eyes.

"Good afternoon," Elsie said, pretending she hadn't heard a thing.

"Oh. Hello, Elsie," Mrs. Reed said, looking behind her into the house. "Would you like to come in?"

"No, she wouldn't," Gabriel said as he came to the door, pulling his jacket on. His face went from a grimace to a smile in seconds. "Good afternoon, Elsie."

He pushed past his mother and closed the door before either of the women had a chance to say goodbye, then took Elsie's arm and marched her down the street.

"Gabriel!" She wrenched her arm out of his grip and came to a stop beside a milk wagon halfway up the block.

"What?" He glanced around at the passersby to see who might be listening.

"That was exceedingly rude. I wanted to speak to your mother about the wedding."

He stood looking at her for a moment. She wondered if he was thinking up an excuse for his behavior.

He took a slow breath and let it out in a rush before he spoke. "I told you not to come to my house. It is rude of *you* to ignore what I want."

"I've asked you to bring your mother to my house, but you have not done so."

"You know I've been busy with preparations on board the ship. I'll bring Mother next week."

"But why can't I come to your house? After all, it will be my home soon."

He reddened slightly and looked away as he spoke. "It needs sprucing up before it's fit to be your home."

Elsie was immediately contrite. His house had been

a source of embarrassment to him when they were children. But he must know she wouldn't judge it.

"Gabriel…" she said softly, taking his hand.

He turned to her with defiant eyes. But something in her gaze seemed to soften his.

"I will make it your castle," he said with a dimpled grin.

"As long as you're with me, it will be perfect."

He relaxed and took her arm. They walked over to the dock to look at the *Kraken*, a grand three-masted schooner. He glowed when he looked at it. She only wished he wouldn't be gone so long. Five weeks at sea!

"Gabriel?"

He looked at her, good humor restored.

She probably should not ask, but…

"Why was there yelling? At your house?"

He looked down and kicked at loose gravel on the street. "Oh, we have these spats from time to time."

"You should try to get along with her." She'd heard it said that how a man treats his mother is an indication of how he'll treat his wife. But surely Gabriel would never be so cross with her once they were married.

"I've seen you with your mother," he said with a shake of his head. "All families argue sometimes."

She could not deny it, but she got along with her mother as well as she could and would never shout, whether behind closed doors or not. They had a mutual love and respect for each other, which was what made honesty—albeit sometimes a trifle uncomfortable—possible.

"Yes, but the yelling…" she began.

"It's nothing to worry yourself about." He wrapped his arms around her and leaned in close to kiss her hair, then moved his lips to her neck.

"Gabriel, not here," she said. "We're in broad daylight."

"Nobody's looking."

She stiffened in his arms. "Someone might see us."

He exhaled loudly and dropped his hands to his sides. "You worry too much what people think."

Her stomach squirmed. "No I don't, but this isn't the—"

"Come, I'll take you home."

They walked in silence to her house. Every time she glanced his way, he was looking straight ahead as if she weren't there.

****

"Elsie?" Charles said now.

"Just lost in memories."

"Not pleasant ones?" he asked kindly.

"Not particularly."

"Do you want to talk about it?"

"No, let's enjoy our day."

Charles seemed to deliberate whether to press her on the matter but after a moment said, "It would be hard not to enjoy a day like this. Look at that sky. And we have a picnic waiting for us. Also," he said, a twinkle in his eye, "we're not in the study." He offered her his arm.

She wrapped both hands around the crook of his elbow and gave him a little tug. "Let's get our lunch. I'm famished."

The picnic basket and a blanket were waiting for them when they returned to the house. Charles carried everything on their short walk to the beach.

Elsie removed her shoes at the end of the garden path, her heart lightening the moment her feet touched the sand. A salty breeze blew past her, taking with it her dark memories.

As usual, they had the beach to themselves. Charles spread the blanket in front of the driftwood log while Elsie unpacked the food: wild strawberries, little cucumber sandwiches, molasses cookies, and a thermos of lemonade with two glasses.

"Judith has forgotten that I'm grown up now," Elsie said. "This is the same picnic she packed for me every summer when I was a child."

They sat side by side, leaning back against the log and watching sandpipers dash along the shore. It was a perfect June day, and the weather matched her mood. The sky was clear and bright, the hot air tempered by a cool sea breeze. Red and gold highlights in Elsie's hair shimmered in the sunshine.

"I should have remembered a shovel," Charles said, rolling onto his stomach. "We could have built a sandcastle."

"Aren't we a little old for that?"

"Of course not. We're only twenty-two."

"We'll remember next time," Elsie said.

After lunch he removed his shoes and socks and rolled his trousers up almost to the knee for their walk along the beach.

"I wager I will find more glass than you," Charles said, walking in the surf while Elsie stayed on the hard, wet sand.

She spotted a glint of white and raced toward it. "I wager you will *not*!"

Charles tried to catch up to her but was too late. She triumphantly held up the bit of glass.

"You were saying?" she said, waving it in front of

him.

"That's only one piece!" He sprinted ahead of her.

She turned in the opposite direction and set off. There was no sense trailing him; he would have found every exposed piece already. From experience, Elsie knew the waves would have carried glass past the high tide mark, and the tide had receded a few hours ago. Following her hunch, she found a number of pieces, even a rare purple one. Every time she discovered one, she wondered where it had come from. A bottle of wine from a wreck on the ocean floor? A dropped glass from a seaside picnic such as theirs? If only they could tell their stories.

She went back to the blanket to wait for Charles, and after drinking a glass of lemonade she lay on her back, listening to the methodical rush of the waves, an arm draped across her eyes. The wind tugged playfully at her hair and ruffled her skirt. She was almost asleep when Charles returned. She smiled lazily but didn't move.

"Well?" she asked. Her lips tasted like the ocean.

"I did all right. You?"

"Fair enough."

"I have the feeling your heart wasn't in this competition," he teased.

"It was, and I'm certain I collected more than you. But I'm too content to move."

"Me too." He lay down beside her, very close, the length of their arms touching. He entwined his fingers with hers.

If it had been anyone else, she would have insisted they get up at once. She scooted a bit closer and glanced over at him, but his eyes were closed. She shut her eyes too and listened to the waves gently breaking on the shore.

After a time, Charles spoke. "Elsie, look at the sky."

He sat with his arms resting on his elevated knees, his feet buried in the sand.

Elsie rubbed her eyes and sat up to look at the vivid orange horizon. The ocean sparkled as though covered in multicolored gems.

"How beautiful!" she said.

"I didn't want you to miss it."

"Did you fall asleep too?" She stretched her arms above her head.

"For a short time," he said.

"And where is your bounty?"

"My bounty? Oh!" He reached into his pocket for four pieces of sea glass.

Elsie arched an eyebrow at him. "That's all?" She pulled out ten.

He leaned into her shoulder. "You always were the treasure hunter."

"You only need to know where to look," she said, handing him the glass.

He put it in his pocket, then gave her what he'd collected.

"I'd like to get into the water," Charles said.

"Someday soon we'll come back and swim."

"I'll at least get my feet wet again. Will you join me?"

His shining blue eyes were just visible through his unkempt hair. Elsie had to laugh. She may as well have been looking at Charles when he was ten years old. She took his hand, and they ran into the surf. The sand gave way beneath her feet as she walked in almost up to her knees, the pulse of the ocean pressing against her legs.

Charles splashed her, and naturally she retaliated. By the time they went back onto dry sand, they were soaked.

"Ugh! Look at my dress!" The blue-and-white gingham was almost transparent.

"Go up to the house and change. I'll clean up the picnic," Charles said, politely averting his eyes.

Elsie went on ahead, collecting her shoes on the way. The carefree afternoon had almost made her forget the dust-covered study. When she reached the front porch, she turned back to see Charles watching her. He gave her a little wave and bent down to collect the blanket and basket.

****

Elsie smiled to herself as she sat at the vanity and prepared for bed. It had been a wonderful day. Only one thing dampened her mood: Charles possibly moving back to California. Had he not given up on Amelia? She put her brush down, a crease on her brow. Just thinking about him marrying someone else gave her a sensation akin to vertigo. She'd missed Charles terribly during their years apart but, for some reason, had never imagined him with another woman. Even when they were both engaged, she believed they still held a special place in each other's hearts. They shared a bond that nobody else could touch. But what would happen to that bond if he married? Naturally, there would be someone else who came first in all things. Their relationship would never be the same again. For the first time, Elsie realized just how much her life had been altered when he moved away.

A startling thought occurred to her: would she have considered Gabriel if Charles had still been in Holderness? Would Gabriel have courted her at all?

What would have happened after that night on the beach if Charles hadn't left for San Francisco the next morning? Would he have spoken to her of his feelings, or tried to kiss her again?

She put her nightgown on and climbed into bed, remembering the night before Charles left for California. Memories came flooding back, as vivid as if it were yesterday. They'd been walking on the beach at sunset. The waves were calm, only a light breeze stirred the air. Charles stopped suddenly. He took Elsie's hand and turned her to face him. She looked at him expectantly, waiting for him to release her hand, but he didn't.

"Elsie, while I'm away, will you write to me?" His deep voice, barely above a whisper, sounded like his throat was dry. Charles had looked at her in a way he never had before.

"I've already bought extra stationery," she said with a smile. "And I'll want to hear from you as often as possible. I'm going to miss you, Charles." She entwined her fingers with his.

His eyes brightened, and a satisfied expression lit up his face. They stood there holding hands for a long moment. Something as obvious as the sun shining above had just been pointed out to her, and she couldn't believe she hadn't seen it sooner.

Charles's gaze softened as he looked into her eyes, and Elsie knew what was coming. He took a step closer. She stood there, heart stampeding in her chest, not sure if she wanted to step forward or step back. In the blink of an eye, she knew.

She inched toward him.

Charles took her other hand and drew her in. He leaned toward her, his face so close she could see his eyelashes. She closed her eyes, waiting for his kiss.

****

In the middle of her recollection, Elsie drifted off to sleep, and before long her thoughts had slipped into a dream:

Charles turned and walked up a tall sand dune. The sun was so bright that Elsie lost sight of him. She tried to call out, but her voice was lost in the wind. Holding her dress above her ankles, she ran after him. Beneath her bare feet, the hot sand changed to cool green grass, the hill covered in a blanket of colorful wildflowers.

She turned in a circle, looking for Charles. She felt rather than heard him call her name. He was standing under the big oak tree at the top of the hill, holding his arms out to her. She took one step and was instantly beside him.

Suddenly it was night, the soft evening lit up by hundreds of dancing fireflies. The wind was warm on her skin. Her skin? Elsie looked down. Her dress was gone. She ran her hands over her body. And then Charles's hands were entwined with hers. She looked up. He was naked. His eyes were blazing as he wrapped her tightly in his arms, his tongue tasting hers, his mouth welcoming her in. He stroked her skin and kissed her over and over until she was senseless. She sighed his name, and then they were lying on the grass. She ran her hands over his chest, his legs, his arms, every inch of him. He moaned softly, and then he was on top of her, his delicious weight pressing her into the dewy morning grass. The sun had risen. His skin on hers was roses and silk and the lick of flames and summer rain all at once. "Elsie, Elsie, my Elsie," he said and began to move.

****

Elsie awoke with a shudder and a sigh. She sat up in bed, her cheeks scarlet, and looked around in the dark. She was not on the hill. Charles was not here. She fell back against the pillows and did her best to hold on to the dream, but it was already slipping away, as all dreams do. With trembling legs, she got out of bed, crossed the room, and opened the windows. The cool night air dried the light perspiration on her face and body.

Charles. In her dream, she had been with Charles. In a deep recess of her mind, she had never given him up, had never stopped wanting him. It had been years since she'd dreamed of him that way. Perhaps the idea of him going away had made that part of her cling to him all the more. After a time, she went back to bed and fell asleep to the echoes of Charles whispering her name.

Chapter Ten

The fossil project kept Elsie and Charles busy over the next few weeks. Every time they finished sorting a box, Max appeared with another one. Elsie took a particular liking to the ancient shark teeth. It was hard to imagine an animal that huge had ever existed, but Charles assured her they had once ruled the oceans.

"I wouldn't go swimming if I knew that was in the water," Elsie said with a shiver.

"Neither would I." Charles picked up a tooth the size of his hand.

She ran her finger along the edge. "It must have been razor-sharp at one time."

He put the tooth back on the table with the others, then took Elsie's hand and pressed her palm against his. "Why Elsie, your hand is not quite as big as that tooth," he said, meeting her eyes over the tips of their fingers.

A little whirlwind flickered in her chest. After a moment, she pulled her hand away and cleared her throat. "And to think the shark had a mouthful of these."

"It would have been formidable indeed." He rolled his sleeves up to his elbows.

She was considering the muscles moving smoothly beneath his skin when he said her name.

"Yes?" she said quickly, looking up.

He motioned to his bare forearms. "You don't mind, do you?"

"No. No, of course not."

"I could roll them back down if you prefer," he said, preparing to do so.

"No, it's fine. The truth is I was noticing how tan your arms are." And how much she would like to caress them.

Charles moved closer and put his arm right next to hers. He was very warm. "You're almost as tan as I am."

The hair on her arm rose slightly. "I'm not sure how. My mother insists I bring a parasol every time I go out." She pulled her arm away, rubbing the goosebumps.

He leaned back against the table and folded his arms. "Funny, I haven't seen you using one lately," he said, his eyes sparkling.

"My mother isn't here." She grinned. "My hat is enough, I'm sure."

"When you wear one. If you don't start soon you'll be so tanned I won't be able to find your freckles," he said, touching his finger lightly to her cheekbone.

Her heart bounded.

"You must be the only person who doesn't think I have dirt on my face." She retreated half a step; it wouldn't do for him to see how much she enjoyed his touch.

"That's because I've been looking at those freckles all my life. Well, shall we begin?"

They set to work, but her mind was far from fossils. It was in a hidden little place where she *had* touched Charles's arms, and he had wrapped them around her, and kissed her, and whispered her name. A few weeks ago, she would never have entertained thoughts of such a scenario.

But this wasn't the first time recently that Charles

had done something that, had it been someone else, she would have considered downright flirtatious. A touch on the small of her back while climbing the stairs, a thoroughly unnecessary arm around her waist when helping her mount her horse. It was as if he was looking for any excuse to put his hands on her. Sometimes she caught him staring at her. When she smiled at him, he would immediately look away. She knew exactly what this would all mean if it were anyone other than Charles. But it *was* Charles.

She tried to convince herself she was not attracted to him. But she had to admit, at least to herself, that she was. No matter how often they were together, it was never enough time. Nearly everything she saw, thought, or did meant more after she'd shared it with him. She'd attributed these feelings to their newly rekindled friendship.

But something else had been rekindled, too.

That hope of something more than friendship, the possibility that his feelings from three years ago remained, sent her heart soaring. Could he still harbor that affection for her? But perhaps, if her own feelings had changed, wouldn't it make sense that she could misinterpret Charles's innocent gestures? He had always been more affectionate than she had, even when they were children. He would hold her hand when they sped along the shore or put an arm around her shoulders when they roamed the woods at night searching for fireflies. It had been entirely innocent, simply a part of who he was. Elsie suspected he got it from his mother, who had always been almost overly—

"Elsie?" Charles was waving a hand in front of her face. "Daydreams?"

If he only knew the thoughts she had been entertaining!

"I was just thinking about the sharks. I still can't fathom how ocean creatures came to be in the deserts of California."

He looked askance at her, as if he knew she hadn't really been pondering the mysteries of ancient seas. "The world has changed very much since those times." And he launched into a long explanation of ice ages and tectonic plates and shifting continents. She tried her best to feign interest, though she already knew it all.

Luna, who had been sunning herself on the windowsill, came over and curled herself around Elsie's legs. Elsie picked her up and kissed her soft, warm head. She'd grown so much in just a few weeks.

"She's getting so big," Charles said. When he reached over to scratch Luna behind the ears Elsie noticed the time on his pocket watch.

"It's almost time for my photography class. Shall I take Luna to the stables on my way out?"

He leaned close to Elsie and took Luna from her. "I like to have her with me."

"I'll see you later, then."

"I'll probably still be here when you get back, buried under boxes of old bones," he said with a good-natured grimace. "But I suspect by the end of the week we'll be just about finished."

"If I can't find you at suppertime, I'll know where to look."

Walking to Mrs. Wright's, Elsie wished she'd stayed home. If this was really the last week of working on Max's project, she wouldn't want to miss it. Well, she wouldn't want to miss having an excuse to be with

Charles. The *Sea Tiger*, beset by numerous delays, was finally due in Sherwood Bay any day, and that would keep Charles and Max busy. She wondered what she would do with all of her free time. Perhaps Mrs. Wright needed help in the shop—she could learn more about the development process and portraiture.

When she arrived, Elsie went straight into the back room and hung up her coat. She waved to Lucy, who was on the other side of the room with Nancy and Grace. Lucy and Nancy waved back. Grace nodded once and turned away. Elsie must be moving up in her esteem; she was usually greeted with a blank stare.

Elsie walked along the wall, searching unsuccessfully for her photographs. She went back into the front room, where Mrs. Wright was sitting at the desk.

"Mrs. Wright?"

She looked up. "Yes?"

"Are my photographs still in the darkroom?"

Mrs. Wright reached into a drawer and pulled out five gray, blurry photos. The schooner, *Trinity Dawn,* was discernible in one of them, if one made allowances for the long, tilted hull.

"Oh, dear." Elsie picked them up to examine them more closely. "What did I do wrong?"

Mrs. Wright took one from Elsie. "Your hand wasn't steady enough here, and in some of the others you didn't take time to focus. It will get easier. Practice as much as you can."

"I will. Thank you." She took the pictures into the back room and sat at a table. She turned them every which way to try to identify the subjects.

"What on earth is this supposed to be?" Grace asked

from behind her and snatched one out of Elsie's hand. Elsie tried to grab it back, but Grace spun around.

"Give it back, please," Elsie said, standing up.

"Why, are you going to put it in an album?" Grace said through her laughter. She wiped a tear from her eye and handed it back to Elsie. "Perhaps you should take up painting."

Elsie put it back in the pile with the others. Her ears were ringing. "I did not ask for your opinion, Grace."

"But isn't that what our class is for?" she asked sweetly. "To advise and support each other? I wouldn't be honest if I didn't advise you to take up a different art form. One that you might possibly master."

"Why must you put me down at every opportunity?"

"I'm not putting you down. Only pointing out that you still don't know how to use a camera."

"Good day, Grace." Elsie turned her back on her.

"I wonder why Lucy spends so much time with you," Grace muttered.

Elsie should have walked away, but this was too much. She turned to face Grace. "Don't tell me you're jealous of my friendship with Lucy. We're not in the schoolyard."

"Jealous of you?" she snorted, then took a step closer and lowered her voice. "But I might caution my friend to steer clear of someone living in such questionable circumstances."

"There's nothing questionable about my living circumstances," Elsie hissed. "You know I'm staying with my uncle. It's not as though I'm doing anything untoward."

"Mr. Rockingham is staying there also. A young, unmarried woman living under the same roof as an eligible young man? Nothing untoward indeed." She raised her overly plucked brows to the sky.

"Mr. Rockingham and I have been friends since birth. We are constantly chaperoned by my uncle and his staff. Not that I need to justify myself to you." She crossed her fingers at the tiny lie. They were never chaperoned in a traditional sense, but it wasn't as though they ran amok alone in the house.

Grace said no more but put her nose in the air and walked to the other side of the room. Elsie sat down, rifling through her photographs with shaking hands. Mrs. Wright began her lecture on the best time of day to use natural light in photographs but Elsie didn't listen at all. She was seething. How dare Grace suggest such a thing! Elsie hoped she was the only person in town to have such thoughts. It wouldn't do to cause a scandal for Max, no matter how trivial.

After class, Elsie gathered her things and was out the door before anyone else. She stopped at Finkelstein's for a sundae. Just as she was scraping the dish for the last bit of chocolate, Lucy happened by. She ordered an ice cream soda and joined Elsie at her table.

"What did Grace do?" she asked, drinking through two straws.

"How could you tell she did anything?"

"I saw you two arguing, and you didn't come sit with us during the lecture. And it's written all over your face. You were looking daggers at Grace."

Elsie told her of Grace's accusations, leaving out the insults about her photographs. Lucy simply nodded as she listened.

"I wouldn't pay her any mind," she said.

"But to say such things to my face!" Elsie said.

"Have you heard such an opinion from anyone else in town?" Her ice cream was churning in her stomach.

"Oh, no. I think Grace is jealous. She'd love to have a handsome man like Mr. Rockingham living with her. Nobody but Grace would even hint at improprieties between you and Mr. Rockingham. The way you tell it, he's more like a cousin than a potential beau." Lucy sipped the last of her drink.

They parted, and Elsie carried her blurry photographs home. She supposed it was true what Mrs. Wright said: her skills would improve with time. Perhaps the film she'd brought for developing today would turn out better than this last batch.

As Elsie approached the house, she saw Charles sitting on the bench on the front porch. He was so engrossed in a letter he didn't notice her coming up the steps.

"Good evening, Charles."

He stood up quickly, and the pages of his letter dropped from his hands. A photograph of a young woman fluttered down between their feet. Elsie glimpsed light hair and a pretty face. They stooped to pick it up at the same time and knocked heads.

"Ow!" She actually saw stars for a moment. She'd always thought that was just an expression. Rubbing her forehead, she sat on the bench, hoping a bump wouldn't appear in the morning.

Charles gingerly touched his head, then gathered his papers and sat beside her. He put the photograph in his waistcoat pocket. The papers he stuffed back into the envelope.

"So you're still in correspondence with Amelia?"

She held her breath while awaiting his answer.

151

Charles, perhaps contemplating whether this was an offensive question, said curtly, "Yes, I am."

"What is she like? She's interested in fossils, right?"

"Yes, she studies paleontology. She's a nice person."

She could have left it there—and should have—but her mouth had other ideas.

"Do you think you'll marry her? Amelia?" she almost whispered.

"How did we get from 'I think she's nice' to you asking if I'll marry her?"

"Would you?"

"She's too far away." He stared at her for a few seconds, then shrugged. "Now that I'm home, I don't think I could bear to leave again."

"But she might come here. Amelia might. If she loves you."

"She might, if she loved me. But I don't think she does."

"Do you love her?" Elsie immediately wanted to go five seconds back in time and hold her tongue.

Charles opened his mouth then clamped it shut, his brows stormy.

She held her hands up in front of her and said quickly, "No, don't answer that. It was terrible of me to ask."

His eyes held none of their usual warmth. "No, I don't think I will answer that," he said, bristling at the question. "You know, Elsie, some things really are meant to be private. Even between friends such as us."

He walked into the house without a backward glance.

Elsie stayed on the bench until the sun went down.

It was hard to believe she'd thought he might have feelings for her when his heart was so clearly elsewhere. His correspondence with Amelia proved it. Yet he'd said they weren't courting. He wouldn't lie, would he? Or perhaps he wanted to court Amelia, but the feelings were not reciprocated?

This was the third time she'd misconstrued a man's feelings toward her. Granted, two times had been the same man—Charles three years ago and Charles now. And then there was Gabriel. How could she even begin to trust her own judgment about men when she'd been so terribly wrong about Gabriel? If she'd been paying more attention, she may have seen sooner that he didn't really love her. And more important, that she hadn't loved him enough to be his wife.

Elsie went inside, rubbing her forehead again. Perhaps she should let her mother marry her off to David Doane after all.

The next morning when Elsie went down to the study, Charles wasn't there. She rang the bell, and Daisy soon appeared in the doorway.

Elsie stepped out into the hall. "Daisy, was Mr. Rockingham at breakfast?"

"Yes, he was."

"Is he in the dining room now?" she asked, ready to go look for him.

"No, he left right after he ate. I can't say where." Elsie nodded, and Daisy hurried down the hall.

Elsie went to the dining room but wasn't in the mood for a big breakfast. She took a few pieces of toast out into the garden and sat on the bench under the biggest apple tree. Her stomach twisted when she thought of Charles's face last night. Should she seek him out or leave him alone? Knowing him, he'd like a few days to stew, and then she could apologize for encroaching on his privacy. Again.

"Lost your partner?" Max called as he ambled down the garden path, carrying two cups of coffee. He gave one to Elsie and sat beside her. "What happened to your head?" he asked, peering at it.

"Oh," she said, reaching up and touching it gingerly. "I knocked heads with Charles last night."

"Does he have a goose egg, too?"

"I don't know. I haven't seen him this morning."

"Maybe because you're picnicking out here," Max said, taking a slice of her toast and biting into it.

"No. It's because he's angry with me. I've been a little too inquisitive about his friend from California."

"Of course you are. You aren't used to sharing him."

She couldn't deny it.

"Do you know anything about Amelia?" She sipped her black, bitter coffee and made a face, then set it down on the bench beside her.

"All I know is she's the daughter of my friend Ned, and she's knowledgeable about paleontology."

"Charles fancies her." She pumped her legs under the bench as if on a swing.

"He may. But I wouldn't assume that, just because they write letters to each other." He tipped his cup all the way back, getting the last drop of coffee. He reached across Elsie and took hers. She wondered if he'd planned all along to end up with two, as he knew very well she took her coffee with cream and sugar.

"I'm not going to ask him about her again, even though I'm burning with curiosity."

"That's a wise decision. If there's anything that

needs telling, he'll tell." He finished off the toast and brushed the crumbs off his trousers. "I've been in touch with Amelia's father. He's coming east and may have time to stop by and drop off a fossil for me."

"I can't fit much more into that study, Max," Elsie said with a grin.

"If I'm lucky, he'll bring a trunk load. In his letter he said he found a tooth from a saber-toothed cat. Imagine that. I don't have enough mammals in my collection. Are you working in the study today?"

"I'm not sure there's any point, without Charles. Do you know where he's gone?" She leaned her head back to look up at the sunshine filtering through the leaves.

"I'd guess the office. With the *Sea Tiger* due, he'll have some preparations to make."

"That will please him. When we were young, he always found some project to do when he was upset. It helps him clear his head."

"How has your head been? Still thinking about Gabriel?"

"Not as much lately. But sometimes things remind me of him, and the loss hits me afresh."

"It will get better with time."

Elsie wasn't sure about that but nodded.

"Max, do you think it's possible to mourn someone you're angry with?" She pulled an apple off the tree and turned it over in her hands.

Max was thoughtful for a few moments. "I don't see why not. Grief is grief, loss is loss, isn't it?"

"I suppose so. But I've discovered some things about Gabriel, and when I think about it all, I'm furious with him. But then I feel ashamed of myself. He's dead—dead! How can I hold a grudge against someone who's gone?"

"They're the same feelings you'd have about somebody who is still here. You can love your uncle, say, and still find him vexing when he won't buy a telephone."

"That is not the same at all. I'm speaking about things that are much more serious than your refusal to install a telephone," she said with a grimace and a shake of the head.

"No, but you see my point. We humans are multifaceted creatures. One feeling doesn't block out another."

"But this problem I have with him—I can never talk to him about it. I can never hear his side or tell him how I feel. How can I forgive him?" She let the apple fall to the ground and started picking at the fabric of her skirt.

"Think about it, Elsie." He cocked his head and looked her in the eye. "Anytime you forgive someone, it isn't about them, is it? It's about you. People can't erase whatever grievance you have with them. You find it in your heart to forgive them or you don't, regardless of what they say or do."

They sat in silence for a few minutes before she spoke.

"I've never thought of it that way before, but you're right. The reason I ask is that Gabriel... He lied to me. About a number of things, I believe. He was not all that he seemed."

"I could have told you that," Max said.

"You could? Then why didn't you?" It wasn't like him to hold back.

He shrugged. "You were happy with him. It wasn't for me to say."

Elsie realized that even if Max had said something to her, she would not have acted any differently. Or would she? Would having an ally have made it easier to call off the wedding? As with most things about Gabriel, she'd never know now.

She sat with Max in the garden a while, then fetched her camera from upstairs. Down at the stable she found Luna scampering about with the other kittens. Elsie tried taking pictures of them, but they definitely wouldn't stay still, so she photographed the house and the carriages. She hadn't been working long when Max appeared.

"Elsie, do come see my new toy," he said, bouncing on his heels.

"Your what?" She put her camera down on a chair in front of the stable door.

"Oh no, bring that with you." He trotted toward the woods.

She picked up the camera and followed Max to the back of the old gatehouse. As she rounded the corner, she stopped in her tracks. A black, shiny motorcar was parked under the trees.

He caressed the hood. "I'm going to have a garage built, but it will stay here for now."

"Max! When did you get this?" Elsie circled it, running her hand over the smooth metal.

"It was delivered last night. Must have been while you were interrogating Charles. Isn't it a beaut?" Max's chest puffed out with pride as he opened the door for her. "Get in!"

She slid onto the soft leather of the passenger seat. Max went around to the driver's side and got in. He put his hands on the steering wheel, beaming like a child on his birthday. Elsie quickly focused her camera and took his photograph.

"Where are we going?" she asked, eyes shining.

"Oh, nowhere yet. I haven't learned how to drive it."

"You must have at least some idea," she said, trying to hold back a laugh. "Why buy it otherwise?"

"Mr. Anderson knows all about motorcars, and he's going to teach me. I do know how to start it."

He jumped out and cranked the handle until the engine stirred to life, then took his seat behind the wheel. He released the brake, and the motorcar pitched forward.

"Wait," Elsie said, clutching the seat. "You said you don't know how to drive!"

"It can't be that difficult."

Max turned the wheel hard to the right. Elsie covered her eyes as they bumped and jostled over the uneven ground, Max laughing fiendishly. She peeked between her fingers. They drove through the stable yard and onto the front lawn. Horses neighed indignantly from their stalls as cats scattered like skittles.

"Max!" Elsie gripped the dashboard and tucked her chin down into her shoulder.

He turned the wheel back and forth as they snaked through the grassy lawn.

On the porch, Mr. Anderson, mouth agape, dropped his glass of iced tea. It shattered on the stairs. He ran onto the lawn, waving his hands. "Mr. Lambert!" he cried, chasing after them.

Max screeched the brakes and brought the vehicle to a halt just before they reached the front gate. Grass and dirt flew out behind them. Elsie leaned back in her seat. Her stomach hurt from laughing. Her hand was at her chest, hat gone, hair undone. She reached over and took Max's hand. He was shaking with mirth and gave the steering wheel a loving pat.

When Elsie turned to look back, the entire household staff was on the porch. Mrs. Holt's face was buried in her hands, Judith's flour-covered arm draped around her shoulders. Elsie didn't want to think of what Mr. Cook, the head gardener, was going to say when he saw his chewed-up lawn.

Mr. Anderson approached the motorcar as if it might turn and attack him. Then, with a distinguished bow, he opened the door and offered Elsie a hand. She took it and stepped out, her legs wobbly.

"Mr. Lambert, if you would allow me to take the motorcar back to the gate house?" he said, his voice quavering only a little.

"Very good, Mr. Anderson." Max took Elsie's arm and escorted her into the house.

Chapter Eleven

It wasn't until four days later that Charles reappeared in the study. Elsie had taken to spending afternoons there, opening the boxes that never ceased to arrive in the mail. Luckily most of them only contained one or two items. Max had told her earlier that day that he was expecting a shipment of fossilized wood. Of everything they'd looked at thus far, this idea perplexed her the most. How could wood be fossilized?

She was sitting on the settee with Luna when she heard someone come through the door. Her heart lifted when she saw that Charles's smile had returned. She'd endured his dour looks across the supper table for days.

"Good afternoon," he said, lifting a deep, rectangular box onto the table.

"Not another one?" Elsie groaned, scooping Luna into her arms and going to join Charles. He took Luna from her, and the kitten started chewing on his waistcoat buttons.

"This one doesn't contain fossils. I wouldn't think so, at any rate. It's from your mother."

She opened the box. Inside was her emerald-green taffeta dress. Elsie held it up to herself.

"It's pretty," Charles said.

"Yes, but why would she send my dress?" She found a note inside the box and read it aloud: "*Dear Elsie. You didn't pack any evening gowns when you went to New*

Hampshire. I thought you could use this in case of any sudden social engagements. You always look lovely in it.—Mother."

Elsie grimaced. "This is what I get for not attending her last party. If she can't force me to look for a husband in Holderness, she'll make sure I'm well-dressed in case I stumble across one here." Courting, husbands—this was the ideal moment for Charles to bring up Amelia.

"Do you really think that's why she sent it?" he asked as she stuffed it back into the box.

She cocked her head and looked at him through the corner of her eye. "You know my mother."

"Yes, I do," he said with a grin. "I'm sure you're right."

"Was there any other mail?" She looked away so he wouldn't see the curiosity written all over her face.

"You didn't get anything else. Were you expecting something?" He put Luna on the floor, and she scampered out into the hall.

An uncomfortable knot grew in Elsie's stomach.

"No, I just wondered. Speaking of letters, Charles, about the other night—"

He held up a hand. "Please, it's not necessary."

"Let me speak."

"Elsie, no more needs to be said." He scanned the room as if seeking a hiding place.

"Yes it does. Listen to me, please," she said, taking a step forward.

He crossed his arms and leaned against the table, giving her a resigned look. She couldn't help but notice the amused expression in his eyes.

"I'm sorry for prying the other night. I was being overly curious about your new friend. But as you said, some things are private. I will do my utmost to respect that from now on."

He nodded. "I appreciate that. And I apologize for being rude. It was easier to walk away than try to answer your questions. Some things are not so simple to explain."

"Of course," she said, holding back questions that such a statement naturally brought to mind. It was as if he was testing her promise to stay out of his affairs.

"Now then," he said, "why don't you show me what's arrived this week."

They spent the next hour going over the new items, and Charles entered them into his inventory while Elsie took photographs of a few of the finer ones. When they were finished, Elsie tried to think of what to do next. A ride through the woods perhaps?

Just as she was about to suggest it, he said, "Would you like to go into town?"

"I'd like that. On the condition that we stop at McGoldrick's."

"I will readily agree to that," he said, offering her his arm.

When she tucked her hand into the crook of his arm, he covered it with his own hand. As they passed the front lawn, Elsie saw Mr. Cook on his hands and knees filling in the last of the ruts the motorcar had left.

McGoldrick's had a line out the door, as could be expected on a Saturday afternoon, and they stood at the end of it. Once they were inside, Charles asked, "Do you want to get a table?"

Elsie was about to answer when she spotted Grace a few people ahead of them in line. "No, it's such a nice day. Let's go to the park."

When they reached the counter, Elsie bought a box of chocolates and a bag of maple-sugar candy. She stood by while Charles paid for two bottles of Moxie. In the corner of the room, she saw Grace sharing a table with a young man. Grace caught her eye, then looked pointedly from her to Charles and gave Elsie a smirk. Elsie clenched her fists at her sides and turned away.

"Here you are," Charles said, handing her a bottle.

She took a long sip through the red straw and left the shop without another glance at Grace.

They strolled through town until they came to a park known for its wild strawberries and sat on a bench overlooking the boats moored just offshore: the *Dona Jean*, the *Jaunty Bobber,* the *Amanda*.

On the way home, they went through the woods instead of taking Birch Street. The forest was deep and quiet. They could have been the only two people on Earth. Here and there, delicate pink lady's slippers bloomed among the trees. Elsie and Charles, stepping carefully so as not to crush the flowers, silently enjoyed the birds calling to one another and the branches rustling in the wind.

They walked alongside a swift-flowing mountain stream, its water singing a sweet, melodic tune, then sat for a while on a mossy granite bolder just out of reach of the splashing current and tossed fallen maple leaves into the water and watched them tumble downstream.

"I'd like to get into those hills," Charles said, pointing to the peak of a mountain range in the distance.

"So would I. Later in the summer perhaps we could go to the White Mountains."

"That's a bit of a trek, don't you think?"

"A bit. But we do like our adventures, don't we?"

"That we do. We could even spend the night. Imagine all the fireflies we would find."

"That sounds wonderful," she said. "I'm certain Max would be happy to act as chaperone. For now, it looks like it's time to head home. The sun is nearly gone."

As they got up to leave, Charles took her hand to help steady her over the slippery rocks, and a warm glow rippled through her. Instead of letting go when they reached the grassy bank, she laced her fingers through his, her heart racing as fast as the stream. He looked at her and his eyes held something like tenderness. She almost tripped over her dress.

The sky was softening to the faintest hint of dusk. She wished it was morning so they could begin their day together all over again. They continued down the trail and turned onto a narrow path that came out behind Max's stables, then walked up the lawn to the front of the house. An unfamiliar motorcar was parked in the drive.

"Who's here, Mr. Anderson?" Elsie asked when he opened the front door.

"An associate of Mr. Lambert's."

Charles's fingers slipped out of hers as they stepped inside. Elsie removed her hat and dropped it on the table beside the soda bottles and the bag from McGoldrick's.

"Let's go see who it is," she said to Charles, tugging on his jacket sleeve.

From the dining room came the sound of laughter: two gravelly chortles and one tinkling, delicate giggle.

Charles stopped in his tracks. Elsie looked up at him. The color had drained from his face. She opened her mouth to ask what was wrong, but Max called out:

164

"Don't hang about in the doorway, you two. Come see what the cat dragged in."

Elsie went first, Charles close on her heels.

Three people sat around the dining room table, having just finished a sumptuous tea: Max, red in the face and as happy as Elsie had seen him since their drive across the lawn; a blond, older gentleman beside him; and a woman with shiny, golden hair facing the doorway. She looked up just as Elsie—a cold sinking feeling in her stomach—realized who she must be.

"Amelia," Charles said under his breath.

"Charles," Amelia said in a wisp of a voice, rising gracefully to her feet. She was petite and willowy, her luminous eyes fixed on Charles.

Elsie cast a glance over her shoulder, catching a slight furrow of Charles's brow as he brushed past. At the table he pulled Amelia's chair out for her, and she sat. He slid into the seat next her, his eyes never leaving her face.

Elsie gave Max a pointed look.

"Ah, yes, introductions!" he said, standing up. "Charles, you know everyone, of course. Elsie, allow me to introduce Mr. Ned Hazen and his daughter, Miss Amelia Hazen."

"How lovely to meet you both," Elsie said.

"We won't stand on ceremony," Max said. "Ned, Amelia, this is my niece, Elsie. Miss Elsie Hayward."

"I'm delighted to meet you," Ned said, smiling.

"It's a pleasure," Amelia said, nodding at Elsie for a split second before turning back to Charles.

"Where were we?" Max said, turning to Ned. "Tell Charles and Elsie about that site that's full of cats and elephants."

Elsie sat down next to Max and served herself a cup of tea, which was stone cold. She drank it anyway to give her cheeks a moment to relax after all the forced smiles.

Amelia. Here. In the dining room.

She hadn't been real until this moment. Elsie's fear of losing Charles rushed in like high tide. Charles had said he didn't think Amelia loved him. Not enough to travel east, at any rate. And yet here she sat, taking birdlike bites of Mrs. Holt's spice cake.

Charles's face was hard to read. He kept stealing tiny glances at Amelia while trying to follow the conversation. His voice had a strained edge evident only to Elsie. She felt his eyes on her more than usual, but when she turned to him, he looked away.

Elsie helped herself to a piece of cake. She'd never felt less hungry, but eating excused her from speaking. Not that she would have had a chance to. Amelia was well acquainted with the excavation site her father was describing, and before long, she, Charles, and Ned were reminiscing about their time out west, effectively shutting Elsie out of the conversation. Max followed along with many a "Well, I'll be!" and "You don't say!" and "Isn't that something!"

After over an hour of this, Ned stood up, his impeccably tailored suit now rumpled. "We'd best be getting along to our hotel."

"Ridiculous! You'll stay here. We have plenty of room," Max said.

Elsie nodded and pasted on a welcoming expression.

"No, no. It's all arranged," Ned said. "We have a room waiting for us at Richardson's Hotel. But we'll be back tomorrow with the bones. There was a mix-up on the train—our trunks weren't ready to leave the station when we were."

Elsie followed the two old friends into the entryway, where Mr. Anderson was waiting to open the door. Charles and Amelia were still talking in the dining room. They were out of earshot, but Elsie caught snatches of laughter.

"Until tomorrow, then," Max said, thumping Ned on the back.

"Amelia, dear. We're going," Ned called out.

Amelia reluctantly joined her father. Her elegant traveling suit had remained immaculate despite what must have been hours on the train today. She wore a sky blue chiffon scarf that accentuated the color of her eyes. She turned to Elsie. "I'm so glad to meet you at last. Charles has told me so much about you."

Not Mr. Rockingham, but *Charles.*

"It's nice to meet you, too. I hope we'll have more time to talk tomorrow," Elsie said.

"We'll be back in the morning. We're only here for a day or so, I'm afraid."

"I assumed you'd be staying longer. That's quite a journey to deliver a few fossils." But not so far to secure a husband.

Amelia let out her tinkly laugh again. "We're going to see Daddy's family in Maine. His Aunt Maria lives there, but he's never met her. Imagine? A relative we've never met." Her eyes were wide, as if this were the most unbelievable thing she'd ever heard of.

"What good fortune that you were able to visit this part of the country."

"Yes, very good fortune," Amelia said. Her attention shifted to Charles, who was talking to Ned and Max.

Elsie stayed in the entryway as long as courtesy required. As soon as their motorcar pulled away, she ran down the length of the porch, through the garden, and out to the beach. She removed the pins from her hair and let it flow down her back as she paced back and forth along the shore, searching for glass peeking out of the sand.

But she didn't see glass.

She saw Amelia's adoring eyes when she looked at Charles. She saw the way Charles gazed at her, like he could barely look into such a bright light. As if she were an angel. Better yet, an angel who knew about dinosaur bones.

A movement out of the corner of her eye caught her attention, and she turned to see Charles walking toward her. When he reached her, he didn't speak but fit his steps to hers. Seagulls weaved and circled above them, their cries carried away on the cool evening wind.

Charles spoke matter-of-factly, in a tone that didn't match the lines on his face: "That was a shock."

"Was it?"

"Yes," he said so fervently that she believed him. "I had no idea Amelia was coming. She might have mentioned it in that vague way people make plans you never think will happen. I didn't expect her to actually come east."

"Are you glad she's here?"

He seemed to debate for a moment, then said, "It's nice to see both of them. And I'm curious about the specimens they've brought. They'll be back tomorrow."

Elsie watched a horseshoe crab make its slow way back to the ocean. Once it disappeared into the water, she said, "Her father reminds me of Max."

Charles laughed. "He always reminded me of Max, too. Not quite so forgetful, though. He definitely would have mentioned that company from across the country was coming."

"Especially important company." Elsie picked up a long stick and trailed a line behind her in the sand.

"Yes," Charles said. Clearing his throat, he turned to the purple horizon.

This morning she wouldn't have guessed that by the end of the day she would have met Charles's…what? Friend? Sweetheart? He'd said they weren't courting, but he looked spellbound when he saw her. Remembering her promise, she did not question him.

She hurled the stick deep into the waves, but the tide carried it right back in. Charles picked it up and threw it even farther, and this time the current caught it and whisked it away. He gave her a mischievous grin.

"Come on," he said. "Let's see if there's any spice cake left. And I could do with a hot chocolate." They went into the house, leaving the gathering darkness behind.

In the morning, Elsie awoke to sounds of arrival. Good heavens, it was early for callers. She got out of bed and cracked her door open. Voices drifted up from the entryway: Ned and Amelia. Max's muffled voice soon joined theirs. Just then, Charles's door opened. His back to her, he straightened his jacket and smoothed his hair before going downstairs. An effervescent voice greeted him when he reached the first floor.

Elsie closed the door and flopped face-first onto her bed. Then she crawled back under the covers and went to sleep. The next time she woke up, bright sunlight was streaming into her room. She sat up and stretched, then took her hair out of her sleeping braid. She went to her vanity and brushed it out, looking at herself in the mirror. Touching her freckles, she remembered Amelia's creamy, perfect skin.

A ball of something hot ignited in her stomach. But such an emotion was pointless. The chance for something romantic between Elsie and Charles had passed years ago. There was no denying how she felt about him, but clearly he did not see her in the same way. If only she'd been able to stop herself from dreaming and hoping... Perhaps it would have made all of this easier.

She should be happy for him. She'd loved Gabriel, and Charles hadn't been jealous of that. He'd probably been happy for her. It was like Max had said: she just wasn't used to sharing Charles. But naturally he'd had a whole other life without her in California, and part of that life had come to call.

She made her way downstairs in an apple-green dress she was particularly fond of, as was Charles. When she went into the dining room, the food was already gone, and Daisy was clearing the dishes.

"Good morning, miss. Would you like breakfast?"

"Yes, please. Bring whatever is left in the kitchen. There's no need for Judith to make something up just for me."

She sat down and looked out the window, her chin resting in her hand. In the distance, a schooner was heading at full sail toward the horizon. She couldn't help but think of the *Kraken*'s final voyage.

****

The day it set sail, Elsie had wakened before dawn. Gabriel had told her to stay in her warm bed rather than venture down to the docks at such an early hour. She resigned herself to waiting until midmorning and took her time dressing. After all, the way she looked today would be how Gabriel remembered her during his weeks at sea. She went down to the balcony off the drawing room and looked toward the harbor, where she could just make out the *Kraken*'s mainmast.

She rang the bell for Sarah, the maid, and asked her to bring some coffee as well as the tin of oatmeal cookies Elsie had baked for Gabriel. He'd told her many times how much he missed home cooking while at sea.

When it was finally time to leave, she wrapped herself in her warmest coat and scarf. On her way to the docks, she caught a whiff of snow in the air.

She hadn't even neared the ship's berth when Gabriel appeared. The sun was gleaming off his black hair, and he was smiling in that way only a voyage could bring to his face. He ran up the street to meet her, his breath visible in the cold air.

"Elsie." He took her in his arms and lifted her high into the air.

"Put me down," she said, breaking into a laugh. Her eyes twinkled as she noticed his rosy cheeks. How she loved to see him this way.

He set her down but kept an arm tight around her waist.

"Oh, I'll miss you," he said. He took her hand and led her around the corner into a quiet, empty yard.

"And I'll miss you." Since nobody was about, she wrapped her arms around him and buried her nose in the shoulder of his cold wool jacket. He rubbed his hands along her back to keep her warm and gave her a swift kiss.

A bell pealed from somewhere on the docks. Gabriel

lifted his head and turned toward the sound. "That'll be for me. Not long until we weigh anchor."

She handed him the cookies. "It's not much, but it will remind you of home. And me."

"As if I need a reminder of my pretty bride," he said, and bent to kiss her once more.

They held hands as they walked to the dock, and when they were within sight of the *Kraken* he let go and ran down the street. Once on board, he beamed and gave her a wave. She stayed on the dock until the *Kraken* disappeared past the horizon.

And that was the last time she ever saw him.

****

Daisy returned with a platter of blueberry pancakes and a pot of coffee, as well as some mail for Elsie. Just one envelope, in her mother's writing. Probably another party invitation. She put it in her pocket to read later. The sweet aroma of spice cake wafted out from the kitchen.

After she finished eating, she rang the bell for Daisy.

"Will you please ask Mrs. Holt when the spice cake will be ready?"

"I'll go ask, miss," Daisy said, taking the breakfast dishes with her.

Mrs. Holt came out herself.

"Good morning, Mrs. Holt. When will the spice cake be ready? I'd love to have some with my coffee, and maybe a bit of whipped cream to go with it."

Mrs. Holt brightened. "Oh, this one isn't for us. Miss Hazen liked it so much at tea yesterday she asked me for the recipe. But you know I never give that out. I told her I'd bake one to take back to her hotel."

"I see. I'll just finish my coffee, then." She managed to maintain the smile on her face.

"I will make one for you tomorrow," Mrs. Holt said with a wink, turning to leave.

"Before you go, Mrs. Holt, where are our guests?"

"In the study, I believe."

Elsie lingered at the table, then walked down the hall. Excited voices were coming from the study. She paused just outside the door, deliberating about entering. Ned and Max were at the desk, passing a magnifying glass back and forth as they studied some artifact. Charles and Amelia stood at the table, both sorting through boxes of tiny bits in that same confident way Elsie had seen in Charles weeks ago. Amelia gasped and held something up to Charles, who leaned in for a closer look.

Elsie was on the verge of leaving to go into town when Amelia noticed her and lit up like she'd just spotted her best friend in a crowd.

"Oh, Elsie, there you are! I did hope to see you today." She placed a massive shark tooth back on the table.

Elsie stepped into the room, which now had the air of a college laboratory.

"Good morning," Charles said.

"Good morning. What are you sorting?" Elsie asked, approaching the table to get a look at the new acquisitions.

"Oh, it's a bit more complicated than sorting," Amelia said. "We're categorizing the pieces by flora and fauna. Then we classify them by era and species."

"I see. What have you found?"

"You may be familiar with some of our finds. Charles told me you've assisted him from time to time." Amelia then began a detailed lecture using scientific terms Elsie had never heard in her life. She had no idea what she was talking about, but Charles nodded along the whole time. After she finished speaking, Amelia put a hand on Charles's sleeve. "Would you be so kind as to bring my sketchbook from the parlor? I want to show Elsie my drawings of the Smilodon."

"Yes, of course."

At the doorway he turned and looked back, his hand on the frame as his eyes darted back and forth between the women. When Elsie shot him a questioning look, he continued down the hall.

"What is a Smilodon?" Elsie asked.

"It's a saber-toothed cat," Amelia said, reaching for a long fossil. "You see? These were the front teeth. This is what we brought for Max. We came with quite a bit more, as well," she said almost apologetically.

"Max can never acquire enough." Elsie glanced at him across the room. He was deep in conversation with Ned. Both their pipes had gone out, yet they continued to bring them to their lips.

"It's like that with fossils," Amelia said. "They're fascinating, and there's so much to learn about them. Discoveries are being made all the time."

"Where did you learn so much about paleontology?" Elsie took the long tooth from her to get a better look.

"From my father," she said, smiling. "He never thought I should be left out of schooling simply because I'm a woman. My mother, on the other hand..." She grimaced and closed her eyes, an expression that Elsie and Margaret must have made a dozen times a week in their youth.

"Your mother didn't approve?"

"Oh, dear me, no. She thought I would be ruining

my chances for a husband. She believes a woman should be less intelligent than her husband. Or," she whispered with a tiny wink, "pretend to be."

Elsie joined in her laughter.

"My mother is of a similar mindset." Elsie handed the tooth back to Amelia. "She didn't want me to attend college."

"I've been tutored by my father at home, but I would have enjoyed going to college."

"I liked it very much. My sister didn't go—she married before she had the chance—but she would have liked it, too."

"Is your sister here?"

"No, she's in Holderness, where we grew up. She had a baby not long ago."

"So you're also an auntie! How sweet. I have four brothers, but none of them are married yet. I'm the eldest, I'm twenty-five." She didn't act the least embarrassed to disclose her age. Amelia was forthcoming for someone Elsie had just met, but she did it so naturally that it was endearing.

Charles returned with the sketch book, and Amelia took Elsie over to the settee to show her the drawings. Charles then joined Max and Ned at the desk, but Elsie caught him glancing in the direction of the settee every so often.

"You're a very good artist," Elsie told Amelia.

"Thank you. Charles tells me you're learning to use a camera?"

"Oh—yes, I am," she said, surprised they would have discussed her.

"It looks difficult. Do you find it so?" Amelia asked with an adorably furrowed brow.

175

"I didn't at first, but the photographs I recently developed did not come out as I'd hoped. My teacher said the only way to master it is to practice."

"Oh, that old adage!" Amelia said, waving her hand. "Practice does make perfect. If you believe it, just six months ago you wouldn't have been able to tell my Smilodon drawing from that of a mastodon."

"That's hard to believe. Your drawings are so realistic."

"Thank you. May I see some of your photographs?" Amelia asked. "Oh! May I see your camera if it isn't too delicate?"

"Not at all. I'll go get it from my room." She went upstairs and pulled out her pile of photographs. She wanted to bring down her best examples and settled on one she'd taken of the *Second Wind*'s figurehead. She also chose two she'd taken of Max's house, and one of the stables.

She went back downstairs, and this time was not surprised to hear Amelia's laughter ringing through the hall. Charles was sitting beside her on the settee. Elsie had an impulse to turn right around and take her photographs upstairs, but she walked in and stood before them.

Charles looked at Elsie with an expression that was difficult to read. If she had to take a guess at it, she'd say he was embarrassed, but she couldn't imagine why. He rose at once so she could take his place. He did not join Ned and Max but went to look out the window.

She sat down and handed Amelia the photographs.

Amelia sifted through them. "These are darling! Especially considering you've only just started."

"Thank you."

"And that's your camera?"

Elsie handed it to her, and she held it on her lap as if it were made of fine porcelain. She gave it back quickly. "I'm afraid I'll drop it."

"It's very sturdy." Elsie pointed out the main components.

Amelia glanced up at her and suddenly focused on her cheek. "Elsie," she whispered, coming closer, "you have a smudge of ink on your face. Would you like to borrow my handkerchief?"

"It's not ink. It's just my freckles."

Amelia leaned in closer. "So they are. How adorable," she said with a giggle.

Charles met Elsie's eyes from across the room, and they shared a smile. She looked back to the camera and showed Amelia how to focus it. Before long, Ned and Max wandered over to have a look.

"Nice piece of equipment, Elsie," Ned said. "We could use one at the site. Then I could send photographs of the excavations to Max here."

"Speaking of equipment, Ned, I want to show you my newest acquisition." Max raised his eyebrows at Elsie and gave her a grin.

Everyone filed out of the study and followed Max outside. Charles and Amelia walked together, while Ned gave Elsie his arm. He chatted to her about their train journey and where they were going next, but Elsie barely listened. Charles kept bending his head down toward Amelia to better hear her. After the third time they burst out laughing, Elsie inhaled deeply and turned her attention to Ned.

When they reached the stables, Elsie excused herself from seeing the motorcar even though she would have liked to hear what Charles thought of it. In fact, she'd give far more than a penny for his thoughts about many things over the last two days. She wandered over to a haystack near the barn and sat down. Within moments Luna leapt onto her lap and began purring.

Fortunately Max didn't attempt a driving demonstration. He gave his guests a tour of the grounds until it was time to go in for supper.

When Elsie carried Luna over to the stables, she found Charles waiting for her. Ned, Max, and Amelia were a little way behind him.

"Do you think Max will ever learn to drive?" Charles asked, reaching over to pet Luna, still in Elsie's arms.

"Oh, yes, he's already tried."

"That's right—I saw the lawn," he said, and they laughed together.

Elsie took Luna to where the other cats were playing. When she returned to take Charles's arm to walk back to the house, Amelia was standing beside him.

Both women looked at him expectantly.

Charles coughed lightly, his gaze hovering between the two women. Elsie glanced at Amelia, but her eyes were fixed on Charles. His arms hung limply at his sides as if unsure what they were supposed to do. He shuffled his feet and stared intently at the ground for what felt like a day before giving Elsie an apologetic look and offering Amelia his arm. Amelia flashed him a dazzling smile and latched on tightly. They started toward the house, Elsie watching after them with a tight throat.

"Come now, Elsie," Max said from behind her and offered his arm. She took it gratefully and walked beside him in silence.

Ned joined them and engaged Max in a discussion about motorcars. When Luna scampered ahead of them Amelia picked her up and nuzzled her nose into the fur. Elsie overheard Charles tell her the story of how they'd found her.

The supper table was set with Max's finest dishes and silver. They had cream of lettuce soup, baked halibut with lobster sauce, braised duck, oyster toast, and cucumber salad. For dessert, Judith had made a sweet lemon sponge cake.

Elsie, seated next to Amelia, found they had much in common and the meal flew by as they became better acquainted. Engrossed in conversation, neither woman spared much time for Charles, and Elsie noted that he looked both nettled and bored.

After port and pipes in the parlor, Ned announced it was time for them to leave.

"Thank you very much for supper and spending the day with us," Ned said to the room at large as everyone rose from their seats.

"I'm glad you came, old chap," Max said. "Mr. Anderson's gone to tell your chauffeur to bring your motorcar around."

Charles took a step forward. "Might I be allowed to show Amelia the beach while you wait?"

There were ten seconds of silence before Ned said, "Yes. Yes, of course. You're such old friends I see no trouble in that." Amelia frowned, but Elsie was the only one to notice.

Elsie said her goodbyes to Ned and Amelia. Before they parted, Amelia said, "It was a pleasure to meet you. I have the feeling we'd be such good friends if I lived close by."

"I have that feeling also. It's unfortunate that you live so far away."

"It is. But perhaps I may be closer than you think before too long." She half glanced at Charles, who was waiting for her at the door.

"Goodbye," Elsie said and hurried to her room. She lay on her bed, trying to read a novel, but she couldn't quiet her mind enough to focus. When she noticed fiery orange ribbons piercing the darkening sky, she got up to close the window and saw Charles and Amelia on the beach, talking earnestly. She would have leaned out the window if she thought she'd be able to hear their conversation. On second thought, maybe she didn't want to hear. Amelia took a step closer to Charles, placed a hand on his arm, and looked up into his face. Elsie shut the window, closed the curtains, and readied herself for bed.

After meeting Amelia, she couldn't disapprove of the match—they would be happy together. Charles would undoubtably have news to share tomorrow.

Chapter Twelve

Elsie awoke to sunbeams streaming through her window. She lingered in bed for far longer than was necessary, not wanting to face Charles just yet. She turned over on her stomach and rested her chin on the back of her hands.

Charles really was lost to her now. She'd already known, but it still stung.

There were other nice men in the world, but after failing twice to properly interpret a man's feelings for her, she wasn't sure she wanted to try again. What would it be like if she never married? Perhaps instead of being swept along by matrimonial plans it was time to decide for herself what to do with her life.

She threw back her covers and paced the room, her mind racing with ideas. She need not marry. She could travel, or become a teacher or go back to school. The possibilities were endless. Many women remained unmarried and still had a good station in life. Her parents would never turn her out, nor would Max. She would always have a home, even if it wasn't her own. But why not her own? She could buy a cottage by the sea, perhaps even open a photography studio.

But then she remembered tiny, newborn Brian in her arms. If she didn't marry, she would never hold her own dear little one. Brown eyes like Margaret's flashed before her, only to be instantly replaced by Charles's blue. She stood in front of the window, her forehead resting on the cool glass.

There was nothing for it. If she wanted a family, she needed a husband. The next time she went home to Holderness, she would not be so quick to spurn the men who called on her. There must be one of them who would support her in fulfilling her dreams. She would need to open herself up to the idea of marrying someone she hadn't known since childhood. That would at least rule out the Rockinghams.

Breakfast was long over by the time she finally entered the dining room, but Elsie had reason to smile. A warm spice cake waited for her on the sideboard. Mrs. Holt had even provided the whipped cream. She sliced a piece and sat at the table to eat it with her coffee.

When she finished, she went to the beach and, much to her surprise, found Charles sitting on the log, leaning forward with his elbows on his knees. She sat down next to him. "Good morning."

"Good morning," he said, turning to look at her.

Her smile faded when she saw his expression. Amelia wouldn't have refused him?

"Is everything all right, Charles?"

"Yes, everything's fine," he said, his attention on the rolling waves.

"Are you engaged?" she asked softly.

"No, I'm not engaged." His voice held no trace of remorse.

"But you asked her?" She moved a bit closer and noticed his eyes were clear and bright.

"No, I didn't."

"But I thought—"

"I like Amelia, but we're only friends. I talked to her

about it last night."

"That sounds like a difficult conversation."

He laughed gruffly. "It was, and not one I wanted to have. But she clearly had some expectations in coming here, and I couldn't let her go on thinking I might propose. But I think I understand why she may have hoped for that. In California, I did consider courting her. There may have been one or two days when I showed more interest than was prudent."

Elsie desperately wanted more details about those one or two days but did not ask. "What made you decide not to court her?"

"She's a kind enough person, but I wasn't drawn to her with any urgency. I could go hours without hearing her voice and not even notice, days without seeing her and not miss her at all. I felt perfectly at ease and enjoyed myself even when I wasn't with her." He was silent for a moment then added, "Essentially, I knew that I would never love her."

"But you seemed so pleased to see her."

"I can enjoy a woman's company without wanting to marry her," he said sharply. "I'd rather not discuss it anymore at the moment."

For once, Elsie listened. She couldn't imagine what he must be going through. She did have an inkling of what Amelia was feeling. Elsie had always thought the way Charles made her feel—like she was the most important person in the world—was unique to her. But perhaps it's the way he was with all women. In their youth, he'd been shy with girls, aside from her. Apparently that, too, had changed while he was in California.

When she got up to leave, Charles lightly wrapped

his fingers around her wrist. She looked down at him and noticed dark circles under his eyes. She resisted the urge to brush the hair off his forehead.

"Don't go," he said. "I know I'm not the most engaging company right now, but I like being with you."

Her heart flipped. "What would you like to do?"

"The study could use some attention after yesterday."

Elsie scrunched up her nose, and he laughed.

"What about that sandcastle you wanted to build?" she asked.

His face lit up. He released her wrist and took her hand, and they ran down to the water's edge.

"A shame I still don't have a shovel," Charles said, sitting down and taking up big handfuls of sand.

Elsie sat next to him, ignoring the water soaking her skirt. She didn't pay much attention to what she was building, either, as her eyes were mostly on Charles. He had a look of deep concentration that seemed out of place for the task at hand.

Her heart melted as she watched him totally relaxed and happy, knowing she had done this for him. She told herself that their special connection was much more important than romantic love. He was her best friend, and perhaps that was enough. It would have to be.

They sat back and assessed their handiwork.

"I'm afraid it's more of a pyramid than a castle," she said. She brushed a lock of hair off her face, leaving her forehead sprinkled with sand. Charles reached over and gently wiped it off. She shuddered.

"Are you cold?" he asked.

"No, not at all. How do you like our castle?"

"I like it. But I think it would look better with a

moat." He started scooping out a circle around the castle-pyramid-mound.

Elsie sat back and wrapped her arms around her knees. "What kind of house do you want some day?"

Charles looked up, squinting a little from the sun. "Something like Max's, with plenty of rooms and a well stocked library. I'd like to live on the coast. You?"

Elsie thought for a moment. "Something cozy and close to the sea. Cozy but big enough for a family. And I'd like to open a photography studio."

"That sounds perfect for you," he said with a grin. "Very ambitious, and I have no doubt you will make a great success of it."

"Thank you," she said brightly as she began deepening the moat.

"And where will you set up this cozy seaside home? Holderness?"

"Perhaps. Although Sherwood Bay has grown on me. Will you live in Holderness?"

"I think so. Unless I go back to California."

She froze in the middle of expanding their moat. "Would you go back? I thought you said you wouldn't go back."

"It was only a thought, Elsie. I didn't mean to alarm you."

"I'm not alarmed. Only—only I would miss you if you went away again," she said with a shrug, attempting an air of nonchalance.

"I would miss you, too. You're my dearest friend, and it's been wonderful spending so much time with you this summer," he said with the sweetest smile imaginable. "At any rate, my mother would never forgive me if I left again."

"Oh, she'd forgive you," Elsie said lightly, standing up and dusting the sand off her skirt. "And we would write to each other."

"Yes, or you could visit. But why even discuss it? It's clear to me that I'll never leave the East Coast again as long as the people I love are here." He bent down and wrote their initials and the date in the sand, then straightened and brushed his hands on his jacket.

"Yes, your family is here. We'll only have to convince James not to go back."

"That won't be difficult. He missed the snow, of all things. That and the White Mountains."

As they started for the house, Elsie found a piece of clear sea glass and gave it to Charles.

After lunch they worked in the study, mostly putting things back in their proper places after Ned and Max had ransacked the cupboards. Elsie found a drawing Amelia had made of a desert close to her home in California.

"Would you like to keep this?" she asked, holding it out to Charles. He took it and gave it only a cursory glance before handing it back. "No, I don't want it."

Elsie didn't want to destroy it but didn't want to display it either. She went over to Max's desk and started opening drawers.

"What are you doing?" Charles asked, hurrying over and standing between Elsie and the desk.

"I'm looking for a place to store this. What on earth is the matter?"

"I keep my private papers in this desk. You shouldn't snoop, Elsie. You've been doing that since we were children."

His voice was too reproving for her liking.

"I wasn't *snooping*. We keep the inventories in here.

I was going to put the drawing in with those, or perhaps in Max's business files. He might like it."

"I'll deal with it," he said, and snatched the drawing from her. He stashed it in a deep drawer at the bottom of the desk.

Elsie put her hands on her hips. "Since when have you considered me a snoop? From what I recall, any snooping I did when we were children was encouraged or assisted by you."

"I'm sorry. I didn't want you to disturb my papers. I have them all organized. I shouldn't have called you a snoop. Am I forgiven?" He pressed his palms together as if in prayer and took on a penitent look.

Elsie put her fingers to her chin, pretending to deliberate. "Yes," she finally said. "Now where were we?"

They finished putting things away, and before long it was time to eat. Max wasn't in, so it was just the two of them. Judith served a simple supper of beef stew, green beans, and buttery rolls, with fresh strawberry ice cream for dessert. Charles and Elsie talked and laughed their way through the meal.

Afterward, Charles leaned back in his chair and closed his eyes, his hands folded across his ribs. She would not tell him how much he resembled his father when he was about to nod off beside the drawing room fire back home.

The house felt peaceful—quiet and homier than ever after the Hazens' departure last night. Elsie wondered if Charles would miss Amelia, and if he would continue to write to her. She'd never asked him if Amelia was the woman Gabriel had mentioned to her last year. She dared not, with the way he'd been reacting to such queries of late. She'd just as soon never bring Amelia up to him again. She liked her, though, and would welcome news of her from Max from time to time.

"Elsie," Charles said, snapping her out of her reverie, "I had a thought the other day. Why don't we take a boat out? We haven't been sailing together in years."

"I'd like that. But I haven't been on a boat since Gabriel's ship went down."

"We don't have to go out very far. We could launch a rowboat from Max's beach if you're not ready to sail in deep waters yet."

"Yes, let's do it." Even though she'd gone sailing hundreds of times in the past, she felt like she'd committed to something positively daring. But she knew she had nothing to fear with Charles at the helm.

"We'll hug the coastline. Max must have a boat. I'll ask Mr. Anderson about it."

"He probably has one tucked away. For a man who wanted his house right on the sea, you'd expect him to enjoy sailing. But he told me he never has, even as a child. 'I want to look at it, not wade through it,' " Elsie said, imitating Max.

Charles laughed. "I have some work to do in the office over the next few days, so let's say we'll go next week."

"That sounds perfect." She pushed her chair back, but before she could stand, Charles spoke.

"Did Gabriel ever take you sailing after I left?" he asked, his eyes on his folded hands in his lap.

"No." She scooted her chair back in and took a sip of water.

"Why not?"

"I suppose because he was busy, or perhaps he just didn't want to."

"But you said he was so attentive," Charles said, now looking directly at her.

"He was. He simply didn't have the time nor the inclination to take me boating." A defensive tone had crept into her voice, but she wasn't sure why. Certainly not to keep Charles's good opinion of Gabriel. She had the feeling that had been lost years ago.

"He should have," Charles said.

Elsie let out a derisive laugh. "What does it matter? He wanted to marry me for my money, yet I should be upset that he didn't take me sailing?" She picked up a napkin and started tying it in knots.

"I'm sorry. Of course that's of no consequence, considering what you've found out about his intentions. But I like to think he treated you well."

"He did, most of the time." Elsie fell back against her chair.

Charles sat up straighter. "*Most* of the time?"

"We didn't have serious problems. Only the sort of squabbles any couple might have. I told you before, he tried to be the man I wanted."

"But was he right? Did he know what you wanted?"

How could she say she wanted Gabriel to act more like Charles? But even if he'd tried, there was no way Gabriel could have given her the same joy, the same stability that Charles did. Though she'd grown to love Gabriel, he could never be her best friend. He wasn't capable of it. There were too many parts of himself he'd kept hidden, and now she knew that he had outright lied to her about certain things.

Elsie tossed the napkin on the table and walked to

the window overlooking the beach. She heard Charles rise from the table and felt him standing behind her.

"He knew what I wanted, to some degree, as though he'd studied me for years and taken notes. He remembered what food I liked, what flowers. But it felt like he was working off a list. Nothing spontaneous, which was odd, considering how he acted in so many other situations."

"It sounds like he did try, in his way, to make you happy," Charles said, resting a hand on her shoulder.

Elsie whipped around to face him.

"What has been vexing me for weeks is how I could have been such a bad judge of character. I feel like such a fool for not realizing sooner he was using me." Her head drooped, and she wiped away an angry tear. He handed her a handkerchief, which she clutched in her fist.

"He was very good at deceiving people," Charles said. "He fooled me."

"You never trusted him like I did. I was so gullible. Believing everything he told me, defending him if anyone spoke ill of him."

"That doesn't make you gullible. It makes you a good friend. You would have done the same for me had anyone been gossiping about me. Gabriel would have done that for both of us. He would have gladly defended your honor."

"Perhaps. But then he dishonored me himself when we were older."

Charles's eyes grew round as pennies and his lips parted.

"Not like *that*!" she said. "You know me better."

Charles nodded and the color came back into his

cheeks. "Of course."

"I only meant he would have made me his wife even though he didn't love me. That isn't honoring someone."

"No. It's despicable."

Elsie wiped her eyes with the handkerchief and inhaled deeply through her nose. As always, she felt better after sharing her troubles with Charles.

"Well," she said, "perhaps it's time I let my mother marry me off after all. She may do better at choosing my groom than I did, and she knows many handsome young men in Holderness."

Charles rubbed a hand across the back of his neck. "I don't think—I mean to say…is that necessary?"

Her eyes sparkled. "I was joking."

"Oh, of course. And who were you saying was gullible?"

They laughed together, and she turned to go.

"I'd best say good night," she said.

"Just a moment. I have something for you."

He reached into his pocket and withdrew a piece of sea glass, distinctly shaped like a heart. "I haven't seen one like this before, and I thought you'd like it," he said, offering it to her. "The color reminded me of your eyes."

She took it and traced its smooth surface with her finger. "Thank you."

"You're welcome. I thought of you the moment I saw it."

"I love it. I'll go put it upstairs with my collection."

She sat on the window seat in her room and cradled the glass heart in her hand. He'd thought of her as soon as he'd seen it. He'd remembered the color of her eyes. Something hopeful stirred in her chest, but she did her best to ignore it. She'd already misread Charles's feelings twice and wouldn't let herself do it again. She put the glass in the Mason jar with the rest and prepared herself for bed, where she could pursue other, more realistic dreams.

Over the ensuing days, Elsie spent plenty of time with Charles. She had the feeling he was trying to make up for something—perhaps when he'd ignored her a few weeks ago, or the days when he'd been so busy with Amelia. Whatever the reason, it was most welcome. She had the old Charles back, and she would enjoy every moment. They worked in the study, went into town, and shared quiet afternoons in the parlor or library. After supper they would talk late into the night. Yet Elsie still wished for more hours in the day.

One evening Charles pointed out the constellations from the rooftop balcony and the next night they went on a quest for fireflies. They walked deeper into the woods than they ever had before and came to a clearing that was enclosed by trees and bushes. The swaying branches overhead could not block out the deep, clear sky bursting with bright stars. Elsie and Charles gazed about in wonder. Every firefly from within a hundred miles seemed to be there, filling the woods with dazzling, twinkling lights.

"Elsie," Charles said suddenly.

"Yes?"

"Do you remember that time I kissed you?"

Her heart set off at a gallop. Remember it? That night on the beach she'd dreamed of so many times? But no. They hadn't kissed *that* night. He was talking about that other night. Long, long ago.

"I do," she said with a soft smile. "We were what…twelve? Thirteen?"

"Thirteen. At the big oak tree, and it was a night like this," he said, motioning to the swirling fireflies. "It's the only other time I can think of where we found so many. We'd raced right up the hill and were out of breath. We sat down against the tree trunk, and I just leaned over and kissed you. You looked at me like I was mad."

"I didn't think you were mad. It was just so unexpected."

"I surprised even myself," he said, chuckling.

"My first kiss," she said, glowing. It hadn't been in the least romantic, but still.

"And mine," he said, grazing his hands along the tops of the tall grass.

"Whatever prompted you to do it?"

Afterward, they'd just looked at each other, smiled, and started back down the hill to the birch wood. The next day they'd gone on as usual, as if it had never happened—he may as well have shaken her hand. They'd never discussed it again until tonight.

"Just one of those moments where I felt especially connected to you. Like now," he said, taking her hand.

"It was only that one time."

"Yes. It occurred to me later that it wasn't entirely proper."

Elsie wondered if he ever thought about that night on the beach. She wanted to ask, but what if he said no? Had it been just another moment where he'd felt close to her? What if, like that first kiss, it had meant nothing at all? She sighed inwardly. He was simply more affectionate than she was, and she should stop trying to read too much into his actions. Like now. His hand was warm and strong in hers. But his face was not flushed, his heart not racing as hers was. Friends. Good friends.

Best friends. But nothing more.

"Let's look for shooting stars," she said and let go of his hand.

They lay down in the center of the clearing and stayed out until well past midnight.

****

The day of their boat outing dawned fair and clear. Max had, after all, owned a rowboat. He had allowed Charles to christen it the *Elizabeth*, in honor of Elsie's full name. She felt somewhat vain going out in a boat named after herself but was pleased nonetheless.

Max's house receded slowly into the distance as Charles rowed the little boat down the coast. After an hour or so, they pulled into a secluded cove to have a picnic. They spread a blanket on the sand and ate lunch, then explored the tidal pools. Afterward they climbed a grassy bank and ventured into the woods, searching for wild strawberries. They picked enough for a refreshing dessert and put some into the picnic basket to bring home. When they arrived back at Max's, they carried the boat beyond the tide's reach.

Elsie was tired in that satisfying way that only a day at sea could make her. Once inside, they met Mr. Anderson in the hallway. He told them a package had arrived and was in the study.

"What could it be?" Elsie asked Charles as they walked down the hall.

"It could be anything, the way Max has been acquiring fossils. But I suspect it's the petrified wood he's been expecting."

"Oh! I've been so curious about that. Let's open it." They found the package on the table. It was big enough to hold quite a few specimens. As Charles opened the box, Elsie heard the cuckoo clock in the dining room strike three.

"Oh, dear, this will have to wait. I'm due at my photography class."

She was tempted to skip it just to examine the petrified wood, but she was anxious to see her latest photos. Mrs. Wright had said she'd develop some of Elsie's film that had been missed earlier in the summer.

"I won't look inside until you get back," Charles said. He sat down at the desk and began sorting through some papers.

She stood watching him for a few moments before remembering she needed to go prepare for her class. Upstairs in her bedroom, she fixed her hair and changed into a long violet skirt and high-necked white blouse. Then she grabbed her camera and hurried into town, her mind full of her day with Charles.

When Elsie entered Mrs. Wright's, she went straight to the back room. She hung her coat on the rack and left her camera on a table with Lucy's, then took a turn about the room, looking at all the new photographs. Max's fossil collection had come out clear and crisp. There were multiple pictures of ships she recognized—the *Soaring Puff,* the *Scouring Maiden* and the *Gertrude.*

Most of the class was clustered around a photograph on the other side of the room. When Elsie approached, they turned to regard her with unabashed curiosity—so intently that she subtly ran her fingers over the buttons of her blouse to be sure one hadn't come undone.

"Oh, Elsie," Lucy said in an awed voice.

When she broke through the crowd and stood before the photograph, her breath caught in her throat.

It was Charles.

Charles, when she had come upon him in the study weeks ago.

Charles in profile, looking at Luna.

Beside it was the other one she had taken that day, immediately after. Charles was facing the camera head-on. He was staring straight into her eyes. His smile was captivating, to say the very least, as though he was seeing the most beautiful thing in the world. His eyes were soft, warm and alight with...love.

Elsie pulled it from the wall and held it against her chest. She crossed the room and put it under her coat. The others watched her, Lucy's eyes begged for an explanation.

Mrs. Wright came in, and everyone took their seats. Elsie hardly heard her lecture on the use of outdoor backgrounds for portraits. When it came time to go outside, her mind was in a whirl. She snapped a few trees and birds but couldn't concentrate.

Lucy, Grace, and Nancy caught up with her on the way back to Mrs. Wright's.

"Elsie, excuse me, but I must know. Is there an understanding between you and Mr. Rockingham?" Lucy asked, practically dancing with anticipation as she awaited Elsie's answer.

Nancy listened raptly for her reply. Grace eyed her shrewdly.

"No, there isn't," Elsie said.

The women shared a glance that suggested Elsie was hiding the truth.

"None at all?" Lucy pressed.

"No."

The disappointment in her voice must have been obvious, because Nancy asked, "But you would like one?"

They had reached Mrs. Wright's. Elsie beckoned them into the deserted back room so they could speak privately. She sat at a table while Lucy and Nancy gathered around as though ready for a fireside story. Grace settled herself on a couch across the room, but Elsie saw her shift in her direction to hear better. She would have liked to shut her out of the conversation entirely, but it was impossible to do so without being rude.

That photograph had brought her such an unexpected hope she couldn't keep it to herself. Soon she was telling them everything. About Charles being her best friend when they were children, about the night she thought he would kiss her, and then the cessation of the letters. She told them about Amelia and her recent visit. She recounted her recent discoveries about Gabriel and her conflicting feelings about him.

"You cannot grieve forever," Lucy said, moving her chair closer and patting Elsie's shoulder.

Grace stretched her hand out in front of her to examine her fingernails. "No, and it sounds as if this Gabriel was something of a cad."

"Elsie—that look on Mr. Rockingham's face in the photo! Have you ever seen it before?" Nancy asked.

"No. Never. It isn't something I would ever forget."

"And you have feelings for him?" Lucy asked.

"Yes, I do. They've been growing all summer. I don't know how I didn't realize sooner that, for me, it's always been Charles," she said, the truth of it overwhelming her.

"What will you do now?" Lucy asked, her face ablaze with excitement.

Nancy leaned forward in her chair. "You must speak to him. You must tell him how you feel."

Elsie blanched at the idea. She'd always been able to speak to Charles about anything. But *this*?

She voiced her greatest fear of all: how could she trust herself to interpret his feelings?

"What if I'm wrong?" she asked. "What if I'm only seeing his behavior as romantic because I want it to be? His mother told me he might be involved with someone. And the woman who visited, Amelia—I thought he may be in love with her. He told me he considered courting her when they were in California."

"You said he didn't propose to her, so he can't be in love with her," Lucy said firmly. "And I think his mother is wrong about the other woman, or perhaps she was talking about Amelia. As for the photograph—a man looks at a woman that way for only one reason."

"He loves her," Nancy practically sang, bringing her hands to her heart.

Grace looked at Elsie for a long moment. She let out a slow breath and said, almost begrudgingly, "You're not imagining it, Elsie. If my beau looked at me like that, I would be choosing my wedding gown today."

This more than anything gave her reason to hope; Grace would never lie just to make Elsie feel better. She took the photograph out from under her coat. His eyes bored into hers. The special smile, the tilt of the head. She would have kissed the paper if she'd been alone.

"If that is true, if he should actually love me…" Elsie said, unable to complete the fantastic and cherished thought aloud. Into her mind rushed all the tiny things he'd done recently that she would have deemed flirtatious had any other man done them. Had Charles been trying to show her how he felt and she'd been too obtuse to understand? Had she been so certain he couldn't love her that she hadn't allowed herself to see the signs?

"Elsie, I think you should go home now. Go talk to Mr. Rockingham," Lucy said, standing.

"I will. Right away." Elsie jumped to her feet and gathered her things from the table.

They left the shop together, each woman turning off at her street. Her friends wished her good luck and extracted a promise to hear about what happened as soon as possible. Even Grace appeared curious. Finally only Lucy and Elsie remained. When they approached Lucy's house, she tugged at Elsie's sleeve to stop her.

"What is it?" Elsie asked, not wanting to waste a moment getting home to Charles.

Lucy looked up and down the street. The nearest people were a block away, outside of Tony's Bakery. "I didn't want to say this in front of Nancy and Grace, but I've seen the way Mr. Rockingham looks at you. I've only seen you together once, and that was weeks ago. But I think perhaps you've been missing something quite obvious."

The thought buoyed Elsie up even more. The sky was full of gray clouds that did nothing to dampen her mood. A brisk, tangy wind came off the sea.

"But why wouldn't he speak of it?" Elsie asked. "He's had no lack of opportunities over the summer."

"How could he possibly share his thoughts? The man who would have been your husband was also his friend. No, if anything, this proves the deep nature of his feelings for you. He's been staying out of the way of your grief, not selfishly making declarations or the like."

Indeed, it was just the type of thing Charles would do. Elsie had to hold herself back from running down the street and flinging herself into his arms.

"I must go, Lucy," she said, slowly backing away.

"Of course. Please call on me as soon as you can and tell me everything!"

"I will."

Lucy gave her an encouraging smile and started up the long drive to her house.

Elsie half ran, half walked toward home. But once she was in sight of the house, she was overcome by a storm of nerves. She pressed her hands to her cheeks. Was she really going to tell Charles that she loved him? Yes. She trusted him enough to talk to him about anything.

She closed her eyes for a moment and listened. The distant waves were a heartbeat, the wind a sigh. The crisp evening air cleared her mind. She was ready.

****

Elsie went straight upstairs to change out of her skirt and blouse. She wanted something eye-catching for this special evening with Charles. She chose an aqua dress that had a tight-fitting bodice with a low, square neckline. The lace cap-sleeves, wide sash, and wispy overskirt were a forget-me-not blue. It hugged her body in all the right places.

After dressing, she brushed her hair until it shone. She wound it up in a loose bun, leaving one lock over her shoulder the way Charles liked it. When she looked at herself in the mirror, her eyes were bright and her cheeks a delicate pink. It was true what they said: love is the most wonderful beautifier of all.

Elsie kept to a dainty walk down the stairs instead

of the gallop she would have preferred. Charles's voice drifted out of the study, sounding like he was reading something aloud to himself. Curiosity piqued, she went in to find him sitting at the desk, absorbed in paperwork.

"Good evening, Charles," she said, relieved that her voice didn't match her fluttering heart.

"Good evening." He glanced up before going back to his papers.

He looked up again, his eyes wide. He took in every detail of her dress, her face, her hair. After staring for a moment, he spoke.

"Special occasion?" he asked, rising from the chair and coming toward her.

"No, I only fancied wearing this. It's one of my favorites."

His trousers brushed against the hem of her dress. She looked up at him and smiled.

"Your eyes look like the ocean on a sunny day, Elsie." His voice sounded sweeter than it ever had before.

"Thank you," she said, her cheeks growing warm.

Now that the moment had come, Elsie realized she couldn't simply blurt out that she loved him and suspected that he loved her too, and would he please propose as soon as possible.

"What were you reading before I came in?"

His eyes lingered on her face as he answered. "I was going over this inventory." He held up a piece of paper. "I feel sure I've misplaced something. I was going to look through my desk to see if there's another list I could have written it on."

"I can check for you." She took the inventory from his hand. A tremor rippled through her when their fingers touched.

"Thank you," he said, his eyes never leaving her.

"Where's Luna?" The kitten wasn't in any of her usual spots.

"She's down at the stables. Why don't I fetch her while you look for that list? And then a walk on the beach?"

"I would like nothing more."

He took one more fleeting glance at her before he left.

Elsie giggled to herself. It would be a wonder if he hadn't noticed her love for him shining from her eyes. An evening stroll would be the perfect time to tell him how she really felt. And how appropriate, given that the last time they had almost kissed had been on the beach.

Sighing happily, she sat in the chair that Charles had just vacated. She began searching for anything that could be an inventory. It was not until she opened the last drawer that she found something.

But it wasn't the inventory.

It was one page of a letter, still open as though it had been hastily stashed away, in Charles's strong, flowing script that she knew so well. As she read down the page, her heart plummeted into her feet. She blinked back tears; the delicate paper shook in her hands. The paper that in one instant changed everything.

And I thoroughly agree with you. But enough of those things. I did not write merely to tell you how much I value your opinion, which you must surely already know.

There is something else that I want you to know. I must tell you what's been on my mind since we parted. More than anything I want to be with you. I want to hold you in my arms and tell you how much I love you.

I want you to be my wife.

Forgive me for mentioning this here, in a letter, first. I simply cannot wait another moment for you to know what's in my heart. Please tell me that you love me, as I love you. Please say you'll marry me. Write to me and I will be with you as soon as I can, and we will begin our life together.

Yours—always yours,

Charles

Elsie fell back against the chair as the room spun around her; she gripped the side of the desk to steady herself. She put a hand to her chest and took a deep, quivering breath. There was no date on the letter. He must have finished writing it recently, maybe even today. She let the paper slip from her fingers.

He was lost to her.

Lost.

She covered her face with her hands, all light and warmth gone. It was a bitter cold, following so soon on the hope that had filled her for the last few hours. She had dreamed of an embrace, and laughter, and wholeness. She had never imagined such an abrupt end to the love that had never been and could now never be.

Elsie searched the desk but found no other pages of the letter, only what must be Charles's personal papers. With trembling hands she picked up a pile and rifled through them, envelope after envelope showing a return address from California. On the bottom of the drawer was a bundle of letters tied with green ribbon. She didn't bother to pick them up—there was no need to look to know who had sent them.

Elsie sat in a daze, hardly able to think. Her mind

flew back to the day he'd been so agitated when she tried to get into the desk. Charles must have had a change of heart since Amelia left and wanted to keep it a secret from Elsie. She pressed her fingers to her eyes, trying to keep the tears in, but it was impossible.

She glanced out the window. Charles was striding across the lawn with Luna. Elsie closed the drawer, taking care to make it look as though it had not been disturbed, and ran from the study; she couldn't possibly face him now. Her foot was on the first stair, her hand gripping the banister, when he entered the hall.

"Here's Luna. Perhaps she would like to come to the beach. We could bring her in the basket."

Elsie closed her eyes and cursed herself for not moving faster. She turned to face him and clasped her hands tightly behind her back to keep them from shaking.

"Elsie! What happened? Are you ill?" He took a step toward her.

"Yes," she managed. "Yes, I'm ill. Quite ill." It was not a lie, for she had never felt so sick in her life.

He took another step closer. "Is there anything I can do for you? Do you want to lie down on the sofa?"

"No, I'm going to my room," she said, trying to keep her voice steady.

"Do you want me to help you upstairs?" He reached out a hand to take her arm.

"No!" She retreated farther up the stairs. His touch would unlock the tears she was barely keeping at bay.

His face was etched with worry as he placed his foot on the first stair. "Wait." He reached for her again.

She turned her back on him and was halfway up the stairs when she heard a meow. She hurried back down the stairs and took Luna.

"Elsie," Charles implored, "please let me help you."

She just shook her head and rushed up the stairs as the tears began to flow.

As soon as she made it to her bedroom she locked the door behind her. She put Luna on the bed and all but tore her dress off. She would never wear it again. Elsie threw herself on the bed in just her underclothes and sobbed for her missed chance at love.

Chapter Thirteen

She'd been in her room for about an hour when there was a soft knock on the door.

"Elsie?" Charles called.

At the concern in his voice, her tears began anew. His footsteps soon retreated down the hall toward his own room. She got under the sheets and pulled the blankets up to her chin, Luna nestled against her.

Elsie lay there, motionless, going over the last few weeks in her mind. How had she deluded herself into thinking that Charles was in love with her? She was grateful she hadn't spoken to him about it before she saw the letter. Her cheeks burned when she thought of how gently he would have rejected her advances.

When Amelia left, Elsie had secretly hoped he would turn to her, that those tender feelings remained. But hope had betrayed her once again.

It wasn't as though she had long suspected that he loved her. True, there had been moments over the past month that had been more flirtatious than friendly. Some actions that—had he been anyone else—she would have taken as a sign of affection, even love. It had only been today, when she saw the photograph, that she had come to believe he loved her. And she hadn't recognized until that moment how strong her love was for him. It was no fleeting thing, no mild infatuation. She loved him so deeply that it was a part of her.

She got out of bed and crossed the room to the washstand. The mirror on the wall reflected a face of misery. Her red-rimmed eyes stood out against the ashen hue of her skin. She splashed water on her face and rubbed it dry with a soft towel.

She sat on the window seat, where she'd dropped her camera and coat earlier that day. Tucked inside the coat was the photograph. Had she known Charles for so long that she had ceased to see the strong jaw, the full lips, the fine eyes that she had convinced herself shined with love? She ran a finger across his brow. What moment, what mood had she caught with her camera? Elsie stashed the photograph on the tallest shelf in her wardrobe, out of sight.

She returned to bed and lay there, strategizing how she should deal with Charles now. Act as if nothing had happened? Avoid him entirely? That would be difficult, living in the same house. She could perhaps move back to Holderness. But no, she had tried running away from her feelings once before, and it hadn't worked. Besides, her heart gave a desperate lurch when she thought of leaving him.

What a fool she had been to let herself fall in love. She laughed to herself. As if she could have helped it. She'd known Charles her entire life. He was an integral part of all her childhood adventures, mishaps, joys. They had spent countless hours together, talking, joking, sharing secrets. They had been molded to each other. He was her first and best friend.

A day popped into her mind, the day she realized just how much he cared about her. It was after she'd broken her elbow, when they were six. James had been pressuring Charles to go away with him on some outing, but he refused. He stayed inside with Elsie every day until she healed. He gave up time with his brother and friends just to be with her, and it confirmed what she'd always known; they had something special.

She had a glimpse of her true feelings for him the night before he moved away, and those feelings had only grown stronger with time. She tried to ignore them then, not because she stopped caring, but because she thought he had.

All at once it was clear that this was the root of her doubts about Gabriel. She had cared for him and had hoped for an agreeable marriage. But he was not Charles.

Another future she had yearned for was now stripped away. Charles would never be her husband. But she need not lose him entirely. She would stand by and watch him marry Amelia and support him as the friend she had always been. And her love, her secret, she would lock away in her heart the way she had the guilt over Gabriel. But this secret she would never unlock.

As the clock struck two, Elsie turned out the lights, Luna still asleep beside her.

Another knock came upon the door.

"Elsie? Are you awake?" Charles whispered.

She was not even tempted to answer. She needed the night to gird herself against these emotions.

"Elsie?" After a few minutes, she heard him sigh and walk away.

Elsie turned over in bed and cried herself to sleep.

****

By the next morning, Elsie had a plan. She would go on as if nothing had happened. As if she had never seen that photograph, or the letter. She would go back to how things had been the day before yesterday. But one thing must change: she must not spend so much time with Charles.

She put Luna in her basket and went downstairs. Halfway down the stairs she froze—Max and Charles were speaking together in the dining room.

"Do you think we need to send for Dr. Braman?" Charles asked. He sounded tired and worried.

"Oh, no. From what you've told me, it came on very suddenly last night. I'm sure she'll be right as rain this morning."

"Did you see her after she went to her room? I went and knocked several times, but she didn't answer."

"No, she stayed in her room all night."

"How can you take this so calmly?" Charles said, his voice rising. "You didn't see her last night. She looked terrible. As if she had had dreadful news or was seriously ill." He paused for a moment. "Did any letters come for her yesterday? Any word from Holderness? Perhaps she did have bad news. I should have asked her."

"She received no letters that I know of. But Charles, isn't it obvious?" Max asked, unperturbed.

Elsie held her breath, worried that Max was about to divulge her secret. Not that she'd told him, but she was beginning to suspect that he was much more perceptive than she'd given him credit for.

"Is what obvious?" Charles seemed like he was barely containing his frustration.

"It's Gabriel. She mourns him still. I've seen this sort of fit take her before. It comes upon her suddenly, usually when something reminds her of him."

"Gabriel?" Charles asked, sounding skeptical.

"She went into town yesterday. Maybe the docks or the boats reminded her of his wreck. Oh"—she heard

Max's fingers snap—"the two of you went rowing yesterday. Perhaps it was that. Something must have brought him to mind last night, poor lamb."

She thought it a good excuse for her behavior the night before, if Max could get Charles to believe it.

"So you don't think she needs the doctor?" Charles asked.

"Of course not. What woman needs a doctor to help mend a broken heart? Funny, though…"

"What's funny?"

"I thought she turned a corner and had let the past go, at least a bit. I thought she'd been through the worst of her grief. It seems I was wrong."

"I thought that, too." His voice sagged, as if he was not only concerned but disappointed.

After a few minutes of silence, Elsie took a moment to compose herself, then continued down the stairs.

"Good morning," she said, walking into the dining room.

"Elsie." Charles rose from his chair.

She smiled at him, hoping it looked much more natural than it felt.

"Charles, here's Luna. Would you be a dear and take her to the stables?" She held out the basket, careful to avoid his eyes and his touch when he took it from her.

"How are you feeling? You looked particularly unwell last night." Charles sat down, put the basket in his lap, and absentmindedly petted Luna.

"I can't think what brought it on so suddenly. In any case, I feel much better this morning."

Charles was watching her closely. She sipped her coffee and nibbled a warm cinnamon donut. Her throat was so tight she could barely swallow.

"Are you finished in the study?" asked Max, looking from Charles to Elsie.

"There's still a bit to be done," Charles said, tearing his eyes away from Elsie to look at Max.

"I'm sure Charles can finish it by himself. I feel I am mostly in the way." She let out a laugh that sounded fake even to her.

Charles narrowed his eyes at her. She stood up, having hardly eaten anything.

"I'm meeting Lucy this morning. I'll see you both later," she said in as cheery a voice as she could muster.

"Yesterday you said you were eager to look over the petrified wood that arrived," Charles said.

"I'll see it when you're finished. Goodbye." She hurried from the room before her voice or tears could betray her.

****

Elsie was winded when she reached Lucy's hilltop home. She rang the bell and looked out to sea while she waited for the butler to answer. The door opened behind her, and she turned to see Lucy herself, eyes bright with anticipation. Her face fell the moment she saw Elsie.

"Elsie, what happened?"

Elsie just shook her head and fresh tears came unbidden. Lucy took her arm and led her into the parlor. Elsie sat down heavily on the sofa, her face in her hands. Lucy rang for tea, and they sat in silence until the maid brought the teapot. Lucy poured out a cup for Elsie. She took it, not drinking but holding the warm cup with both hands.

"Last night I found a letter that Charles wrote. A romantic letter. To someone else," she said, unable to speak of the details.

"Oh, how shocking!" Lucy said, her hands pressed to her cheeks. "Who was it written to?"

"There wasn't a name on it, but it has to be Amelia." Elsie put her tea down and picked up an embroidered pillow, hugging it against her stomach.

"You're sure the letter was for Amelia?"

"Who else would it be? I don't know of any other woman he's involved with."

"Did you ask him about it? Then you would know for certain."

The possibility had not even crossed her mind. To be caught snooping around his desk, and then admit to reading that letter? She could only imagine how furious he would have been.

"No. I was much too upset. I went straight up to my room."

"We can only assume you're right about Amelia, then." Lucy sounded as dejected as Elsie felt.

"But he told me he wasn't going to propose to her."

"He must have lied to spare your feelings."

Elsie cringed inside. That hurt almost as much as the letter. But what other explanation was there? She thought she and Charles were as close as they'd ever been, and all along he was lying to her face about Amelia. First Gabriel and now Charles. Could she trust any man besides her father? Gabriel's lies had been shocking, but Charles's cut her to the core.

"I've been afraid to let myself love him, and this is exactly why! This is the third time I've misread his feelings. What is wrong with me? When will I finally get it into my head that he does not love me?" She wiped her eyes impatiently, sick of tears.

"It can be hard to understand men," Lucy said,

shaking her head. "Who knows what they're thinking? They say one thing and mean another."

"But Charles is different. At least I thought he was, I thought I knew him better than I know anyone."

"Well, you could have knocked me over with a feather," Lucy said, "I was certain he loved you."

"I was too, until I saw that letter."

"How did you leave things with him?"

"I barely spoke to him this morning. He's confused about my behavior and will no doubt ask me about it later when we are alone."

Lucy gripped Elsie's hand and looked into her face: "You must not be alone with him! It will be too much for you."

"How can I avoid him? We live in the same house."

"See him only at mealtimes. Did you often spend time alone before all this?"

"Yes. Hours alone each day." She looked out the window at the perfect, mocking blue sky.

"That must stop," Lucy said in a businesslike manner. "You will spend as little time at home as possible. You will under no circumstances see Mr. Rockingham alone."

"I know you're right. But—"

"But what?"

"I'll miss him so much," Elsie said, sniffling.

"Oh, no, you won't! I'll keep you so busy and entertained you won't have time for missing him."

Lucy was as good as her word. Over the next few weeks, she took Elsie everywhere with her—to the dressmaker, to Cantwell's, to the library, to Bennington Square, and to call on her friends. Lucy had confided in Grace and Nancy, and they helped with her endeavors to keep Elsie occupied.

One day while they were at Grace's house, she pulled Elsie aside and showed her the rose garden while Nancy and Lucy were busy in the parlor.

"I'm so sorry this has happened," Grace said. "I do understand. You see, I've been in your shoes before." She met Elsie's eyes briefly before looking away.

"Thank you, Grace," she said, unsure of what else to say.

Grace had been much more civil since she'd heard about the letter. She'd taken to chatting with Elsie whenever they had the chance and tried even harder than Nancy and Lucy to find new distractions for her.

"I'd like to apologize for the way I've treated you this summer," Grace said. "I've been in a foul mood since my beau broke things off with me. I thought he was about to propose, but he left. Just left. And I haven't heard from him since."

She looked sadder than Elsie had ever seen her. Elsie tentatively put out a hand, and Grace took it for just a moment before letting go.

"You arrived just days after it happened. I was in no mood to make a new acquaintance, but it was no excuse. I behaved abominably. What would you say to starting over?"

"I'd like that," Elsie said. "And thank you for telling me."

Grace sniffed a delicate pink rose, then turned back to Elsie. "I hoped it would help to know that you are not the only woman to be so scorned by a man she thought she could trust."

"Oh, I do trust Charles," Elsie said, raising her chin a notch.

"Elsie, don't be so naïve," Grace said. "He obviously lied to you about this Amelia person. He said he wasn't courting her, and he was. He even went so far as to propose."

Elsie suppressed a shudder. *Proposed.* The word made her sick to her stomach. "He probably has a good reason for not telling me. Perhaps he didn't want to mention it until he had an answer from her."

"Perhaps he wants to have two women on the hook. He must know how you feel about him."

"I hope not. I've been so careful not to let my feelings show, and I haven't been spending much time with him since I found the letter."

"I hope not too, for your sake. Men who act charming and kind can be even more dangerous to a lady's heart than a rogue."

"He's no rogue," Elsie said, hackles raised.

Grace looked like she wanted to argue. "It's no matter," she said. "You needn't trouble yourself over him any longer. Come, let's join the others in the parlor."

Elsie followed her inside but couldn't stop thinking about what she said. Charles—a rogue! No. She couldn't believe that. It was true he had lied, and a tiny piece of her could not let it go. Yet there was no point being angry with him. It was like Max had said: she could forgive him regardless. Whatever Grace said, Elsie knew Charles. Perhaps he wanted to spare her feelings. In any case, he had a right to his privacy.

One afternoon, while Max and Charles were at the office, Elsie was driven by an impulse to go back and read the letter. Perhaps there was some clue as to when he'd written it, or if she searched more thoroughly, she might find the missing pages. It was possible the letter had been written long ago. It could even be his original proposal to Amelia, the one she had rejected, although why he'd have kept it, she didn't know.

Elsie tiptoed into the study. She sat down and stilled her shaking hands before opening the drawer.

The letter was gone.

She rifled through the drawer to no avail. The pile of letters from Amelia was still there, as was the bundle tied in green ribbon. But there was no sign of the letter she'd seen the other day. She closed the drawer slowly. So he'd sent it. But what had she expected? Once his mind was made up about something so important, he would take action right away. She was surprised he wasn't on a train to California right now to ask for Amelia's hand in person.

Elsie told her friends that she'd looked for the letter, and after some chastising from Lucy for snooping, they all agreed that, sadly, he must have mailed it. After that, they tried even harder to boost her spirits. On the rare days they weren't busy in town, they would go out riding or go to one of their houses for the afternoon. Grace taught Elsie some new embroidery patterns, which she used to make gifts for Margaret and her parents. She even embroidered some tiny slippers for Brian.

Every day she expected and dreaded an announcement from Charles. But perhaps Amelia had not replied yet. As Charles had told her, the post took a long time to cross the country.

Elsie spent a few evenings each week at the photography studio, where Mrs. Wright was teaching her about portraiture. Elsie liked these evenings because she didn't have to sit at the supper table with Max and Charles, talking animatedly and pretending that she was happy when every time Charles smiled at her it bruised her sore heart. All she really wanted was to stare into his eyes or say something to make him laugh.

Why was it that the days took so long to pass when she wasn't with him? Her friends did their best to keep her occupied and distracted, but Charles had taken up residence in her thoughts. Constantly she saw things that reminded her of him, and the empty ache inside would only grow worse. At home she was always anxious, knowing that Charles could come into any room at any time. She would start when she heard a foot on the stairs, and if ever it was Charles that appeared she would make some excuse and flee the room. The only peace was in her bedroom, where she could shut out everyone else.

In early July, Elsie received an invitation to a soiree hosted by Nancy the following week. She and her friends combed the shops in Bennington square to find perfect gowns for the big night. The morning of the party they met at Grace's for tea and gossip about the gentlemen who would attend, guessing who would dance with whom.

Elsie wore a long gown of midnight silk with short sleeves and a scooped neckline. The cornflower-blue overskirt shimmered like a waterfall when she moved. Sapphires sparkled at her throat and ears, and her hair was piled high, held in place with a glittering amber comb. Her eyes picked up the color of the dress, making them almost the same deep blue as Charles's. After pulling on her opera gloves, she was ready.

On her way out of the house, she encountered Charles, who had just come in from the beach. He was wiping the sand off his trouser legs when he looked up and saw her. He grinned, but then something shifted in his eyes, intentionally shutting her out. The pain that coursed through her must be what he'd been feeling daily.

"You're going out?"

"Yes, to Nancy's." She gripped the clasp of her beaded handbag much tighter than necessary.

"Enjoy your evening," he said flatly as he passed.

He'd stopped asking her what was wrong after the first week. She hadn't ignored him but had denied that she was acting differently. He knew she was lying, which made it worse. They still talked at mealtimes, but something vital was missing, and they both knew it.

Elsie wanted to follow him into the library. She would rather not go to the party at all but sit quietly with him and read. She missed even the silences with Charles. A sharp tug in her heart reminded her why she was doing this. It was too difficult to be close to him now that she knew she loved him.

Tears sprang to her eyes, but she blinked them back. After one last glance behind her at Charles, she went outside, where Tom waited with the carriage. Max still had not mastered the motorcar.

Lamps were coming on all over town, twinkling like earthbound stars. Elsie played with the strings of her purse as the carriage made its way to Nancy's—a stately, octagonal mansion made of brick. Lights glowed from every window, and people were already dancing inside. This was what Nancy considered a little party! Motorcars and carriages lined the street, and Elsie had to wait to alight.

A footman helped her out of the carriage and told Tom that a message would be sent when Elsie was ready to be taken home. At the front door, Lucy greeted her, wearing a mauve gown with matching flowers in her hair.

"Good evening. You look splendid," Lucy trilled.

Elsie's gown had seemed extravagant while in her bedroom, but compared to what some of the other women wore, it verged on plain.

"Is my dress all right?" she asked, touching the bow at her waist. "I should have worn something more formal."

"No, it's perfect for you," Lucy said, waving a hand. "I wouldn't have let you buy it if it didn't make you look magnificent."

"Thank you. You look beautiful."

"Thank you!" Lucy said, doing a little twirl. She pointed out Grace on the dance floor, in a dress the color of ripe plums. She was in the arms of a tall dark-haired man who couldn't take his eyes off her. Elsie recognized him as the man she'd seen Grace with at McGoldrick's.

"I had no idea the party would be so grand," Elsie said, taking in the crowd.

At least fifty couples were dancing in the cavernous ballroom. Most of the lights had been replaced with candles in chandeliers. Shimmering candelabras stood on tables and on the sills of the tall, arched windows. It was clearly one of the social events of the summer. She wondered whether Max and Charles had been invited.

Nancy stood out in the crowd, wearing a tangerine-colored gown that accentuated her figure. She beckoned them over from across the ballroom. They waded through people on the edge of the dance floor, delayed by Lucy stopping and saying hello to almost everyone.

"Good evening, Nancy," Elsie said when they joined her.

"I'm so glad you came," Nancy said. She handed Elsie a full dance card.

"So many!" Elsie said, scanning the names before slipping the card onto her wrist by its yellow ribbon.

"Yes. I've filled it out for you, and I guarantee you will like them all," Nancy said brightly.

"Elsie, this will do you a world of good. And perhaps you will meet someone to take your mind off of…well, you know who," Lucy said with a nod.

It was true Elsie had met hardly anyone since coming to Sherwood Bay. And what better way than at a ball? Since she was here, she would do her best to enjoy herself. An irksome voice inside reminded her that she'd promised herself she'd be open to meeting eligible men. Who could say? Perhaps the card dangling from her wrist held not only the names of her dance partners but her future husband. She shushed the tiny voice.

The music began, and a handsome man with glossy brown hair approached the group. He looked to Nancy first.

"Elsie, may I introduce my cousin, Captain John Falla? John, Miss Elsie Hayward." Captain Falla nodded politely and, taking her elbow, led Elsie onto the dance floor.

Kind and very talkative, he told her about his ship, the *Terrapin*, and his latest trip. Elsie hardly listened, having developed a habit of ignoring stories about sea voyages.

She was halfway through her dance card when she began thinking longingly of the settee she'd seen in Nancy's drawing room. After finishing her dance with one Mr. Stockmayer, she went to the refreshment table.

Elsie was about to refill her silver punch cup when

it slipped from her fingers and clattered to the floor. She stooped to pick it up, her eyes on the door.

Charles stood just inside the ballroom, resplendent in a black tuxedo. A gaggle of women surrounded him, dance cards in their hands.

Elsie refused to be one of those women.

She turned on her heel and strode out to the garden to get some air, following a path lined with rhododendrons. The air swirled with their heady scent. The path led to a patio enclosed by tall hedges.

Elsie perched on the edge of a cast-iron bench, then jumped up again, wringing her hands, unable to sit still. It was as though every woman in that ballroom had snuck into her bedroom and read her diary, or gone through her jewelry box and picked out her favorite gem. She laughed to herself. Could she really think of Charles as *hers* anymore?

"What do you find so amusing out here?" Charles asked from behind her. She wondered how he'd managed to fling off all the eager dance partners.

"Oh, nothing," she said, turning. "Why didn't you tell me you were coming?"

"I wasn't going to, until I saw you in that dress," he said, now within arm's reach. His eyes took in every inch of her with one appreciative glance.

"But you don't even like balls," she said, her words coming out in a hoarse whisper.

The moonlight softened his features and brightened his eyes. He looked like a storybook prince.

"How could I pass up a chance to prove myself just as good a dancer as James?" He held out his arms and she went to him without a moment's hesitation.

He held her hand lightly, the other one pressed

against her back. She slowly reached up and rested a hand on his shoulder. There was no space between them, and the heat of him seared through her dress. The scent of his cologne mingled with that of the flowers intoxicated her. All her senses were alive, and she wondered if he could feel her heart throbbing against his chest.

"The Blue Danube Waltz" floated out the open ballroom windows. They didn't speak but looked into each other's eyes as the minutes slipped by. Elsie would have liked to stop time—Charles felt perfect, smelled perfect, *was* perfect. He was solid and strong as he swept her across the patio, their steps fitting perfectly together. She closed her eyes and let him lead.

It was some time before she noticed the music had stopped. The sound of voices snapped her back to reality. Lucy and Grace stood beside the hedges, watching them, whispering to each other behind their hands.

Elsie pulled herself away from Charles and stepped back a few paces. She put a hand up to tuck in a loose strand of hair, only to find that, for once, it had all stayed in place. Charles hadn't moved. His eyes flicked back and forth between hers, he looked like he was on the verge of speaking. Elsie waited breathlessly. Then he broke into a roguish grin.

"Better than James?" he asked, a barely perceptible tightness in his voice.

"No, but you're giving him a run for his money," she said lightly. She smoothed down her skirt and turned to face Grace and Lucy.

"It's time for the supper dance," Grace said, pointing over her shoulder to the house. "You're supposed to be dancing with Mr. Moore."

"Yes, of course," Elsie said, not moving.

Lucy's shoes clicked on the flagstones as she walked across the patio to join them. The look she gave Charles was far from friendly. "You arrived late. I'm not sure who to partner you with."

"I don't need a partner. I'll enjoy my own company for supper," he said with a grin.

"We can't have that," Grace said coolly. "I'm sure somebody needs a partner. Come with me." She tucked a hand into the crook of his arm and led him away into the house. He glanced back at Elsie, but his grin was gone.

Before Elsie could follow, Lucy stepped in front of her.

"Do not dance with him again, Elsie," she said, her voice uncharacteristically stern. "You should have seen yourself in his arms. You looked…enraptured."

"Because I was," Elsie said, looking down the path he'd taken.

Lucy's brows knitted together. "I wish he'd stayed at home. He shouldn't be attending balls if he's on the cusp of becoming engaged."

"We don't know that he is. Perhaps Amelia hasn't gotten the letter yet. Perhaps she said no," Elsie said, painfully aware that this was wishful thinking.

Lucy shot her a disbelieving look. "Would *you*?"

Elsie shook her head. "But still, I don't believe he's engaged yet. My mother would have told me, even if he wouldn't have. At any rate, engaged men are allowed to attend balls."

"Yes, they are, but they shouldn't look like"—Lucy waved her hands in the air, searching for words—"like they are in love with someone else."

Elsie blushed to the roots of her hair and looked at the ground. "He didn't look like that."

"You didn't see it because your eyes were closed. I don't know about this Mr. Rockingham." Lucy directed her glare toward the house. "Perhaps *he* is the cad. He clearly acts besotted with you at times, and then he proposes to another woman! I'm not surprised you're confused. What is a person to think? He needs to sort out his feelings and stop playing with yours."

"He doesn't mean anything by it. He's affectionate by nature."

It wasn't as if he toyed with women's feelings on a regular basis, as Lucy was clearly suggesting, as had Grace. A cad, a rogue. Were other people seeing him for what he was but she refused to? Perhaps she no longer knew him as well as she thought she did. Was she naive, like Grace said, or merely blinded by love?

They went inside, where Elsie was introduced to Mr. Moore. He was a friendly gentleman, polite and chatty.

Close to midnight, she danced with Mr. Cordes and after him, there were yet more men to dance with, until Elsie's feet ached and she longed for nothing but her bed or perhaps a soft chair and a tub of warm water for her toes.

She only saw Charles once more, as he was leaving. She was dancing with a Mr. Owen when she noticed Charles standing by the ballroom door, scanning the crowd. She knew he was looking for her. He finally spotted her, and their eyes held briefly before he turned and walked out.

Chapter Fourteen

Finally the last dance was called and everyone filed out of the house, loud chatter emanating from all sides. When Elsie reached the front steps outside, close to five o'clock in the morning, the sky was a dark, velvety blue. She and Tom exchanged sleepy greetings, and he helped her into the carriage. She took her shoes off immediately and massaged her feet. It wasn't as satisfying as dipping them in the ocean and letting the surf wash over them, but it would have to do.

Dancing all night had been wonderful, but the plan to find someone to take Charles's place in her heart had backfired. Making forced conversation with her dance partners had only reminded her of how easy it was to be with Charles.

She sank into the plush seat, watching the town come to life through the window. When the carriage came to a stop in front of Max's house Tom jumped down and opened the door for her.

"Thank you," she said, taking his hand.

She went upstairs to her bedroom, where Luna was asleep on the bed. After giving her a little pat, Elsie sat at the vanity, took off her jewelry, and removed the comb from her hair, not thinking about much of anything but wondering if Charles, too, was awake just down the hall.

Elsie was exhausted but knew she couldn't settle to sleep yet. She went to her wardrobe and picked out her bathing costume. After changing, she grabbed a towel and went downstairs. The rising sun filled the silent rooms with soft yellow light.

Revitalized by the cold morning air, she sprinted to the beach. At the shore, she dropped her towel and jumped into the surf, gasping in its icy embrace, her aches and fatigue instantly washed away. She adjusted to the temperature and swam past the breaking waves. After swimming laps parallel to the beach, she floated in the water with her eyes closed, and before long the sun was fully up.

After a few more lazy laps, she went back to the beach. She sat on the driftwood log and used the towel to dry herself, then combed her fingers through her hair. Gentle waves broke on the shore.

She'd learned something last night: staying at Max's house with Charles was unbearable; it was time to leave. Avoiding him hadn't helped anything. Not only were they not sweethearts, they had almost ceased being friends altogether. Their dance at the ball was the closest they'd been in weeks. What was the point of it all if she was going to hurt the person she loved most? There was pain in his eyes every time she pulled away. The best thing to do was to put some distance between them, and hopefully, over time, her feelings would dull. Perhaps they could restore their old, comfortable friendship if they corresponded. Writing letters, she wouldn't constantly have to stifle her urge to touch his face or kiss him.

Elsie would go home to Holderness. She would become a devoted auntie to little Brian and even attend some of her mother's parties. She would never fall in love with anyone but Charles—of that she was certain.

But perhaps she could find a kind man to share a life with, have a family. Her heart shattered at the thought.

Back at the house, she sank into a hot bath and let the warmth seep into her muscles. She closed her eyes, luxuriating in the steamy water, and lay there until the water was almost cold. She wrapped a towel around herself and left the bathroom.

She was almost at her bedroom door when Charles exited his room. His eyes widened, then he looked away, his face a dark pink. She blushed furiously, tugging at her towel in a vain attempt to make it bigger.

"I was just going back to my room," she said, stating the obvious.

"Have you just arrived home?" he asked, looking at the ceiling.

"Not too long ago. I went for a swim. It was refreshing but cold." A little puddle was forming on the carpet. Water dripped from her hair down between her breasts.

"I can imagine, at this hour." He shifted his attention to a spot on the wall behind her.

"Did you enjoy yourself last night?"

"I enjoyed it as much as any ball. I haven't danced that much in a long time." He pivoted so that she saw only his profile as she imagined stunning dance partners in his arms.

Elsie stood there, exceedingly conscious of her near nakedness. She reminded herself that he'd seen her in her bathing costume before, which covered only a bit more than this towel.

"Well, I'd better go to my room."

"Oh, yes. I'm just going down for an early breakfast," he said to a spot on the carpet.

"I'll see you in the dining room, then, after I'm dressed." She went into her room, brushing his arm as she passed. Once inside, she was overcome with a fit of laughter.

She changed into a lilac-colored dress and pinned her hair up. Luna was on the bed, trying to catch patches of sunlight in her paws. Elsie lay down for only a moment. She had every intention of going downstairs for breakfast, but sleep soon carried her away.

****

The gray light in Elsie's bedroom told her it was close to dusk. She sat up and stretched, uncomfortable from sleeping in her corset all day. Someone must have come in while she slept, as a blanket had been tucked around her and Luna was nowhere to be seen. She got out of bed, her head still foggy. If she went downstairs right away, she'd be in time for supper. She didn't bother to change out of her wrinkled clothes.

Max and Charles were sitting at the table, the remains of their meal in front of them.

"Good morning, Elsie," said Max with a snicker. "I trust you slept well."

"Good *evening*," she replied, taking the seat across from Charles.

Charles nodded to her.

Elsie filled her plate with sliced ham, asparagus, baked beans, and a warm slice of brown bread dripping with butter. She listened to Charles and Max discuss their latest shipment while she ate. After she finished, it was time to break the news that she was leaving Sherwood Bay.

"I have a book I want to get back to in the library," Charles said, standing up.

"Please wait a moment, Charles. There's something I need to tell you both." She cleared her throat and took a sip of water.

He sat down and drummed his fingers on the table.

"What is it, Elsie?" Max asked, folding his hands across his stomach.

"It's time for me to leave Sherwood Bay."

"Another visit to Holderness already?" Max asked and chuckled.

"No, this time I'm going back to Holderness for good. I can't tell you how much I've loved being here. But it's time I went home."

Nobody spoke. Elsie could almost read the arguments for her to stay flashing through Max's mind. Charles looked out the window, his thumbnail between his teeth. Somehow it made her love him even more. Her heart seemed to skip a beat, and she resolved to follow through with leaving, no matter what.

"But why?" Max finally asked. He regarded her as if waiting for her to answer an exam question.

She said the first plausible reason she could think of. "I miss my parents and Margaret."

"I'll be sorry to see you go, but I understand. Home is home, eh?"

"Yes. And of course I'll visit. Perhaps next summer." She chanced a look at Charles. Now he was scowling at her.

"When do you intend to leave?" Max asked.

"Next week." She hadn't had a date in mind, but now it seemed a good idea to leave as soon as possible.

"I'll have Mr. Anderson make the arrangements." Max pushed back from the table and left the room.

Elsie and Charles sat in uncomfortable silence. He

stared at her as if he couldn't quite place her.

"What?" she finally asked, throwing her hands up.

"Elsie, what is this really about?"

"What do you mean?"

"I thought you liked Sherwood Bay." He left his chair and came over to sit right next to her. His knee bumped hers beneath the table.

"I do like it here. But I miss home."

Charles scoffed, which irked her.

"Why shouldn't I miss home? You know how close I am to Margaret. And I'd like to spend more time with Brian." She scooted her chair a few inches away from him.

"I know you love Margaret, and I know you love babies. But that seems to be all I know about you right now."

"What is that supposed to mean?" she snapped.

"It means you've changed, Elsie. I don't know why, but you have. You act as though you can't stand to be in the same room with me." His voice broke, but he kept his eyes on hers.

A cold knot settled itself in Elsie's chest. "Don't be ridiculous, Charles. Of course I still like to be with you. We danced together just last night at the ball."

"But I had to follow you there. That's the first time you've willingly spent time with me in weeks. You spend whole days out of the house. I hardly see you anymore, and when I do, you barely speak to me."

"You've been so busy with your work for Max, and I've been busy too."

"Being busy never used to get in the way of our time together."

"That's true, but we can't always be holed up in

Max's study," she said with a light laugh, as though the whole thing was of little consequence.

He glared at her. "Stop pretending. I know you're avoiding me, and I wish you'd tell me why. We've never kept secrets from each other before."

"Charles, it's—"

"Don't lie to me anymore, Elsie. I can't bear it!" He raked a hand through his hair. "I'll be honest even if you won't. I miss you, and I know you're hiding something from me."

"No, I'm not! I don't know why you would think so." This was of course a lie, but what else could she say? Admit that she was avoiding him because she wanted to either kiss him or start crying whenever they were in a room together for more than five minutes?

"You don't think *I* can tell when *you* are keeping secrets?" he asked, his voice rising to an impressive pitch.

"Maybe you don't know me as well as you think you do." Pain shot across his face and she immediately regretted her words.

"No. No, maybe I don't," he said quietly. "The Elsie I know wouldn't hide things from me."

"I am the Elsie you know," she said, working hard to keep the pain out of her voice. "But we've both changed since those days in Holderness. And perhaps you are not the only one who has things to keep private now."

He looked shocked for a moment but then laughed quietly. "Yes, we have both changed. But not *that* much. If you ever feel like telling me the truth, you know where to find me." He shoved back from the table and stalked out.

Elsie laid her head in her arms on the table. It went against everything she felt to let him storm off and not chase after him. But if she explained why she'd been avoiding him, it would be humiliating for her and awkward for him. And who was he to accuse her of keeping secrets? For all she knew, he was already engaged. His anger would burn itself out as it always did, and then she'd try to be just a little friendlier so they could part on good terms.

During the next week Elsie spent most of her days with Lucy, Nancy, and Grace. She told them she was leaving, and why. They were very understanding and hoped she would come back to Sherwood Bay soon. They exchanged addresses and promised to write and trade photographs through the mail.

A few days before Elsie was to leave, she took tea on the patio overlooking the beach. The lilac bush was free of flowers, but bees lazily circled the orange daylilies nearby. The morning was sunny, yet with a promise of rain in the air.

She heard a sound and turned to see Charles standing in front of the French doors.

"Elsie?" he said tentatively.

"Hello, Charles," she said, her face lighting up.

Encouraged by her reception, he took the chair beside her.

After a few minutes he said, "I'm sorry."

"For what?"

"I haven't been the best friend of late. I should have respected your wish to put some distance between us. And I think I know why you were avoiding me." He looked right into her eyes.

A wave of panic washed over her.

"I think," he went on, "that it's Gabriel."

"Gabriel?" she asked, barely keeping her jaw from dropping.

"Yes. Being with me reminds you of him because the three of us spent so much time together. And that must, understandably, cause you pain."

If this explanation made him feel better, perhaps that was all that mattered.

"It has been difficult," she said.

"I could tell. You didn't need to hide it from me," he said and nudged her knee with his.

They sat together in silence, watching a flock of cormorants glide above the water. It was so easy to be with him.

After a while, he turned to her. "I know you're leaving soon and I thought we might have one more adventure before you go."

"What sort of adventure?" she asked eagerly.

"Do you remember Max and me talking about Star Island?"

"Yes, you mentioned it some time ago." She tilted her head and watched him closely while he spoke. She liked the way his lips moved. She brought her attention back to his eyes so she wouldn't miss what he was saying, but they proved to be even more of a distraction.

"We could take the ferry from Portsmouth and go out for the day. I think you'd enjoy seeing the hotel, and there are birds and trees you could photograph. There's a restaurant where we could have lunch before we come back."

Elsie considered Charles's plan. A whole day alone with him!

"I'd love to."

"I was almost certain you'd say yes, so I bought tickets for tomorrow morning's ferry," Charles said, pulling them out of his pocket.

"What if I had said no?" she asked with a laugh.

"I would have gone alone, I suppose."

"Well, there's no need for that now. Tomorrow is perfect."

The sooner the better, as far as she was concerned.

****

Elsie met Charles in the dining room for a quick breakfast of scrambled eggs, cinnamon toast, and tea. Afterward they had a pleasant ride to the pier in Portsmouth, where Tom dropped them at the dock with plenty of time to spare. The bright morning sun promised a hot, clear day, and Elsie was glad for her straw hat.

A fair number of people were waiting to board the ferry, the *Pelican*. At a quarter to eight, the gangplank was lowered and passengers were allowed to board. Elsie and Charles climbed a steep staircase to the top deck and found seats at the bow. Ten minutes later, men on shore untied the ship from the pier.

"Here we go," Charles said and took her hand in an old, familiar gesture that warmed her heart. She held on tight as the ferry pulled away from the dock.

The *Pelican* made good headway through the harbor, and soon they were out in open water. The wind freed strands of hair from Elsie's pins and made her skirt flutter like a sail. She laughed when the sea spray sprinkled her cheeks. Charles handed her one of his handkerchiefs. It smelled like him, and she wondered if he would notice if she didn't give it back. She wiped her face and slipped it into her pocket.

After about an hour, a group of islands appeared on

the horizon. Charles pointed out Star Island, which was easily identified because of the enormous white hotel on it. The ferry continued steadily until they reached a small harbor, where it pulled up against the dock that held men waiting with heavy ropes to tie up the boat.

Elsie and Charles made their way to the middle deck and were directed to the gangplank. She held tight to his arm as the *Pelican* bobbed on the tide.

A crewman on the pier shouted repeatedly, "Three hours ashore! Last ferry at noon! Only three hours ashore!" He was waving his cap for good measure, but Elsie couldn't imagine that anyone would miss his announcement.

They walked down a stone pier and across the wide, sweeping lawn to the hotel. They climbed the wooden staircase to a wraparound porch, where a woman, sitting in one of the many rocking chairs, was using a wheel to turn wool. She offered a friendly smile as they passed. The porch ran the entire length of the hotel and gave them a respite from the wind.

"Shall we?" Charles asked, motioning to the chairs.

Elsie followed him to the far end of the porch, marveling at the beauty of this place. From their vantage point, she had a good view of the harbor. A lighthouse close by sounded its horn.

"I had no idea such a place could exist out in the ocean like this," Elsie said, taking a seat.

"That's why I wanted to show it to you, before you go back to Holderness."

A chill settled in her at the thought of leaving. "Let's not speak of me going away."

"But I thought you were anxious to get home."

"It's more that I feel I must," she said with a sigh

and ceased her rocking.

"But why? Because of Gabriel?" Charles looked at her closely, as if trying to decipher the true meaning of her words by the look in her eyes.

She looked away, out to where the ferry was moored, knowing she had to steer this conversation into safer waters.

"It's complicated. Please, let's not speak of it today. I want to enjoy the island."

"But I think I—" He paused and said, "What would you like to see first?"

"What are our options?"

"The last time I was here, I walked around on the rocks and looked at the tidal pools. I didn't see much of the hotel."

"You said there's a restaurant?" She glanced over her shoulder at the windows lining the front of the hotel.

"Yes, let's go see what they have." He offered his arm, and they went inside.

In the expansive, cool lobby, guests checked in at the front desk while bellhops scurried up the wooden staircase, luggage in tow. Women in deep discussion and couples holding hands lounged on several round sofas, and men sat reading newspapers in cushy chairs in front of a stone fireplace. Boisterous voices emanated from the meeting hall off the lobby.

A sign above double doors indicated the dining room, which was full of long rectangular tables and a few circular ones for more intimate parties. Through a door in the back of the room came the clatter of dishes, while windows on the right offered a view of the sea, and from the left a gray, rocky hill.

The main restaurant wasn't open yet, but a shop

called Hathaway's sold snacks. Charles and Elsie went over to see what was offered. Numerous pastries and a few sandwiches were displayed on the counter, but what interested them both was the smell of fresh popcorn.

They approached the counter, and a man stepped up to help them. "Hello, I'm Mr. Hathaway. What can I get for you?"

"We'd like two popcorns, please, Mr. Hathaway. What do you have to drink?" asked Charles.

"Our most popular drink is the lime rickey. We also serve seltzer, lemonade, coffee, and ice cream soda." He pointed to a painted sign on the wall that listed the ice cream flavors.

"Let's try the rickey," Elsie said. "I've never even heard of it before."

"I'm sure you'll enjoy it." He handed them two boxes of warm, buttery popcorn, then set to work making their drinks.

"Here you are," he said. The red, fizzy drinks came in tall glasses and had lime slices floating on top. Elsie took a sip while Charles paid. The bubbly seltzer tickled her nose. It was sweet and refreshing, and tasted like raspberries.

They found a table next to the window. Charles was more at ease than Elsie had seen him in weeks. Perhaps the strain on their friendship had affected him more than she'd realized. Even his posture was more relaxed. He leaned back in his chair and draped a leg over the opposite knee, as if he hadn't a care in the world. He chatted about their ferry ride and all the things they could do together on the island. Fortunately, he said no more about her return to Holderness.

After they'd finished their refreshments, Charles led

the way to the stony beach down by the pier. A number of sailboats swayed on their moorings in the harbor, and people rowed small wooden boats, heading to neighboring islands. At the tidal pools, they saw a few starfish and a sea urchin, as well as tiny fish scuttling around. Next, they took a leisurely walk around the island.

While the front lawns and area around the hotel were pristine, the back end of the island was decidedly wild. Elsie had never seen so many seagulls in one place. After walking for a quarter of an hour, they entered a sheltered path bordered by bushes and trees. Elsie could see nothing but green. From every direction came whispers of wind and waves, and the sun shone brightly overhead. It was her idea of paradise.

They scrambled over the craggy rocks and came to an opening in the trees. Soon they had reached the very edge of the island.

Elsie gasped: they were on a towering cliff, waves pounding against the rocks below. "It's magnificent!"

"I knew you'd love it," he said, turning to smile at her.

She sat down on the edge, her feet dangling. The ocean spray managed to sprinkle her shoes. She closed her eyes and lay back on the sun-warmed rocks.

Charles sat beside her and his hand unexpectedly covered hers. She entwined her fingers with his and turned to find him leaning back on his elbows, his eyes closed, his face tilted toward the sun. He looked utterly content.

Her eyes strayed to his slightly parted lips. Her pulse quickened, and she had to hold back the sudden wild urge to kiss him. His eyes flickered and opened. The look on his face almost made her believe he felt the same desire that she did.

He gazed at her for a long time. "I think we'd better go," he finally said.

"Why?" Elsie whispered, the word catching in her throat.

"It must be lunchtime. We don't want to miss it," Charles said, making no move to stand up.

She pulled her eyes away from his and looked at the watch pinned to her blouse.

"Yes, it's lunchtime," she said and stood up too quickly, teetering on the rocks.

He was beside her in an instant, reaching out to steady her. "Be careful, Elsie. You're far too close to the edge." He paled as he looked down at the churning waters and put an arm around her, pulling her back.

"I've found my balance now. I can manage," she said, stepping away. He moved with her, his hand still on her waist.

Once they'd gone a few paces he dropped his hand. "Go slowly and follow my steps."

"I will." She gave him a little nod. It was much too difficult to keep a clear head when he was so close.

They made it back to the restaurant in time and sat at a table overlooking the rocky hill. They both ordered clam chowder, club sandwiches, and another round of lime rickeys. For dessert, they each had rhubarb pie with a scoop of vanilla ice cream.

Gazing out the window, Elsie spotted a steeple in the distance and pointed it out to Charles.

"That's the chapel I was telling you about," he said. "I'd like to go up and see it after lunch. I didn't make it last time I was here."

"Let's make a point of it. When does the boat go back to Portsmouth?"

"Twelve o'clock."

She glanced at her watch. "We should have just enough time."

Elsie was almost too full for pie but managed to eat half her slice. Charles had no problem eating all of his as well as the rest of Elsie's. After seeing to their bill, they left the dining room via the back door, which left them at the rear of the hotel, where they followed a path that ran parallel to the dining room. It curved, then went up a steep hill. They turned a corner, and there was the stone chapel with deep, white-paned windows. Its wooden steeple was topped with a shining copper weather vane in the shape of a fish.

"Can we go inside?" Elsie asked.

Charles tried the door, and it opened easily.

Elsie was immediately taken with the cool, quiet peace of the place. Her footsteps echoed on the stone floor as she walked around the chapel, looking out the windows. Along the walls glass lanterns hung on metal hooks.

She joined Charles, who had taken a seat in the front row, and rested her arms on the back of the pew. Her hand lightly brushed against Charles's shoulder.

They sat in companionable silence for a little while before Charles turned to her. "Are you looking forward to going home?"

His voice was quiet, but there was an intensity behind the question.

"It will be nice to see my family. If I'm lucky, James will still be in town," she said. "I'll miss Sherwood Bay, though."

She put her hands in her lap and fidgeted with her purse strings.

"Could you only go for a visit?" he asked.

"No, I need to get back. This has been a respite of sorts. I never meant to settle in Sherwood Bay permanently. Max only suggested I come because, well…"

"The wedding," Charles said gravely. "The canceled wedding."

"Yes, it was just too much to be in Holderness at the time." Talking about it felt like poking an old wound. Though there was still a twinge of pain, it was nothing like the heartbreak she'd felt in the beginning.

"How are you feeling now about Gabriel?" He dropped his eyes and played with the chain of his pocket watch.

Elsie took a moment to gather her thoughts. "Honestly, it's confusing. I planned to marry him, but now I've found out he was using me. It's hard to believe he would have treated me so poorly. At this point, I grieve more for the friend I lost than the husband I almost had."

"And your heart, Elsie?" Charles said, and took her hand. "It's not too bruised to love again?"

She met his earnest gaze, which was a mistake because all the words she knew fled her mind. After looking away for a moment she cleared her throat and said, "My mother seems to think I'm running out of time to secure a husband."

He wrapped his arm around her shoulders, holding her close. He surely heard her wild heart echoing through the chapel, or at the very least saw every beat hammering under her blouse. His cheek was almost resting against hers when he spoke quietly in her ear. "And what do you think?"

But Elsie had no chance to answer—a loud, shrill whistle blasted from the harbor.

"The boat!" Charles said.

Elsie looked at her watch. Twelve o'clock!

"But won't they wait for us? They know we're here," she said desperately.

Charles grabbed her hand, and they ran out the door. They raced down the hill, but at the hotel porch they saw the *Pelican* pulling away from the dock.

"Wait!" Elsie cried uselessly.

They dashed down the stairs, Elsie clutching a stitch in her side. By the time they reached the pier, the ferry was well out in the harbor.

Chapter Fifteen

A man was gathering up mooring lines at the edge of the pier.

"Won't the *Pelican* come back for us?" Charles asked him, gesticulating wildly to the ferry steaming away.

"Once she's gone, she's gone. She'll be back tomorrow noon," the man said, not looking up from his work.

"Tomorrow!" Charles cried.

Elsie stepped forward. "Is there another boat that could take us back to Portsmouth?"

"No, miss. Sorry," the man said and turned away.

Elsie and Charles took their time walking down the pier, neither speaking. Halfway up the lawn, they entered a gazebo and sat on the bench.

"What are we to do?" she asked, trying to hide the panic in her voice.

"It seems we have little choice, Elsie," he said calmly, as if he were left behind on an island every day. "We'll have to see if there are rooms at the hotel. I doubt we'll be turned away. Where could they send us?" He unsuccessfully tried to hold back a laugh.

Elsie had to laugh, too.

"We shouldn't have tarried so long in the chapel," she said, and took her hat off. She'd nearly lost it several times during their sprint across the lawn.

"No, but we did want an adventure, didn't we?" Charles leaned back and clasped his hands behind his head.

Elsie couldn't help thinking he looked a little too pleased with the prospect of a night on the island. Perhaps it would be fun. They hadn't seen the entire island yet, and this would give them a chance to do so. And it would give her a few more hours alone with him.

"Let's go see about rooms," Charles said.

They walked up the stairs and into the lobby. At the front desk a clerk said, "Good afternoon. I'm Mr. Baya. How can I help you?"

"Well, Mr. Baya, we've missed the boat," Charles explained, "and we want to book two rooms for the night. One for me, one for my…sister."

Mr. Baya looked from Charles to Elsie, seeking a resemblance he wouldn't find. He seemed to deliberate for a moment, then shrugged. His finger moved down the page of his ledger.

"I'm afraid we've only got one room, sir." He reached under the desk and brought out a brass key.

"But that's impossible," Charles said. "We need two rooms." He leaned across the desk to try to see the ledger.

Mr. Baya turned it away from him. "There's only the one. You will need to share, as siblings so often do."

Charles looked like he was about to argue.

"Charles, could I have a word?" Elsie asked, placing a hand on his sleeve.

"Yes, of course."

"Let's step outside."

"Excuse us for a moment," Charles said to Mr. Baya, who went back to work.

Elsie led Charles out to the front porch.

He put a hand on his hip and let out more of a huff than a sigh. "What is it?"

She stepped closer and whispered, "How will it look if we stay together overnight here? There could be gossip."

Charles shook his head, barely keeping his voice down. "Don't worry, nobody here knows us. As far as anyone is concerned, we *are* brother and sister. And we might as well be, after all."

"You think so?" She crossed her arms and looked up at him, her brows raised.

He rolled his eyes. "Oh, you know what I mean, Elsie," he said, and ruffled her hair. Actually ruffled her *hair*.

She turned away. It was as she suspected—she was like a sister to him. She let out a slow breath before turning to face him. "You're right. We'd better take the room."

"I don't think we have much choice. If you're worried about people finding out you spent the night here we could register you under a different name. I could use Elizabeth instead of Elsie. You'll have to borrow my surname, though."

"I'm sure you're right; nobody will take any notice of us."

They went back into the lobby. Charles signed the ledger and took the key from Mr. Baya. He had written her name as Elizabeth Rockingham. How she wished it were so!

"You're on the second floor," Mr. Baya said. "You'll have a nice view of the lighthouse and be only a few doors down from the washroom. Miss Krause and Miss Hutchins are the second-floor chambermaids. You may ring for them if you need anything."

"Thank you," Elsie said. Charles just nodded and turned on his heel.

As they crossed the lobby to the staircase, Elsie said, "Charles, it won't be so bad. I won't talk to you or disturb you while you try to sleep, I promise."

"What are you talking about?" he asked as they mounted the stairs to the second floor.

Elsie ran her hand along the soft wooden banister. On a landing halfway up the staircase stood a table with a porcelain pitcher full of wildflowers on it.

"I can see that sharing a room is very disagreeable to you," she said to his back.

"I only hoped to spare you from an uncomfortable situation." He stopped so she could catch up to him.

"What's the room number?"

He looked at the key in his hand. "Two hundred and eight."

A carpeted hallway ran the length of the second floor. Most of the doors were closed, but sunshine streamed into the hall through a few that had been left open.

Charles unlocked the door to their room and held it open for Elsie. White curtains fluttered at the open window, sunshine and a fresh breeze filled the room. There was a tall bureau, a washstand and ewer, two chairs, and a nightstand beside the bed.

Beside the *one* bed.

Her heart did a little flip. Her stomach may have joined in, too.

Charles leaned against the wall and rubbed his chin with his hand.

Elsie crossed to the window and looked out. White

sheets swayed lazily on a clothesline close to the hotel. The lighthouse nearby stood out against the sky like a rook. She turned to Charles, her hands behind her back. "It's a pleasant room."

"Yes." His forehead creased as his eyes strayed to the bed.

"We'll manage," she reassured him. She wasn't sure how, she only knew they must.

"Perhaps I could spend the night in the lobby. There were some chairs near the fireplace. I noticed a parlor downstairs that looked comfortable. I think there's even a sofa in there."

"Charles, really! How can you sleep in the lobby?"

"I'll sleep in one of these," he said, sitting on a hard-backed wooden chair.

"If it makes you feel more comfortable, then please do. I'll give you a blanket and pillow from the bed."

He looked relieved that she had accepted this proposal.

"Well, nothing to unpack. Shall we explore the island some more?"

"I'd like that," she said.

"I saw some rowboats at the dock. Let's see if we can take one of those out."

Elsie took a moment to put her hat back on and left her purse on the bureau since she didn't need it for now. Charles locked their door, and they went back downstairs, stopping at the front desk to inquire about the boats.

"Yes, they're for anyone to use," Mr. Baya told them. "Mr. Fisher will help you. He's down at the end of the pier."

They left the lobby and walked down the porch

stairs. Elsie paused midway to take in the view: the harbor glistened in the sun, and the sea was calm for miles around. It was hard to imagine a more idyllic place to be stranded. They continued on and found Mr. Fisher, who directed them to a boat and showed them where the oars were stored.

The tide was low, mountains of seaweed floated on the surface.

"You'll have to be careful of that," Elsie said, pointing it out.

"I will. I've captained a ship before, if you remember," he said with a grin, clearly speaking of their childhood craft, the *Flying Catfish*.

Their boat, the *McGill*, was moored at the end of the dock. Charles helped Elsie in, then took the oars. He rowed them right into the middle of the harbor, where there were four more little boats. Elsie leaned back in the stern, letting her hand trail in the cool Atlantic waters. She couldn't help but notice the muscles working beneath Charles's shirt as he pulled on the wooden oars. He certainly was strong. How marvelous it would be to run her hands along those muscles, or to be held in those arms. She looked away quickly before he caught her staring.

Charles rowed around the island for a couple of hours. Elsie spent most of the time taking covert glances at him as they chatted about nothing of great consequence. Just the simple banter they'd shared their whole lives. She could listen to him talk forever; his voice was more beautiful than the wind or waves.

After returning the boat, they sat in rockers on the front porch until it was time go in for supper. Seated at a table beside the window, they enjoyed creamed onion soup, baked cod with lemon sauce, green peas, and baking powder biscuits with fresh butter. For dessert, Elsie picked a slice of apple pie, while Charles chose rich fudge cake.

Somewhere around Elsie's third bite of pie, her appetite disappeared. It would soon be time to retire to their room. Visions of them together in the quiet darkness filled her mind. She'd been alone with Charles a thousand times before, but this was different. From a hopeful corner of her mind, she imagined the impossible.

Before she knew it, Charles was taking care of the bill and pulling her chair out for her.

"Would you like to go for a walk? The sunset must be spectacular from here," she asked.

"I was thinking the same thing." He offered his arm, and they left the dining room.

On the front porch, people enjoyed the rocking chairs, and down on the lawn children played with balls and trundling hoops. Their laughter echoed off the walls of the hotel.

They meandered through a field of tall grass and found themselves at a spacious, red-roofed summerhouse perched on the very edge of the island. A few other people were sitting on the benches inside, so Elsie and Charles stood against a railing, facing the mainland.

They looked out over the water, not speaking, as gentle waves broke softly against the rocks. The island held a certain magic, as if nothing else existed beyond its shores. The days of worry, doubt, and confusion were a distant memory. She sighed, feeling refreshed, as if she'd slept for three straight days. She felt Charles shift beside her. He, too, held a certain magic.

"When all is said and done, I'm glad we missed the boat," she said.

"I am too. I feel as though I left all my concerns somewhere out there on the ride over," he said, sweeping his arm to encompass the whole ocean.

"Do you have many? Concerns?"

"No more than the next man, I'm sure."

"Do you want to talk about it?" Perhaps he'd received a letter from Amelia.

He laughed softly. "No, it's nothing, really. Look, the sun is just about gone." He pointed to the horizon.

The sun, enormous before them, was almost too bright as it descended to meet the ocean, shrinking as the minutes passed. First a fiery orb that melted into a golden pool, finally a shining pebble that sank beneath the waves. The sky was a symphony of red, orange, pink, and purple. Elsie and Charles stood side by side and watched until the sky faded to a star-filled inky blue.

They crossed the lawn to the hotel, where lights were coming on in one window after another, giving the place a warm, homey glow. One of those gas lamps was in the room she would share with Charles. A light shiver ran through her.

The lobby was full of people mingling and talking, but the second floor was relatively empty. Laughter and muffled voices could be heard from behind a few closed doors. When they reached their room, they found the chambermaids had been in to light their lamps and turn down the bed. Elsie was surprised to see a bottle of wine reclining in a bucket of ice on the nightstand, with two wineglasses beside it.

She rested her hand on the bottle, her eyes on Charles. "Did you order this?"

"Just a little nightcap before bed," he said, standing next to the door with his hands in his pockets.

An awkward silence filled the room as they looked at each other, unsure of what to do next.

"Well," Charles finally said.

"Well," Elsie repeated.

Their eyes met, and they instantly started laughing.

"Nothing we can't handle, eh, Elsie?"

"No."

"I suggest that I use the washroom first so you can have some privacy. When I get back, you can go."

"That's a fine idea."

Charles closed the door behind him, and Elsie paced around the room, trying to compose herself before he came back. She rubbed her hands together to stop the little tremors shooting up her arms and took a deep breath, then let it out slowly. She rolled her shoulders to release the tension in her neck. She could get through this night without giving her feelings away.

What to wear to bed was a quandary. Her chemise alone was her first choice but would be far too risqué. She'd need to sleep in her clothes. Fortunately, she'd worn a square-collared cotton blouse and a walking skirt, instead of a more confining dress. She untucked her blouse and loosened her corset, then undid the top two buttons of her skirt. She was reasonably supported and now had at least the possibility of a comfortable night's sleep.

There was a soft knock on the door.

"Come in."

Charles entered the room, his hair combed and his face pink from washing. "It's just down the hall."

"I remember," she said, smiling, and left the room.

Lamps illuminating the hall threw comforting shadows on the floor. In the ladies' washroom she washed her face with one of the orange-flower scented soaps in a basket on the counter. She unpinned her hair and braided it. Her mother would not approve of her leaving it down, but Charles had seen it before, and it was much more comfortable this way.

When she returned she knocked on the door and Charles opened it within seconds.

"Good evening," he said, bowing as if he were the maître d' at a fancy restaurant.

Elsie laughed and stepped into the room. Charles's jacket, waistcoat, and collar were neatly placed on top of the bureau. He had unbuttoned the top two buttons of his shirt. The thin fabric accentuated the muscles that had done all the rowing that afternoon. Elsie averted her eyes and sat on the edge of the bed to remove her shoes. She placed them beside Charles's, next to the nightstand.

"Wine?" he asked.

"Yes, please," Elsie said at once, eager to douse her wild nerves.

He handed her a glass, and they sat facing each other in the flickering light. Sipping her wine, she tried to look out the windows, but it was as dark as midnight. The lamp from the lighthouse occasionally swept the ocean and illuminated their room.

Charles seemed as content as she was to sit in silence. A few times she looked up to find him staring at her. His eyes had a warm, dreamy look—perhaps it was the wine.

The sound of waves breaking upon rocks helped Elsie to relax even more than the wine. A tiny yawn escaped her.

"Time for bed?" Charles asked, stretching his legs out in front of him.

"Yes, I feel like my eyes are going to close of their own accord. Are you tired?" She set her glass on the nightstand.

"Yes, but I don't feel like sleeping," he said, his voice mellow.

"Perhaps it's the strangeness of being in a new place. Or is something on your mind?"

"Not especially. Perhaps you're right about the new place."

"Once we're settled, with the lights out, you'll fall right to sleep. You're certain you want to spend the night on these chairs?" she asked, standing up.

"That seems to be the best arrangement."

"They look very uncomfortable."

"I'll be fine. It will be the same as sitting up all night on a train," he said, eyeing the chairs ruefully.

"If you insist."

He carried the chairs as far from the bed as possible—not far, given the room was scarcely half the size of Max's study. Elsie stepped over to the bed and pulled back the covers. She removed the fluffiest pillow and brought it over to Charles with a thick blanket.

She turned off the overhead lamp and lowered the flame of the bedside lantern, then crawled into bed and covered herself with the downy blanket. Across the room, Charles was trying to fashion the chairs into a bed. First he leaned back, his legs out in front of him. Then he turned himself sideways and propped his feet up on the other chair. At one point he tried to curl up on both chairs, but he was much too tall for that.

"Are you all right?" Elsie asked.

"Oh, yes, quite comfortable," Charles said in a clipped tone.

"Good night, then, Charles."

"Good night, Elsie."

****

Elsie lay in bed—drowsy and warm—but couldn't sleep despite the wine and the late hour. If not for the constant creaking of Charles's chairs and the grating sound of wood scraping the floor, she would have been asleep long ago.

Glancing over at him now in the dim light, she saw that his eyes were closed but too tightly to be asleep. His arms were crossed on his chest, his legs stretched out in front of him. His feet rested on the other chair but with a wide gap between the chairs, leaving his long legs unsupported. The floor may have been a better place for him after all.

After deciding she'd offer to switch places with him halfway through the night, she turned over and faced the wall. Elsie lay there for a long time, not looking at Charles yet acutely aware of his every move. After a while, his breathing changed to the deep, steady sound that could only mean sleep. Focusing on that, she finally managed to drop off herself.

A loud thud jolted her awake.

She bolted upright and jumped out of bed. After one glance at the floor, she burst out laughing.

"It's not funny, Elsie!" Charles's muffled voice came from the floor, somewhere under a pile of blankets and chairs. He was stuck with one chair under his legs and the other on top of him. Fumbling with the blanket wrapped around his head, he was trying to get out.

"Here, let me." She pulled the chair off him and

helped untangle the blanket, unsuccessfully trying to keep a straight face. "What happened?"

"I don't know," he said grumpily. "I finally managed to fall asleep on these accursed chairs, and the next thing I knew I was on the floor being laughed at."

She gave him her hand and helped him to his feet, her eyes shining with mirth.

"I suppose I can see how it would be a bit funny…" He started laughing with her as he bent to pick the chairs up off the floor. He was really going to attempt it again!

"Oh, that's enough, Charles." She planted her hands on her hips.

"What?" He turned, a surprised look on his face.

"You are not going to sleep on those chairs."

"I might try the floor. I wouldn't fall off the floor."

"Nonsense." She grabbed his pillow and blanket.

"I need those!" he said, reaching for them.

She pivoted quickly so he couldn't take them. "And you will have them. You will sleep in the bed with me," she said, her voice shaking slightly.

He gulped. "In the bed with you?" He looked from Elsie to the bed.

"Yes. We've dealt with worse."

"I know, but—"

"How do you expect either one of us to get any rest with you squeaking and creaking all night?"

"And here I thought you'd slept through my racket," he said.

She pressed her lips together and shook her head slowly.

"I have an idea that will make this less vexing to you," she said, walking backward toward the bed.

"It isn't vexing, but—"

"And I won't tell anyone, I promise."

"I know you won't. But I'm still not sure it's entirely…proper." He turned a faint shade of pink.

"Listen. I will get into the bed, under the sheets. You will lie on top of the blankets. You can use the spare blanket to cover yourself," she said, proud of her solution.

This should soothe his—what? Embarrassment? Guilty conscience? Awaiting his answer, she tried not to smile as he looked from the chairs, to the floor, to the bed, and back again. He winced when his eyes fell on the chairs.

"Yes, that will work. Thank you." He held up a finger as if checking the direction of the wind. "But under no circumstances will we ever, *ever* tell our mothers."

Elsie blanched at the very idea. "No. We will never tell anyone." Why was it that keeping it a secret made it feel even more intimate?

Elsie climbed into bed and pulled the blankets up to her chin. Once she was settled, Charles lay on top of the blankets right next to her and covered himself. He stretched out on his back and let out a sigh of pleasure. "I can stretch out my legs," he said so appreciatively that Elsie laughed.

They both quieted down, making small adjustments for their comfort. She saw that his eyes were closed, a sleepy smile on his face. Her heart felt twice its usual size, and her stomach danced with butterflies. She may as well enjoy being so close to him, because nothing like this would ever happen again. She shut her eyes, relishing the warm comfort of his body pressed against hers. Her nervousness had evaporated, as it was natural to be so close to him.

She was almost asleep when he spoke.

"Elsie? Are you awake?"

"Barely," she whispered, opening her eyes.

He turned over on his side and propped himself up on one elbow. The lamp cast a soft light on his face. "Do you know what this reminds me of?"

"What?"

"That night we stayed out late looking for fireflies. Remember? We decided to go up to the grassy hill, the one with all the wildflowers," he said, his breath warm on her face.

"And we fell asleep outside in the grass, under that big old oak tree," she said, smiling at the memory.

She reached up and touched his bangs. "Your hair is darker now." She lightly pressed her hand against his cheek. He leaned into it and closed his eyes, inhaling deeply.

She moved her hand to his shoulder and shifted a little closer to him.

"And me?" she said. "Do I look different?"

He gently stroked her cheek. She closed her eyes, savoring his touch.

"Perhaps, if possible, you are more beautiful."

Heat rushed from her chest to the tips of her toes.

He was impossibly close. Her lips parted, and she raised her chin just a bit. She let her hand slide from her shoulder to his back. Charles tilted his head and looked at her mouth. She'd seen that expression once before. Just once. That night on the beach three years ago. He leaned toward her.

Her breathing stopped.

So did Charles.

He silently searched her eyes. Elsie kept still, trying to convey with a look how much she wanted him. After a moment he closed his eyes and shook his head slightly. He stretched out on his back again, hands folded across his stomach. She waited for him to say something—anything.

Her heart gradually made its way back to its usual pace. The moment she'd been hoping for had come and gone. She shut her eyes tight to stop the prickling tears and pulled him back to their reminiscing. "We slept under the tree all night, and your brother had to come find us in the morning."

Charles took so long to answer she thought he had fallen asleep. When he spoke, his voice was hoarse. "I remember. James was furious with us and scolded us all the way to your mother's parlor."

"And both our mothers were there, looking as though they had been awake half the night."

"We will look like our worried mothers tomorrow," Charles said, "if we don't get some sleep."

They settled down again, his heat radiating through the thin layers of cotton that separated them. Before long, his breathing changed and she knew he slept. She turned on her side to face him. His eyelids fluttered, and she caught his scent without even trying: spicy, sweet, and homey. She closed her eyes, falling into a deep sleep.

When she woke in the morning, Elsie didn't want to open her eyes. During the night, Charles had turned over, and his arm was now draped over her back. She nestled against him, delighting in the closeness.

The lighthouse horn blared, and Charles woke up. He looked blearily at Elsie for a moment, then hastily let go of her and jumped out of bed. He stood there, looking at her. Was it regret she saw in his eyes?

"Good morning," he said gruffly.

"Good morning," she said, getting out of bed.

"I must say, that was far more comfortable than the floor would have been."

"It was very comfortable," she agreed, enchanted by the memory of last night's conversation. His word danced around in her mind: *beautiful, beautiful, beautiful.*

She went to the window and opened the curtains. "It's foggy."

"It will clear soon, I imagine." He gathered his things from the bureau, then shrugged into his waistcoat and jacket.

"In time for the ferry to arrive?"

"I'm sure it will. You'll be home soon enough." He stared blankly out the window while he reattached his collar.

"Charles? Is anything wrong?" Elsie advanced a step closer.

He simply sat on the edge of the bed, put his socks and shoes on, and marched to the door.

"Charles?" she said again, reaching out to him.

He stepped away so she couldn't touch him. "I'll leave so you can dress," he said, already halfway through the door.

"Will you meet me back here?"

"I'll be in the dining room," he answered, not looking back. He walked swiftly down the hall and soon turned the corner and was out of sight.

Elsie sat for a time, gazing into the mirror on the washstand. Perhaps Charles regretted sharing the bed and would have felt better if he'd stayed on the floor. She straightened her clothes as best she could. The hem of her skirt looked like she had indeed sprinted across the island, and her blouse was wrinkled beyond the help of the hottest iron. She did not even want to consider the state of her shoes. Her hat, at least, looked respectable, but she had mislaid her hatpins, so could only carry it. She fixed her hair and went downstairs.

Elsie looked around for a while before she found Charles in the crowded dining room. He was sitting alone, staring out the window with his chin in his hand. He didn't move when she sat down across from him.

"Have you already eaten?" she asked, pouring herself a cup of coffee.

He didn't answer.

"Charles? Have you eaten?"

He looked up as if surprised to see her there. "I'm sorry, what did you say?"

"I asked if you've already eaten." She sipped her coffee.

"Not yet," he said, "But I ordered." His eyes were puffy and, if she didn't know better, she'd guess he hadn't slept a wink last night.

The waitress came over with a platter of waffles and bacon. While Elsie ate, she kept up a steady stream of conversation, but she may as well have been talking to herself. Charles was usually the chatty one in the morning, but today he barely acknowledged her before lapsing back into silence.

After only a few bites, he put his fork down and stared vacantly around the room, biting his thumbnail. The thumping of his heel against the floor rattled the whole table. He stood abruptly, almost overturning his chair.

"I'm going for a walk," he said over his shoulder on the way out the back door.

"Wait!" she called, but he was gone.

She rushed outside, but there was no sign of him behind the hotel. She climbed up to the chapel to get a clear view of the whole island and finally saw him jogging east. Making her way cautiously down the hill, she followed him to the wild end of the island. More than once, she lost sight of him and had to run to catch up. The terrain became more barren the farther she went. She trod gingerly over the uneven ground, watching for unexpected dips and crevices. At length the grass gave way to granite. The rocky terrain ended abruptly at the edge of the island and formed cliffs towering over the sea.

Charles stood on one such cliff. She walked over and stood beside him. There was nothing ahead of them but ocean. The waves swelled, climbing up the sheer rock face.

"Elsie, I need to ask you something," Charles said flatly. "And I need you to be honest with me."

"Of course I'll be honest with you."

"I need to know why you accepted Gabriel's proposal." It was a statement, not a question.

Elsie's stomach dropped. "But we've been over this."

Charles closed his eyes, as if praying for patience. "Please. Tell me why."

"As I told you before, I hoped we could be happy."

"Max told me Gabriel proposed several times before you said yes." His hands were in fists at his sides.

"He came back four times before he got the answer he wanted—the answer I shouldn't have given him."

"What made you finally accept him?"

"Why are you asking me this? I don't want to talk about Gabriel anymore." She turned around but had only gone a few steps when his words rooted her to the spot.

"Because I need to know why you agreed to marry him instead of waiting for me."

Chapter Sixteen

Charles hadn't shouted, but his words reverberated in her ears. She spun back around, not even noticing the wide-open sky and heaving waves. All she saw was Charles. It was as close as he could get to a declaration.

"Wait for you?" she asked, her eyebrows shooting up. "There was nothing to wait *for*. You left. You left and you barely even wrote to me. And I did wait. I waited for months for a letter."

He took a step forward. "I told you, the post—"

"Yes, yes—you *wrote*. But never a word about that night on the beach. You never said anything about waiting for you. I didn't even know when you'd be back—if you'd *ever* be back!" She stomped her foot, even though she knew it made her look childish.

"I was planning to come home. But not after I heard you were marrying *Gabriel*," he practically shouted, pain clouding his eyes.

"But I was only marrying him because he told me you were engaged to someone else!" she blurted out, then covered her mouth with her hands.

His eyes widened. "That's why you said yes? That's why you agreed to marry him?"

She looked down at her muddy shoes, unable to meet his eyes. "Yes."

"If I were engaged, don't you think you would have heard about it? My mother would never have been able to keep such a secret."

"After Gabriel and I were engaged, he told me it had been called off."

She glanced up at him. He didn't look like a man on the verge of declaring his love. He looked like a man trying to teach math to a baby.

"I never told Gabriel I was going to marry someone," he said with a slow shake of his head.

"Why would he say that if it wasn't true? And why are you still trying to hide it from me?"

"You're going to believe Gabriel over *me*? I swear to you, there was no engagement. I don't know why Gabriel told you such a tale."

"Have you heard from Amelia? Did she give you an answer yet?" she asked, crossing her arms tightly across her chest.

"What does Amelia have to do with anything? What answer?"

"Isn't she the one—the one Gabriel told me you proposed to when you were in California? She said no then, but it seems she's had a change of heart."

"I've already told you there's nothing between Amelia and me. And I never told Gabriel I was getting engaged to someone. I barely even wrote to him."

"Charles, I don't know why you're still lying to me. I know what Gabriel told me is true."

"No, it's not!" he yelled, throwing his arms wide.

"I saw the letters! I saw them!"

"What letters?"

"The letters you wrote to her! In the study, the day you were going over the inventory. I was looking for that list for you, and I found the letter in a drawer. And below that, a whole bundle of letters." She glared at him, daring him to deny it.

"And you read them?" He somehow managed to blanche and turn green at the same time.

"I only read one of them. It caught my eye, and I was curious." She paused. "The one where you...you proposed. I'm sorry, I shouldn't have read it." How dearly she wished she had never seen it!

Charles let out a moan and ran a trembling hand across his brow. He was silent for an eternity, staring out to sea. When he turned back to her, his voice was steady. "Elsie, I believe it's time you did read that letter."

"I assure you, Charles, I have no desire to pry into your personal affairs." She clasped her hands in front of her to keep them from shaking as much as her voice.

"But you don't understand." He took a step closer to her. "That letter is yours. I wrote it to you."

"To me?" She asked incredulously, recalling the love, the longing that came through the page.

"Yes, to you," he said in a sweet tone she'd never heard him use before. He stepped closer still.

"You weren't going to marry someone else? Gabriel truly lied?" She placed her hands over her throbbing heart.

"He knew before I went away that I always planned to come home. Home to you."

"I thought you forgot me," she said quietly.

"I could never forget you. It would be like forgetting myself." His eyes held that same look she'd captured in the photograph.

"You were gone for so long."

"I only stayed away because Gabriel said you were deeply in love with him. He said you could scarcely wait to get married."

"He told you that? But when? You'd already been gone almost two years when Gabriel proposed."

"He told me that just a few months after I left. That's why I stayed in California."

"But he was lying. We didn't start courting until a year later. We were engaged just this past September." She frowned. "If only you'd asked me about it in your letters."

"I did, more than once. But you never replied."

"I don't recall any letters that mentioned it. Perhaps they're among those that were lost. I know I replied to every letter Gabriel brought to me."

"Gabriel brought them to you?" Charles looked suddenly alert.

"As soon as you left, Gabriel offered to collect my letters from you and bring them to my house. He lived just around the corner from the post office, remember? He said he would save me the trip. And every time he saw me, he would ask if I had any letters to send out. He would always post them with his, on the same day."

"Wait," Charles said, holding up a hand. "Gabriel mailed all of your letters and collected mine for you? They were not delivered to your house by the postman?"

She nodded.

He looked off into the distance. "How often would you say you wrote to me?"

"Are we going to start that again?" she asked, raising her eyes to the sky.

"No, but I'm wondering how many letters I may have missed. Or how many perhaps were not *sent*."

Elsie felt like something sticky was caught in her throat. "I would say I wrote to you at least once a week for the first year, and after that it varied from month to month. Never less than twice a month, even last year when I stopped hearing from you. I always held out hope that you would reply."

"I wrote to you just as often, possibly more," he said. "Like you, I held out hope."

"I do admit I stopped writing after he died. As I told you before, I was distraught. I wasn't corresponding with anyone at that point."

"Naturally I didn't expect a reply then, in fact that's why I stopped writing after I sent the condolence letter. I knew you would need some time to yourself. But before that, we were both writing to each other at least once a month."

"Yes. And I asked Gabriel almost every time I saw him if any letters had come. All last year he said you must have been too busy with your fiancée to write."

The truth was so obvious—how had she not realized? She was about to voice her suspicions, but Charles spoke first.

"I think he was doing much more than saving you a trip to the post office. It sounds like he was holding back our letters!"

"So I would never know how you felt," she said, bringing a hand slowly to her lips.

"I should have come home to speak to you. But I couldn't bear to see you with someone else, least of all Gabriel." He inched toward her and closed his hand around hers.

"That's why you stayed away so long, because he lied to you about us," she said.

"With you engaged to someone else, there seemed no point in hurrying home. But how I regret that now."

She almost reeled with joy.

But no.

She pulled her hand out of his grasp and took a step back.

Confusion flashed in his eyes. "Didn't you hear me? The letter was for you. The…love was for you."

Her heart stampeded in her chest. It was like a dream. But a dream she'd had too many times before.

"No. No, no, no," she said almost to herself, holding her hands out in front of her and backing away.

"Elsie?" he said, moving closer.

She retreated another step. The only sound was waves crashing upon the rocks as they stared at each other.

"I thought you loved me three years ago," she said, "but you never mentioned it again. I suspected your feelings may have returned earlier this summer, but then Amelia arrived. I practically threw myself at you last night, but you weren't interested."

"Last night I wanted you so much. You have no idea how much! But I couldn't take advantage of the situation we found ourselves in. It wouldn't have been right."

"You wouldn't have been taking advantage. I've wanted you for such a long time, Charles." Her heart was in her throat as she finally told him the truth. He may as well know it all now.

"Then we can be together," he said with a trembling voice. He took a step closer and held his arms out to her.

She twisted away, moving back a few more paces. "I can't let myself do this again. I can't let myself believe you love me. It hurts too much when you turn away from me."

"When have I ever turned away from you? You say I didn't write to you—I did. Gabriel was apparently keeping my letters from you. All summer I've tried to be close to you, even when I despaired that you could never love me." He paused and looked directly into her eyes. "I can't stay away from you, Elsie."

"But you did stay away—for more than three years."

"Only because I thought I'd already lost you. I came home as soon as I could, after I heard that Gabriel died. Even if I could never have what I desperately wanted— you as my wife—I had to be here because I knew you needed me the same way I need you."

"But what about Amelia?" she asked, wringing her hands.

"There is no Amelia! There is only you. There has only ever been you."

"But…but I keep thinking you love me, and I'm proved wrong," she said, barely holding back her tears.

"You're not wrong," he said. "You've never been wrong. Every time you thought I cared for you, I did. It's these circumstances that have been keeping us apart. Why have you convinced yourself that I would lie to you, stop writing to you, ever dream of leaving you? Can't you convince yourself that I love you? You can trust me. I'm telling you right now that I love you. I've loved you my whole life. Don't shut your love away from me. I can see in your eyes and feel in your touch that you care for me."

"I do care. You know I do. But if you cared about me, why didn't you come home?" she asked, wiping her eyes on her sleeve. "You said Gabriel told you I was in love with him, but why would you believe him without even asking me about it?"

"I told you. I tried to write to you," he said, pressing his fingers into his temples and then letting them drop to his sides.

"You should have come home for me instead of taking his word for it."

Charles glowered. "The thing I wanted most in the world was your happiness. What kind of man would I be if I came home and tried to break up your relationship with Gabriel?"

"A man who wanted me," she said softly.

"I yearned for you every single day in California. I wrote to you the day I left Holderness and told you that I love you. I asked you to wait for me. But you didn't. You never even replied to my letter."

"But—you did?"

"How can you possibly doubt that I wanted you, Elsie? I asked you in a letter to marry me years ago!"

"I didn't know that. You clearly never sent it, as I found it *in a drawer.*"

"I was going to mail it after I had your reply to my first letter. But it never came."

"I'm sorry," she said. And she was. She was sorry for the missed years, for the misunderstandings, for Gabriel's lies. But most of all, she was sorry for doubting him. How could she ever have doubted Charles? But then, in a flash, she knew—this wasn't about doubting Charles. It was about doubting herself. Once she'd realized she'd been a fool to trust Gabriel, she'd stopped trusting herself. She'd stopped trusting anyone.

As they stood there facing each other, she realized it didn't matter what he said; it mattered what she knew about him. He hadn't lied to her, and she knew in her heart that he never would. If Charles said he loved her, then he loved her. It was too fantastic to believe, and yet she did.

Her fear melted away.

She stepped forward, but in her haste she twisted her ankle and lost her balance. Charles was there to catch her. Falling into his arms was like coming home.

"You love me," he said quietly. The certainty brought a slow, sweet smile to his face.

She slipped her arms around his neck and pulled him closer.

"You love me," he said again, searching her eyes.

"Yes," she said, "I love you, Charles."

She trembled in his arms, the pounding of her heart matched the surf below.

"Oh, Elsie, I've loved you for so long," he said, his voice breaking with emotion, "And I've dreamed of kissing you for years."

"Kiss me now, Charles," she whispered and lifted her face to his. "Kiss me."

He kissed her.

When their lips touched, everything disappeared but the frantic beating of her heart and his body pressed against hers. Every hidden part of her revealed itself to him, and a sensation she'd never known before coursed through her. He stroked her back and whispered her name, leaving her breathless with searching kisses. She opened herself to him, kissing him with a passion that left her reeling. His lips were warm, soft, and perfect; they had been made for her alone. All of his love flowed into her, filling her up. In that moment, she understood everything—they were destined for each other.

He picked her right up off her feet and spun her around. Elsie laughed with pure joy.

Suddenly Charles's expression grew concerned, and he became still. "Are you hurt?"

"What?" How could that kiss do anything besides cure any woe she had ever had?

"Your foot. Can you walk?"

She gingerly tried to take a step but stumbled.

"My ankle!" she cried, holding on to him.

"Only one thing to do," Charles said, and swept her into his arms.

"Do you mean to carry me all the way back to the hotel?"

"I do, and I will enjoy every moment. I've waited a long time to hold you," he said tenderly.

"Well, do watch your step, or we will have more than one injury to worry about." She secured her arms around his neck.

"I will have no more worry. I've had enough to last a lifetime these last few weeks."

He stepped nimbly over the stones as though she weighed nothing at all.

"What have you been worried about?" she asked, nestling into his arms.

"About you. Here I've been thinking you're still in deep mourning for Gabriel. And worse, you haven't wanted to spend time with me. I've been driving Max mad, talking to him about you all the time, trying to sort it out."

"I thought that any chance I had with you was gone. It hurt to be around you—to finally understand how much I love you, and at the same time to find that you had given your heart away to someone else!"

"I gave it to you, Elsie, long ago." He kissed the top of her head.

She was suddenly warm all over despite the cool morning breeze.

"I remember that night." He squinted as if running it through his mind again. "You were so bright, so open. I thought you'd come to see what I learned long ago. We are meant to be together." Almost in sight of the hotel, he slowed down.

"I had. I was going to tell you that I love you, but then I read that letter. Oh, how we have been plagued by letters gone amiss!"

He stopped walking. "The moment I saw you again this summer, it was clear I would never love anyone but you. You're the only one for me, Elsie. You always have been, and you always will be. I love you so very, very much." He leaned in and kissed her softly.

Elsie's heart swelled at these words. As sure as she was that the sun would rise tomorrow, she was sure of Charles's love and devotion to her.

After a moment she asked, "But why was that letter in your drawer? Why didn't you throw it away?"

Charles looked embarrassed. "I never wanted to part with it. I was going through my old papers the day before you found it. I wish you'd found the first half of that letter—you'd have known it was for you."

"I wish that also." To think of all the melancholy she would have been spared if she'd seen her name on the letter.

"I wrote it when I arrived in San Francisco. It was ready to post as soon as I had your reply to the letter I sent the day I left. The one where I asked you to wait for me."

"But I never received that letter."

"More of Gabriel's handiwork."

"But how? How could he have gotten our letters and known what was in them?"

"I don't know, but I mean to find out," Charles said firmly.

"We'll find out together."

Elsie rested her head on his shoulder. The past didn't matter now, only their future. The proposal in that letter would come again, and Elsie knew exactly what she would say when it did. Charles walked on, and they spoke no more for the moment. There would be years for talking.

Chapter Seventeen

As soon as they stepped into the lobby, a woman standing behind the front desk looked up and gasped, then ran over to meet them.

"What happened?" she asked.

"I fell on the rocks." Elsie's ankle was hot and beginning to throb. She'd been so distracted by Charles that she hadn't noticed it until now.

"Come sit here while I fetch the doctor," the woman said, motioning to a long green bench under the window. Charles put Elsie down and sat beside her.

After a few minutes, the woman came striding through the dining room with the doctor in tow.

"Hello, I'm Dr. Watts." He was the youngest doctor Elsie had ever met. His confident air and friendly eyes immediately put her at ease.

"I'm Miss Hayward, and this is my friend Mr. Rockingham."

Too late she remembered their ruse of being siblings. However, Dr. Watts hadn't seemed to notice, as his attention was fixed on her leg. He sat down beside her on the bench after Charles stood up to give them room.

"Miss Walton tells me you're injured. Can you explain what happened?"

"I was out on the east end of the island and slipped on the rocks, and now my ankle hurts. I can't walk or stand on it." She pointed to her left ankle and tried to turn it from side to side, but it was too swollen.

"Mm-hm. Yes, that happens often, out on East Rock. The ground there is so uneven. I'd like to give you a proper examination, but I don't want to move you down to the infirmary."

"The pink parlor is free, Doctor," Miss Walton said.

"Yes, the pink parlor will suffice," Dr. Watts said, gesturing to a room off the lobby.

"We must be in time for the boat," Elsie said.

Dr. Watts looked at his pocket watch. "You have half an hour, and I will send word for the *Pelican* to wait for you."

Leaning on Charles, she limped to the parlor. The wallpaper, chairs, lamp shades, and even the long sofa on which Dr. Watts directed her to lie down were all in various shades of pink. Charles pulled up a chair and sat close to Elsie.

Dr. Watts removed her shoe. She winced in pain during the examination, though he was exceedingly gentle.

"Fortunately, it isn't sprained," he said. "It's swollen, but that will go down in a day or so with proper care. Keep ice on it and rest as much as you can. I'm going down to my office for a bandage to wrap it up." He strode out of the room.

Charles closed the parlor door after the doctor and sat on the edge of the sofa. Elsie took his hand, enjoying the fact that she could.

"I can hardly believe it," he said, stroking her hair.

She didn't need to ask what he meant, because she was in the same state of mind. He put a hand on her shoulder and rested his forehead against hers. Elsie's breath quickened as she looked into his eyes. How many times had she looked into those same eyes? But they had never been as tender as they were now. He leaned forward and gave her a soft, lingering kiss that left her wanting more. A sigh escaped her lips, and she sat up, holding him closer. His mouth curled into a smile, and they broke apart as they heard footsteps and voices drawing near.

"Dr. Watts is returning. I'd better get out of his way," Charles said.

"Don't go too far."

"I won't." He lightly kissed her freckles. "I've always wanted to do that," he said, then moved back to the chair.

Dr. Watts entered the parlor, followed closely by a striking woman who wore a long white apron over her dove-grey dress. "This is Nurse Thurlow. She will bind your ankle for you. The stretcher we'll use to carry you to the boat is being brought up from the infirmary. The *Pelican* is here, and Miss Walton has delivered the message that they are to wait for you. I'm going to find some men to help us carry your stretcher."

"Eli and Edmund Church were just in the lobby, Dr. Watts," Nurse Thurlow said.

"Thank you. I'll go look for them." He hurried out of the room.

Nurse Thurlow wrapped Elsie's ankle tightly in a bandage. By the time she finished, Dr. Watts had returned with the stretcher and two young men.

Charles went to fetch her hat, which she'd left in the dining room that morning, while Elsie waited on the sofa, vacillating between extreme joy and utter disbelief.

Charles loved her.

She was going to marry him.

She looked up just as he stepped into the room, her chest feeling light and bubbly. Charles beamed at her. Their eyes met, and it was as though they were alone.

Dr. Watts cleared his throat, breaking their little interlude. "We'd better get going."

"Of course," Elsie said, turning away from Charles. "What should I do?"

"Stay still. We'll help you onto the stretcher and then carry you down to the *Pelican*."

Once she was secured on the stretcher, they lifted her easily—Charles and Dr. Watts at her head, Eli and Edmund at her feet—and carried her slowly through the lobby, across the porch, and down the front lawn.

The walk up the gangplank onto the ferry proved nerve-racking, as the ocean swell caused some jostling of the stretcher. Once on board, Nurse Thurlow helped Elsie settle on a bench the crew had reserved for her. She then placed a bag of ice atop her ankle, which felt better now that it was bandaged. Dr. Watts went to have a word with the captain before coming back to wish Elsie a good voyage.

"Captain Meyer said you may alert the crew if there's anything you need on the trip home. Take care of yourself, and perhaps I will see you on the island again one day under more pleasant circumstances."

She couldn't imagine happier circumstances than the morning she'd just had.

There was so much she wanted to say to Charles, but it would need to wait until they were alone. Every so often she would meet his gaze, unspoken words in both their eyes. Elsie was so full of emotions she didn't know how she would express them even if she had the opportunity.

When the ship docked in Portsmouth, Charles left her alone to send a message to Max explaining what had happened and to request the carriage. Elsie sincerely hoped he wouldn't risk bringing the motorcar instead.

After waiting until everyone else had disembarked, the crew carried Elsie down the gangplank on the stretcher. She was allowed to stand up, though she leaned heavily on Charles for support, his arm tight around her waist.

Tom was pacing back and forth in front of the carriage, twisting his hat in his hands. When they approached, he looked at her with wide eyes. "We had a message you're hurt."

"It's only my ankle."

"We'll get you home quick so Mrs. Holt can fix you up proper," he said, holding the carriage door open.

Charles helped her in, then climbed up beside her.

As the carriage started with a lurch, Elsie turned to look at Charles, who was staring at her, and their eyes met and held. Elsie wanted to say something, but her mouth was too dry to swallow, let alone speak. She wiped her moist palms on her skirt.

A sultry anticipation had followed them into the carriage. Charles reached across her and slowly drew the curtains, leaving them in semi darkness.

"Elsie," he said in a ragged whisper.

She slipped her arms around his neck and kissed him. He wrapped her in his arms, his lips never leaving hers, and a delicious fire spread from her mouth to her stomach to the tips of her toes. She kissed him deeply, openly, oblivious to everything but him.

"Oh, Charles," she said, her head on his shoulder,

her hand over his heart. He pulled away just enough to look into her eyes, still keeping hold of her.

"Elsie, what would you have replied, had you received my letter?"

She didn't need to be told which letter he spoke of. "I would have said to hurry home, because I'm waiting for you."

His chest rose palpably, and his eyes brightened. He was about to speak, but just then they pulled up in front of Max's house. After a few moments, the carriage door opened, and there stood Tom.

"Come along in, and Mrs. Holt will see to you," he said, gesturing toward the house.

"Can you walk?" Charles asked.

"I think I'd better not."

"I'll carry you, then," he said, looking very pleased, and lifted her.

Max waited for them in the entryway. His expression cleared of worry when he saw Elsie in Charles's arms and he looked at each of their faces in turn.

"At last!" he said, clapping his hands together and laughing loudly.

"Have you been dreadfully worried, waiting for us to come home?" Elsie asked.

"No, Elsie. I've been impatient for you two to see what I saw months ago. Years ago!" he said and disappeared into the house.

Mrs. Holt rushed out of the dining room. "Oh, my dear! Look at your poor ankle. Shall I send for Dr. Braman?"

"No, I've just seen a doctor on Star Island. He said my ankle will be better in a day or so. Perhaps I'll call

Dr. Braman in tomorrow if the pain hasn't subsided."

"Very well. You'd better go rest while I fetch some ice for you." She bustled off, calling for Mr. Anderson.

Charles carried Elsie into the library and settled her on the sofa, then gathered pillows from the surrounding furniture and piled them under her ankle.

"Maybe not quite so many?" she said, her leg almost at a right angle.

"Oh. Right." He tossed all but the two fluffiest onto the floor.

"Could you help me sit up?" Smiling at his flustered demeanor, she took his hand and pulled herself up.

He retrieved a few of the discarded pillows and slid them behind her back.

"That's much better. Thank you."

"I'm going upstairs to change. I'll be back soon." Charles leaned down and gave her a soft kiss.

Elsie heard him taking the stairs two at a time, and then his bedroom door closed.

Before long, Mrs. Holt came in with a tray of food and drinks, Mr. Anderson following with ice for Elsie's ankle. He placed a porcelain bell within Elsie's reach, and they left the room.

"So, you're home," Max said, striding into the library. He settled into the chair opposite the sofa.

"Did you worry last night when we didn't return?"

"I didn't hear you were missing until after supper. I guessed you'd decided to stay the night but neglected to send a message."

"We missed the boat. We couldn't come home until this morning." She shifted on her pillows, listening for footsteps on the stairs. Could she really miss Charles already?

"And some things have changed?" Max asked, his hazel eyes twinkling.

Elsie's cheeks turned pink. "How is it that you are so observant with certain matters and yet so neglectful of others, such as sleep and keeping your appointments?"

"It so happens that the former are much more interesting than the latter. Are things settled yet?"

"Settled?"

"Between you and Charles. From the looks on both your faces, I'm expecting wedding bells soon."

"Ssh! No, nothing is settled." Elsie turned to see if Charles was on his way back.

"But it will be soon?"

"I hope so, Max, but please don't mention this in front of Charles."

"Why not? He knows as well as I do he is going to propose to you."

"Uncle!" she said exasperatedly.

He straightened up and spread his hands wide. "Elsie, some things in life stare you square in the face. What's the point of looking the other way?"

"No point at all," she said and sighed. "I tried to deny my feelings for Charles all summer. I think if I had not loved him so much already, as a friend, I might have noticed sooner that I was in love with him. Once I did, it was as though I had always known. But I was so convinced that he didn't love me…" She paused and said wonderingly, "But he did. He did love me, all along. Perhaps if I had been brave enough to tell him how I felt, we would have been together months ago."

"What matters is that he knows now. No need looking back and regretting."

"I suppose you're right." She turned once again to

glance at the doorway.

"'Course I am. Keep your eye on what's to come. The destination is all the sweeter because of the journey it took you both to get there." He sat forward, elbows on his knees.

"I'd rather have skipped the long journey, no matter how sweet, and married him years ago." At that thought, she burst into simultaneous laughter and tears. It was almost too much to believe. After all they'd been through this summer, all her doubts, her fears—Charles was in love with her, and she would spend the rest of her life with him. When she considered how many years they would have together, those lost three did not sting quite so much.

Max handed her a handkerchief that smelled of musty tobacco, then stood and crossed the room to open the French doors.

Elsie wiped away her tears, but the smile stayed fixed on her face. She looked up when she heard Charles's footsteps in the hall.

"Elsie," he said in a velvety voice as he hurried to her side. He'd changed into clean clothes and brushed his hair. He brought her hand to his lips, then pressed it to his heart.

"Good afternoon, Charles," Max said.

Charles started. "Good afternoon," he replied, his cheeks red. He kept Elsie's hand in his as he sat on the edge of the sofa and reached for a glass of iced tea.

"You've had quite an adventure," Max said, returning to his chair and taking a glass for himself.

"Yes, it was a surprise to be stuck on the island, but we managed to enjoy ourselves," Charles said, looking at Elsie.

"Indeed," Max said, giving Elsie a sly look. She rolled her eyes at him.

They ate lunch while Elsie and Charles told him what they'd seen and done on Star Island. Leaving out, of course, the night alone in the hotel room, and what had transpired on the rocks that morning. Some things were simply too precious to share.

****

Two days after Elsie's return, Lucy, Nancy, and Grace called.

"Tell us everything!" Lucy said as soon as she'd settled herself on the arm of the sofa.

Elsie took her time with her story, but she, of course, could not reveal *everything*, deciding that a little white lie was in order. She'd overheard Mrs. Holt telling Max that if people suspected she and Charles had been alone together overnight, it would ruin Elsie's reputation. Max had laughed it off, but Elsie understood her point. She had a feeling that even Max would have disapproved of them sharing a room, let alone a bed. Nobody on Star Island knew them—the only way a rumor could ignite was through gossip in Sherwood Bay.

"I see that I was right about you two, after all," Grace said without a trace of bitterness.

"I'm happy to say that you were," Elsie said, exchanging a warm smile with her.

Daisy brought in lemonade and slices of blueberry cake, which they enjoyed while they chatted. After an hour or so, they left, Elsie assuring them she would be back at Mrs. Wright's as soon as she could. She walked them to the door, pleased to find that her ankle didn't hurt at all.

She returned to the library and lay on the couch, her

arm behind her head. A few minutes later, Charles came in, sat beside Elsie, and took her hand. "How are your friends?"

"Curious. They wanted to hear all about our night on Star Island, and they especially wanted to know what's going on between us."

"What did you tell them?"

"I told them we were stranded together overnight on the island. They thought it was very romantic." She propped herself up on the pillows.

"Did you tell them anything else?"

"I told them that I like you."

"You like me?" he asked with a slightly raised brow.

He put a hand on the pillow behind her head, and the other traced a burning path from her hip to just below her breast. He hovered over her, eyes alight with a mischievous challenge.

She cleared her throat. Tiny beads of sweat were gathering in the most unlikely places. "I do, Charles. I like you very much indeed."

His lips grazed hers, not enough to be called a kiss but enough to leave her wanting more. She wrapped her arms around him, pulling him close. She kissed him deeply, not caring that they were in the library in broad daylight and that anyone could come in at any time. After a few moments, they pulled apart and sat in blissful silence before he stood.

"Where are you going?" Elsie asked.

He laughed at the crestfallen look on her face.

"I have some work to do at the office."

He bent down and kissed her, pulling away much sooner than she would have liked. She had the feeling she could never see, touch, or hear enough of him to satisfy her yearning.

"I'll see you at supper," he said.

"Very well, then. Until this evening."

As soon as the front door closed, she rang the bell beside the sofa.

Becky entered. "Yes, miss?"

"Becky, I wish to bathe and dress," she said, already rising from the sofa.

"Of course. Are you going out?"

"No, I just feel like freshening up," Elsie said with a conspiratorial look.

Becky glanced at the spot Charles had just vacated on the sofa. "Yes, I understand completely."

Elsie went upstairs to her room and threw the windows open, breathing in the sunny afternoon air. A few ships were coming in from their day of fishing, and one or two yachts as well. Star Island was out there, somewhere beyond the horizon. Perhaps on an especially clear day she'd be able to see it from town.

"Your bath is ready, miss," Becky said from behind her. "And what have you decided to wear?"

Without hesitation Elsie said, "My aqua dress." The one she had worn on the night she read the letter.

"I'll press it for you while you bathe."

Elsie had spent a languid half hour in the tub when downstairs the cuckoo clock struck six. She would need to hurry to be in time for supper. She wrapped herself in her dressing gown and walked down the hall, humming a nameless tune. In her bedroom the aqua dress was laid out on the bed.

"Luna!" she reprimanded affectionately. The kitten had curled up on her dress, getting fur all over the bodice. She tutted at Luna, who merely looked at her. She picked her up and carried her to the window seat. After dressing and fixing her hair, she fastened her grandmother's opal necklace around her neck. When the matching earrings were in place, she was ready.

Chapter Eighteen

Though she had said goodbye to Charles only hours ago, it felt like a week, and the staircase had never seemed so long. The fragrance of the flowers hit her before she even entered the library—Charles had placed bouquets on the window sills, book shelves, tables and mantel. He was standing in the middle of the room waiting for her.

"Have you emptied the garden of flowers, Charles?" she asked as she approached him, unable to suppress a grin.

"Yes, but you're putting the flowers to shame. You are so beautiful, Elsie."

She could say the same about him. It was hard to take her eyes off him to appreciate his efforts with the flowers. He had changed into the tuxedo he'd worn to the ball and had never looked more handsome. He took her hand and kissed it, then led her into the dining room.

The table was set for two, as Max had been conspicuously absent from meals over the last few days. Supper was creamed onion soup, roast duck with tarragon, fresh rolls with butter, and cabbage salad. A bottle of wine stood between two tapered candles in the center of the table.

Charles held a chair out for her, then took his own seat. She inched over to close the space between them. They ate their meal, quietly discussing their day.

"Wine?" he asked.

"Yes, please. The last time we drank wine was in our hotel room. You said it would be relaxing."

"I hoped it would be. I was such a bundle of nerves," he said. "That night was so difficult. You were acting so tense—cold almost—I feared you were mortified having to spend the night with me."

"I was trying hard not to give away my feelings. When we were in bed, I wanted to kiss you, I wanted to—well, never mind that. But I'd like to have seen your face had I kissed you."

"I would have been shocked, but over the moon."

She leaned over and gave him the kisses she'd held back that night. She kissed him now because he was hers. She kissed him with all the joy she had within her, knowing it was only one of the thousands of kisses to come.

"I'm so happy," she whispered, before she could help herself.

"I am too, my love." He stood abruptly. "I believe it's time for an evening walk."

The pounding of the surf greeted them when they stepped out through the back door. As soon as they were on the sand, Charles put an arm about Elsie's waist.

"I believe you're looking for reasons to put your hands on me," she teased. "My ankle feels fine. I'm capable of walking on my own now."

"We can't take any chances," Charles said, in mock seriousness.

As they approached the shore, Elsie caught sight of something in the sand. It looked as though someone had left a pile of rocks on the beach. As they came closer, she saw that it had a definite shape.

A heart.

"What…" She looked up at Charles, who was beaming at her. "You did this?"

"Yes, for you."

"But when?"

"This afternoon."

The heart was outlined in smooth rocks from the sea, but the inside was filled with hundreds of pieces of sea glass. Tears sprung to her eyes. He'd been collecting glass during those long weeks when she'd been trying to ignore him.

"Oh, Charles, it's beautiful."

He took both her hands in his and looked earnestly into her eyes. "I want you to know, Elsie, that you have my heart. I'm in love with you, now and forever. I want to be with you every day for the rest of my life. Will you marry me?"

"Yes, I will marry you. A lifetime is not enough to show you how much I love, cherish, and adore you."

Her voice did not tremble as she answered. But her knees did. Her soul did. She felt radiant, like a flame had been lit from within. She stroked the back of his hands with her thumbs and leaned in to kiss him softly.

He drew from his pocket a gold ring, set with an exquisite round-cut diamond in the center and two perfect sapphires on either side.

"It's beautiful," she whispered, watching it catch the light of the setting sun.

"Like my bride." He slipped the ring onto her finger.

Charles wrapped his arms around her and gave himself to her in a deep, binding kiss that melted her from the inside out. She surrendered herself utterly to his embrace. Elsie wanted to stay in his arms forever. He had been part of her life—part of her—for as long as she could remember. And now she knew he would be with her always. Behind them a full moon emerged, casting sparkling ripples on the waves and setting the sea-glass heart aglow.

****

A bright shaft of sunlight streaming in through the curtains greeted Elsie when she woke the next morning. She looked at her ring and sighed happily. It was official now. She would be Elsie Rockingham. She would share her life, her children, and her name with Charles, her best friend, her love.

Her heart raced when she thought of him waiting for her downstairs. She threw off the covers and went to the window. Holding her ring up to the sunlight, she turned it this way and that to see the stones sparkle. Charles had told her he'd bought it as soon as he arrived in San Francisco. He had known for so long that he wanted to marry her! She cursed those lost years.

She washed her face and put on a clover-green day dress embroidered with roses. Her only jewelry was her ring. She had just finished lacing her boots when there was a knock on the door.

"Come in," Elsie called, expecting Becky.

"Good morning," Charles said brightly. He had somehow grown more handsome overnight.

"Good morning," she said, beaming.

"Lovely as always," he said, offering his arm.

"Where are we going?"

"To the garden. There are some things we must discuss."

They strolled down the porch, enjoying the fresh morning breeze.

Elsie pointed to the beach. "Do you think the heart is still there? The glass heart?"

"No, I went back last night and brought the pieces in," he said, sliding an arm around her shoulders.

"That's a shame. It was beautiful."

"I kept the rocks and, of course, the glass. I thought we might put it in our garden one day when we have a house."

"That's a perfect idea." Her heart soared at the thought of setting up a home with him.

They went down the stairs into the garden. Under a canopy of apple trees stood a table set with the silver coffeepot, a platter of cinnamon muffins, and a warm spice cake.

"You are full of surprises," she said, smiling.

He pulled Elsie's chair out for her. "I thought you might like breakfast since you were abed so late this morning."

"That's very sweet. Thank you," she said, sitting down.

He brushed his lips on her neck before taking the seat next to her. She shivered with delight. Birds chirped in the trees above, and sunlight filtered through the leaves onto the grass.

"I have another surprise." He handed her a thick bundle of letters tied with green ribbon.

She recognized them at once as the ones she'd seen in the desk.

As she took them, he said, "The one on top is the rest of the letter you found in my drawer. The others are letters I wrote to you in California."

"And you neglected to send them, knowing how eager I always was to hear from you?" she teased.

"I never mailed these. I said in these letters what I wished I could tell you in person." He blushed. "About how much I love you."

"Oh, Charles," she said, and leaned over to kiss him softly. "I will cherish them." She resisted the urge to read them that moment and held them in her lap all through their meal.

When they'd finished eating, Elsie leaned back in her chair and took Charles's hand. "When will we go to Holderness? We must tell our parents our news but we can't put it in a letter."

"No, we can't. And I need to ask your father for your hand."

"Is it not a bit late for that?" She held up her ring, which caught the sun and flashed in that way that only diamonds can.

"Nonetheless, I shall speak to him."

"I think you'll be safe. There is no way my mother would allow him to stand between this match." She moved her chair a bit closer to him until their legs were touching.

"If I didn't know better, I would think our mothers had contrived it somehow."

"Oh, if it had been up to them, we would have been together years ago," she said. "We've lost so much time."

"Yes." He put a finger under her chin and lifted her eyes to his. "But we can't think of that now. We must look to our future."

"In order to do that, I need to know some things about the past. I need to see Gabriel's mother."

"Why would you want to see Mrs. Reed?"

"I want to find out if she knows what Gabriel did,

and why."

"But we know why." His mouth began to harden. "He meant to keep us apart."

"Nevertheless, I must see her. I can't go forward without knowing more. He's turned into someone else for me. Now it's clear that I talked myself into marrying him, ignoring the doubts in my mind. He played upon my loneliness and convinced me that I had no other choice but him. It was so cruel."

"I should never have left without telling you how I felt," he said. "Then there's no way Gabriel could have come between us."

"Looking back, I obviously should have spoken to your mother about those engagement rumors. No, we cannot blame ourselves. It's Gabriel who is to blame."

"We'll go together to see his mother when we get to Holderness," Charles said.

"I'm glad to know that I have you by my side for this."

"And for everything. For the rest of our lives."

They reached for each other at the same moment. Their passionate kisses swept away the regret of the past and basked in the pledge of their future.

****

The trip to Holderness the next day couldn't have been more different from her solitary journey months before, when she'd been trying to escape the past. Now she sought to discover it and finally put it behind her.

When the train pulled into Holderness, they disembarked and took their luggage to a waiting cab. They'd decided there was no use in putting off their interview with Gabriel's mother. They stopped for a moment at Charles's house to drop off their luggage and then set out for Mrs. Reed's from there.

Elsie was quiet as they made their way through town. She held Charles's hand tightly, contemplating what she would ask Mrs. Reed. Hopefully, she would have some answers, but it was entirely possible Gabriel had been working in secret. Elsie tried to remember other friends of Gabriel's she might be able to ask if Mrs. Reed couldn't help. Most of his friends were sailors and would not be easy to find. She supposed she could try Matthew Newkirk again, if need be.

When they reached Mrs. Reed's, Elsie rested her hands on the front gate and looked up at the house. This would have been her home if she'd married Gabriel. It was modest and two-storied, covered in light brown shingles that had not been painted in some time. Stray buoys were strewn about the rocky yard, and an old net that had never been repaired was lying in a heap next to the front door. A broken lobster trap peeked out of the overgrown bushes.

Elsie and Charles walked hand in hand down the brick walkway, but she hesitated on the doorstep. She wanted answers but wondered if she really needed them. She knew basically what Gabriel had done. Couldn't they just leave this place, go on and forget that he had ever wronged them? But then she thought of all the pain and confusion Gabriel had caused. She remembered his smiling face, his persuasive words, and wanted to know how he could have spoken like that, looked at her like that, when all along he was playing her for a fool.

A wave of anger consumed her. If Gabriel had succeeded with his dastardly plans, she would have spent her life without Charles. To think that she could have been separated from the only man she truly loved, for her entire life.

Elsie kept her eyes on Charles's as she reached up and knocked on the door. They waited a few moments, but nobody came. She knocked again, louder this time. Scuffling sounds could be heard from inside the house, and at last a silhouette was visible through the mottled glass of the window beside the door.

"Who is it?" came Mrs. Reed's voice.

"It's Elsie. Elsie Hayward and Charles Rockingham."

Mrs. Reed opened the door, appearing a little disheveled, as though she had just woken up. A petite woman with Gabriel's green eyes, she had the look of someone who had been beautiful before life's challenges had taken their toll on her. One hand remained on the doorknob while the other adjusted her black shawl.

"Elsie. Now this is a surprise," she said with a forced smile that faded quickly.

"Hello, Mrs. Reed. You remember Charles Rockingham?"

"Yes. Yes, of course," she said with a small nod, one hand still on the door handle.

"Good morning," Charles said, stepping forward and tipping his hat.

"May we come in?" Elsie asked.

"Oh, I wasn't expecting company," she said, looking over her shoulder into the house.

"Please, it's important," Charles said.

Mrs. Reed hesitated, and Elsie sensed that she would rather refuse.

"It's about Gabriel," Elsie said. "Please let us have just a few moments of your time."

"Well…yes, come in, then," she said, opening the

door.

She led them into a sitting room. It was well cared for, but all of the furniture was out of date. Above the fireplace loomed a large portrait of Gabriel, smiling benignly down at them, with an expression Elsie was quite certain she'd never seen him make in real life. She turned her back on it.

"Please sit down," Mrs. Reed said.

Elsie and Charles sat side by side on the brown sofa. Mrs. Reed faced them from a faded floral armchair.

"Would you like coffee? Tea?" She reached for a bell.

"No, thank you," Elsie said. She held her hands together tightly in her lap.

Mrs. Reed regarded her for a moment before asking, "What can I do for you?"

"I hardly know how to begin. But the fact of the matter is…I have found out some things about Gabriel recently, unsettling things, about the time before the wedding was to take place." She glanced up at the painting and wished she could turn it to the wall.

"What sort of things?" Mrs. Reed drew her shawl tighter around herself.

Elsie looked to Charles, unsure how to go on. He took her hand and gave it a reassuring squeeze.

"Well," Elsie said, clearing her throat, "I ran into Matthew Newkirk, from the *Kraken*."

Mrs. Reed paled but nodded for Elsie to go on.

"Matthew told me some things about Gabriel's intentions toward me."

"Such as?"

How could she come right out and blatantly accuse this woman's deceased son of marrying her for money?

There must be a softer way of putting it.

"Matthew implied that the match was not necessarily one of love for Gabriel, but of convenience."

When Mrs. Reed would not meet her eyes, Elsie was certain that what Matthew had told her was true. A chill ran through her.

"I know that Gabriel was very fond of you, Elsie," Mrs. Reed said. "He would have made you happy, I'm sure."

Charles shifted in his seat but did not speak.

"Fond of me, yes, but he planned to marry me and then stop sailing? He expected my father to support him?"

She had to hear it from Mrs. Reed's own lips before she could be certain Matthew hadn't misunderstood. She could hardly fathom Gabriel truly wanting to give up life on the sea.

"He would have been family then. And I'm sure he would have helped your father in any way he could at the bank." Mrs. Reed's attention drifted up to the portrait.

"Gabriel was not the type to work at a bank. He knew that. And so do you," Elsie said in as polite a voice she could manage. Gabriel at the bank would have been like Elsie commandeering a schooner.

Mrs. Reed looked down at her hands as they twisted a black-edged handkerchief. "The sea is a hard living. He only wanted a better life. He didn't want to go the same way as his brothers and father. All gone down in one stormy night! Gabriel escaped that, the one voyage he missed all that year. Ever since it happened, he dreaded that fate. He wanted to get away from sailing and find a new trade to support us."

"By claiming to love me? By marrying me? That

was his new trade?" Elsie said, her cheeks flaming.

Mrs. Reed could only nod.

"And you knew about this? You condoned it?" Elsie gripped the arm of the sofa.

"Who am I to condone?" Mrs. Reed sniffed. "He is—was—a grown man and wouldn't listen to me even if I tried to change his mind."

"But you approved," Elsie said coldly.

"Many people marry for reasons other than love. He would have made you happy," Mrs. Reed insisted again.

"But *I* would not marry without love. I was tricked into believing that he loved me. I would not knowingly enter into a marriage with a man who was lying to me, using me. He had no right," Elsie said, her voice trembling.

"No harm was done! It seems you are at no loss now for a husband," she said with a significant look at Charles and the ring upon Elsie's finger.

"What I do with Mr. Rockingham is none of your concern." Elsie glared at her.

Mrs. Reed stared right back.

Elsie took a moment. She would get nothing out of antagonizing Mrs. Reed. "You have no other explanation for why he did it?"

"No. Only what I told you. He fancied you and thought to marry into a good family, improving his lot. It has been done before! And by worse than my Gabriel," she said, her chin held high as though proud of him for this clever plan.

"But your Gabriel has done worse to me. And to Elsie," Charles broke in.

"What has Gabriel done to you?" Mrs. Reed asked him, gripping her elbows.

"We're not sure how he did it, but it appears Gabriel intercepted letters that Elsie and I wrote to each other. Do you know anything about that?"

Mrs. Reed's eyes swept the room, as if searching for answers.

"He has many letters, but I don't know who they're to or from. He was a great letter writer," she said, glancing at his portrait again.

"May we see the letters?" Charles asked.

She didn't answer at first but looked out the window. Finally she said, "I don't see how it would help you. Gabriel is gone, and you are together. What can the past matter?"

"Gabriel was our friend—we thought—since childhood. You know how it was with the three of us. And now we find out that he meant to use Elsie in the most heartless way, and we suspect that he kept us apart intentionally for years. So yes, the past does matter," Charles said.

Mrs. Reed slumped down in her chair, a hand over her eyes.

"His letters are in his bedroom, down the hall on the right," she said, pointing vaguely toward the other side of the house. "You may see the letters, however much good it will do you, and then show yourselves out." She rose from her chair and went through a door on the opposite side of the sitting room. A lock clicked behind her.

Charles looked at Elsie. "Ready?"

She nodded.

They walked hand in hand down the hall to Gabriel's room. Everything was spotless, like Gabriel had just walked out the door after packing for his last voyage. The wardrobe, whose doors still hung open, displayed empty shelves. There were unfinished letters on the desk, and a mug and plate sat on the bedside table. It looked as though Gabriel could return at any moment to finish his meal or sit behind the desk and take up his pen. But he was never coming back.

"Where should we look first?" Charles asked.

"The desk, I suppose. But I do feel strange looking through his personal things," she said, wrapping her arms around herself and scanning the room.

"If the letters we sent to each other are here, then we're looking through our own personal things. We needn't pry too deeply into anything else."

"You're right," she said. "Let's get this over with."

"I'll look in his trunk." Charles sat on the end of the bed and lifted its creaky wooden lid.

A hint of Gabriel's aftershave wafted over to her. She closed her eyes and took a brief, steadying breath, then went to the desk. Elsie lowered herself gingerly into the wooden chair. She pictured Gabriel sitting there, his hand touching the wood that was now beneath her hand. She looked in the drawers, which were mostly empty but for the oddments that one might find in any desk: spare paper; pens; a dry inkwell; one of his pipes; a mother-of-pearl penknife.

Elsie was about to help Charles look through the trunk when she noticed the letters peeking out from under a pile of blank sheets of paper: one addressed to Elsie, the other to someone named Imogen Baxter. She opened the letter addressed to herself first.

Dear Elsie,

The Kraken leaves today, as you know, for you will have seen me off at the dock this afternoon. I long to see you soon and to be with you. The days cannot pass fast enough for me. I will search for you in the stars as I sail at night, dreaming of your smile.

Love,

Gabriel

It was typical of letters he would write before a voyage. He would send one out the day he left so Elsie would receive it a few days later. He had apparently forgotten to mail it on the hectic morning the *Kraken* set sail. She read it again, his last words to her. She folded the letter and put it back on the desk. She almost left the letter to Imogen Baxter alone, but something compelled her to read it. At the first line, she let out a gasp.

"What is it?" Charles asked, beside her in an instant.

She read the letter aloud, her hands and voice shaking.

"*My Darling Imogen,*

The Kraken leaves today, as you know, for you will have seen me off at the dock this morning. This could be the last time we're parted for so long. Once I marry Elsie I can give up these voyages. We will finally set up the house in Sandberg you've been waiting for. I long to see you soon and to be with you. The days cannot pass fast enough for me. I will search for you in the stars as I sail at night, dreaming of your smile and tender lips.

All of my love,

Gabriel"

Elsie crumpled the letter in her hand. Hot, angry tears bubbled to the surface.

"Who is Imogen?" Charles asked, taking the letter from Elsie and reading it to himself.

"The woman he loved, apparently," she said through gritted teeth.

"But—"

"Read this," she said, thrusting the other letter into his hands.

"What is it?"

"The letter that he wrote to *me*. On the same day. The same morning!"

Elsie paced the room while Charles read, the furrow in his brow deepening with every line. He seemed momentarily at a loss for words.

"That—that scoundrel!" he finally exclaimed, throwing the letter onto the desk.

Elsie could not bring herself to speak. To think how she had mourned him! And this confirmed what she had suspected—known—for months.

She had been nothing to him.

A means to an end. A way for him to get away from the ocean, to be with his Imogen. She was so angry she didn't even know what to do. And yet as she stood there, surrounded by his things, his memories, she could not help but feel a bit of relief. Anger, yes, but also clarity.

She had not been in love with him, either. Had he known? If only he had spoken to her of his feelings! They could have parted as friends, and he need never have gone on that last voyage. His whole life might have changed had he been honest with her. Honest with himself, perhaps. They had gone through years of courtship, planning, pretending.

Had Imogen been there all along, waiting? Elsie remembered the woman on the street with him. Had that been her?

"Elsie? Have you heard of this woman before?" Charles asked, breaking into her train of thought.

"He never mentioned her, but I think I may have

seen him with her on the street one day."

Charles pulled her into his arms.

She leaned on his chest, holding him tight. "It doesn't matter anymore. We're together now," she said.

They stood quietly for a few moments, wrapped in each other's arms.

"Elsie, I found a letter, too."

"I'm not sure I can read any more letters today."

"You'll want to see this one." He gave her a letter written in his own hand. She sat down on the bed. He sat beside her, holding her hand and reading over her shoulder.

My Dearest Elsie,

I'm writing to you from the train station in Boston. Soon I'll make the connection that will take me far from you, to California. Far from you is the last place I want to be. If I hadn't been planning this journey for months, if my uncle was not relying on me, I would never leave your side again. I tried to tell you last night on the beach, but we were interrupted, and I had no chance to speak to you before I left this morning.

What I'm trying to tell you, in my clumsy way, is that I love you. All day I've been remembering the way you looked at me last night. I know you well enough to read your eyes, and I think you might love me, too. Please write to me and tell me that I'm right. Tell me that you will wait for me, and I'll find a way of coming home to you as soon as I can. I love you.

Yours—always yours,

Charles

Elsie read the letter twice. Her heart could burst from the sweetness of it, and from the pity she felt for the Charles of the past.

"To never get an answer! To this!" she cried, looking at Charles. "What must you have thought?"

"That I was wrong," he said with a sad shrug. "That I had imagined you felt the same way."

"How on earth did Gabriel get hold of this? How dare he!"

She threw her arms around his neck and held him close.

"If I'd gotten that letter, I would have been on the first train to California."

"I found your letters, too. The ones you sent. But it's odd. I remember everything you wrote to me, but these letters look like they've been altered."

"Let me see them."

They sat at the foot of the bed, poring over the letters.

"Here," Charles said, handing her one that she'd written soon after he left Holderness.

Dear Charles,

How do you find California? It seems a world away. Please write to me soon and tell me all about it. I will be waiting eagerly for your news. Things here are much the same. After all, you only left five days ago. It feels like longer since I usually see you every day.

You've been on my mind so much. I imagine where you might be and what you're seeing. I want to hear about all of it. I miss you and am already impatient for your return.

I've been thinking about the night before you left. I wish we hadn't been interrupted while saying goodbye. You were so sweet, and I had the feeling you wanted to tell me something, or do something important, before Gabriel came upon us. I will say no more here. If I'm correct, you will know what I'm referring to. Nothing could delight me more than to know I'm right about what you wanted to do.

Do write soon,

Elsie

"You never received this, obviously," she said.

"But I did," Charles said, perplexed. "I read it over and over. The letter I received said nothing of the beach, or of you thinking of me at all. My copy ended after the first paragraph."

"You're certain it was this letter?"

"I still have it. I saved all your letters," he said. "I could never mistake it. I waited so eagerly for it for weeks, and then to see no reply to my own letter…"

"Gabriel must have taken it from me and changed it." She was aghast anew at the lengths he'd gone to, keeping them apart.

"That explains why some of the letters I received from you were so short. He must have altered them. And I think he held back even more than we thought. Especially in the last year. Almost everything I wrote to you is in his trunk."

Elsie glanced down at the pile of envelopes and saw one that she had addressed to Charles, postmarked over a year ago.

She opened it and read it aloud.

"Dear Charles,

I'm writing to tell you how sorry I am that your betrothal was called off. Gabriel told me that you don't want to discuss it, but I couldn't help writing to ask if there is anything I can do for you. I hate to think of you suffering, and I wish you were home so we could talk. I still think of you often, though have not heard from you in some time. Gabriel says you must be too busy to write…"

She stopped reading.

"Did you ever see this letter?" she asked, holding it out to him.

"No. If I had, I would have written back and asked what betrothal you were talking about."

"How did he manage to do this? I can see how he altered the letters that I foolishly sent through him. But how did he intercept the other ones?"

"Perhaps his mother would know."

"Let's get out of here," Elsie said disgustedly. "I can't stand being here another minute."

"We must take our letters."

"Yes, of course."

"It's impossible to think that our friend—or who we thought was our friend—could be so deceitful," Charles said.

"We never knew him." Elsie shuddered at the thought of her near union with him.

Several empty mailbags were piled in a corner of the room. Elsie and Charles stuffed all the letters into one of them.

Elsie was surprised to see Mrs. Reed back in the sitting room.

"We are taking our letters," Elsie told her in a sharp tone. Charles carried the bag, which was almost bursting at the seams.

"You were good friends to him. And you would have been my daughter," Gabriel's mother said to Elsie.

All Elsie wished to say was how grateful she was to be disconnected from that family. Yet it would sound as if she was glad Gabriel had died. No matter what he had done to her and Charles, she could never be glad of his death. She said nothing.

"Mrs. Reed," Charles said, "we'd like to find out how Gabriel has so many of our letters. Do you know anything about that?"

"You may as well know it all. Gabriel had a…a friend who worked at the post office. It was she who helped him."

"That's illegal!" Elsie cried.

"Imoge—his friend was only trying—" Mrs. Reed stopped herself mid-sentence, flustered.

The name had not gotten past Elsie. Her mouth went dry.

"And what of my letters? How did she help him with those?" Elsie demanded of Mrs. Reed.

"She didn't need to. You gave them to him yourself. He would say he was going to post them for you, but he kept them. He would rewrite them, or copy them. He had a fine hand."

"But why did he keep them for so long?" Charles asked.

"He would sometimes look back at what you said to each other. So he would know if he needed to omit anything later, or add anything."

"And you let this go on!" Elsie said.

Mrs. Reed said nothing, but hung her head.

"I think we've heard all we need to," Charles said curtly, taking Elsie's hand.

"Indeed we have," Elsie said. She strode to the door with Charles, anxious to leave this house and never come back.

"Wait," Mrs. Reed said. "Please, can you find it in your heart to forgive me, Elsie? Both of you?" She cast an uneasy glance at Charles.

Mrs. Reed looked so pathetic, so distraught that Elsie was filled with pity. What else could she say? "Yes, of course, Mrs. Reed."

"I'm sorry. I know it was wrong, and I should have tried to stop him. I have no excuse but that I wanted him safe."

Elsie forced out a reply. "I understand."

"We know you couldn't have stopped him, even if you'd tried," Charles said.

"No, I couldn't. And now he's gone, and it's partially my fault," she said, sniffling.

Elsie didn't argue the point. "Goodbye."

"Take care of yourself," Charles said.

They opened the door and were startled to see a young woman standing there, one hand raised, about to knock. Elsie at once recognized her as the woman she'd seen with Gabriel on the street. The sleeping baby she held had black hair and there was no mistaking the resemblance to Mrs. Reed.

"Imogen!" Mrs. Reed cried.

"You said you wanted to see Gabe today, remember?" she said, shifting the baby to her other arm.

Elsie's stomach lurched.

Had Gabriel not done enough to her without also fathering a child, clearly at the same time he was engaged to her? Imogen wore a thin gold wedding band. After Gabriel's death she must have hoodwinked some other man to take care of her and the child. Elsie felt nothing but pity for the baby in her arms.

Elsie met Mrs. Reed's gaze and fixed her with a withering stare. She was at a complete loss for words at this final betrayal.

"I'm sorry," Mrs. Reed stammered and started to cry.

Imogen looked Elsie up and down, not even sparing a glance for Charles.

"Excuse us," Elsie said icily to Imogen. "We are leaving."

She quickly stepped inside, making room for them to exit.

"Is that her?" Imogen asked Mrs. Reed in a haughty voice.

"Shh!" was the reply.

Charles closed the door behind them, and Elsie heard no more of their conversation. With the closing of the door, whatever tenuous hold Gabriel had held upon her was gone. The childhood friendship, the affection, the false promises, her guilt, the anger—all gone in the blink of an eye. The Gabriel she had thought she knew, believed she had loved, had died long ago. And she had no tears left to spare for him.

Chapter Nineteen

Elsie and Charles walked toward home. The sky was a clear, crisp blue. Bright sunshine warmed the chill that had settled over Elsie at Mrs. Reed's house. In the distance was the small birch wood that surrounded the hill with the big oak tree. Elsie took Charles's hand and led him in that direction, and they climbed up the steep grade, not stopping until they stood together under the rustling branches of the oak. Patches of wild violets, buttercups, and bluets spread over the grass like a quilt.

"How are you?" Charles asked, dropping the mail bag and leaning against the trunk of the tree.

"Better than I would have thought," she said serenely, standing beside him.

"After all we've just discovered?"

"It's hard to explain. Everything I suspected, and worse, has proven to be true. The Gabriel of my childhood truly is gone now. He's been replaced by this man who schemed, and lied, and tricked me. I never really knew *that* man. He was pretending to be someone else the entire time."

"You can really go on from here and leave your anger behind?"

"It will be difficult, but I have to try. Otherwise he'll hurt me even more. Staying angry at him, holding on to that pain, it only keeps him with me. But I've cast him off. I'm finished with him."

"You're a wise woman, Elsie."

"And you? Are you angry with him?"

"Yes, and I probably will be for some time. It's difficult to comprehend the damage he's done, the sheer cruelty of his betrayal. It is hard to forgive." Charles closed his eyes and took a deep breath.

"Perhaps, with time, forgiveness will come."

He exhaled. "I hope you're right."

Elsie couldn't even count how many times she and Charles had stood in that exact spot, looking over the unobstructed view over the tops of the trees, all the way to the ocean. The wind sweeping up the hill ruffled their hair and clothes. Elsie leaned into it, basking in the scent of sweet flowers and lush grass.

She wrapped her arms around Charles. "The past is over, and now we must look to the future. We have our whole lives ahead of us."

Charles held her close as they looked out over the field.

"This is where I first knew I wanted to marry you," he said in a soft tone.

"Here?" she said and laughed.

"It was a few months before I left for San Francisco. It was the first big snow we'd had that winter. You careened down the hill on that toboggan of yours—"

"Not very ladylike," she interrupted.

"Perhaps not. But when you reached the bottom of the hill, you stood up and looked at me, laughing. Your jacket was rumpled, and you'd lost your hat and one mitten. You had snow in your hair. I was blinded, as if the sun had just come out for the first time. I swear, Elsie, my heart stopped. From that moment, I knew I was in love with you."

"The day I knew was this summer. Do you remember the photograph I took of you in the study? When it was developed, the look on your face—oh, Charles!" She paused, a rush of emotion bringing tears to her eyes. "The look on your face told me that you love me. It wasn't the moment I fell in love with you. It was the moment I realized I'd fallen deeply in love with you long ago."

They leaned toward each other at the same moment. Their lips met in a soft, tender kiss.

"Let's go home," she said. "Let's go tell our mothers our news."

She bounded down the hill. He caught up with her easily, laughing with her as they ran.

When they reached Elsie's house, they stepped inside, leaving the bag of old letters in the foyer. The chatter of their mothers' voices came from the parlor. Fingers entwined, they stepped into the room. But neither mother noticed them in the doorway, they were so engrossed in conversation. Elsie and Charles shared an amused but exasperated look. They might have been five years old and waiting to be invited in for tea.

"Mother?" Elsie finally said.

Both women stopped mid-conversation and turned to her. In tandem, their eyes traveled from her face to her hand linked with Charles's. They lit up with knowing, satisfied smiles. Without a word to Elsie or Charles, they turned back to each other at once.

"We'll have to go speak with the pastor first thing in the morning," Mrs. Hayward said.

"Maybe even this afternoon, Laura. He should be at the parsonage later today," Mrs. Rockingham countered with a glance at the clock.

"For a late summer wedding, we may have a long wait before the church is free. Perhaps a fall wedding would be better. The leaves would have just turned. It could be beautiful," Mrs. Hayward said, and sipped her tea thoughtfully.

"Mm-hm, you're right about that. We'll want to set a date as soon as we can."

"Perhaps we could stop by the dressmaker after we visit the parsonage. Jenny still has Elsie's measurements. She should start on the dress right away."

"That's an excellent idea. I'm picturing something with a lower neckline, not buttoned up too high."

"Yes, Elsie's neck is one of her finest features," Mrs. Hayward said, tracing her own collarbone with her fingertips.

"And perhaps a bit of a fuller skirt. This trend for tighter skirts—I don't think they're appropriate for a wedding," Mrs. Rockingham said, shaking her head as if watching a parade of ill-fitted brides in her mind's eye.

"No, certainly not."

"We'll have to decide which church. The one in Dortin is grand, of course, with those stained-glass windows. Although the one right here in town has a homey feel, don't you think?"

"It's where they were both christened, Lily! It would be ever so sweet to have the wedding there."

In the hall, Elsie's giggles were teetering on the edge of hiccups. Charles walked right up to his mother's chair, still holding Elsie's hand.

"Mother, Elsie will wear a dress of her own choosing. We wish to be married as soon as possible. And as for the location, we wish to be married in Portsmouth. If that is agreeable to Elsie, that is," he said, casting her a radiant smile.

As always, he had known what would make her happiest without even having to ask. "That is exactly what I want," she said, traces of laughter in her voice. "In the chapel on Star Island."

"Portsmouth!" Mrs. Rockingham gasped, her hand fluttering around her chest. "It's so far—everyone would have to travel by train!"

Mrs. Hayward didn't skip a beat. "You know, Lily, Max's house is in Sherwood Bay, and it would be an ideal place for them to be married from. The house has a covered porch that wraps all the way around, and the gardens are exquisite. You can walk through the back garden right out to the beach."

"Perhaps a reception in the garden, overlooking the ocean. Oh, Laura, that does sound perfect."

"Yes, and don't worry about the journey. We could arrange to have a private train car for the wedding guests," Mrs. Hayward said.

"We could serve champagne on the train. That would be quite elegant." Mrs. Rockingham beamed.

"Max's house has more than enough room. He could put up all the guests."

"Of course, there will be wind coming off the ocean. We will need to make sure we have extra pins for our hats, and for Elsie's veil, of course." Mrs. Rockingham put a hand to her hair.

"We had better speak to Jenny about our dresses, too. It would be fun to match. Different shades of the same color, or even matching, but with different designs."

They didn't notice when Elsie and Charles wandered off to the library. Charles sat on the sofa and pulled Elsie onto his lap. She put her arms around his neck.

Charles reached into his jacket pocket and handed her an image of him taken at a photography studio. He was so young, and with that certain look in his eyes Elsie herself had captured once before: Charles in love.

"Where did you get this?" she asked, taking it from him.

"I found it among our letters."

"You're so handsome," she said, touching his cheek.

"I had that done when I arrived in San Francisco. I sent it to you that week."

"I never saw it. But I will treasure it now."

"It's yours, like everything I have." He ran his hand down her back and drew her in closer.

"And all that I have is yours." She pressed the photograph to her heart. "Everything is settled." She gave a contented sigh.

"Yes. Although I feel sorry for you with all the fittings our mothers are sure to put you through."

"It will be worth it," Elsie said.

"It has all been worth it."

Their lips met in a soft, sweet promise.

****

Three weeks later, Elsie and Charles were married in the chapel on Star Island in an intimate ceremony shared with close friends and family. The wind was mild, so there was no need for extra pins. Margaret was beautiful as Elsie's matron of honor, and James stood up as best man. Lucy, Nancy, and Grace were bridesmaids, and while Elsie stood in the receiving line with Charles, she noticed them all vying for the attention of Dr. Watts.

Charles had not let go of her hand once since the

pastor declared them husband and wife.

Max had chartered a ferry to take the wedding party to the island, and after the ceremony they all boarded the boat for the trip back to Portsmouth. When they docked, Elsie and Charles were the first to disembark and went straight into a carriage to take them to Max's house. Elsie drew the curtains as soon as they were settled in their seats.

"Not long now," Charles said, running a finger along her arm. Several other places tingled at his touch as well.

"Until what, my love?"

"Until we can be alone." He put an arm around her shoulders, his hand resting tantalizingly close to her breast.

Her pulse quickened. "Our wedding night."

"Yes, our wedding night."

"Charles, have you ever..." She couldn't quite finish her question.

"No, never," he said quietly.

"I haven't, either," she said, "but I expect you guessed that."

"Are you nervous?" He caressed her shoulder.

"No, because I'm with you."

She put her hand on his neck, touching that soft, silky skin and leaned in close enough to smell his sweet breath. His fingertips traced the edge of her bodice. She trembled beneath his touch. Her hand ran up his thigh, bringing a sound of surprise and eagerness from his throat, his eyes smoldering with desire as he gathered her into a sensual embrace. Their lips met in a deep, bold, passionate kiss that would have brought Elsie to her knees if she'd been standing. She had expected the fire within her to be quenched when they kissed, but it now burned hotter and brighter, offering a promise of what was to come in a few short hours.

Elsie's head was swimming when they finally pulled away from each other. Charles cleared his throat, his hand massaging her hip. They stared into each other's eyes, both reflecting a yearning that made Elsie wish they could skip the reception altogether.

"We're just about there," he said and rested his cheek against hers.

She put her hands on his shoulders, holding him closer.

They both took a moment to compose themselves, straightening their clothes and smoothing down their hair. The carriage came to a stop in front of Max's house.

"Until tonight." He took her hand and kissed that delicate spot on the underside of her wrist.

"Tonight," she said breathlessly, her skin singing beneath his touch.

Inside, their wedding guests were waiting to greet them. Elsie was pulled into one embrace after another, given congratulations and compliments on the ceremony. Mrs. Hayward and Mrs. Rockingham were in their element, having planned everything exactly to their liking. Elsie had given them free rein over the wedding and reception, telling them they could do whatever they pleased as long as she was married to Charles by the end of the day.

Max's house was stunning, every surface sparkling like new. Candles flickered in his finest silver candlesticks, casting a delicate, romantic light on every face. The scent of hundreds of flowers permeated the air. Greenery and colorful blossoms had taken over the banisters, tables, doorways, and even climbed up some of the walls.

In the dining room, a lavish buffet awaited the guests—a myriad of hors d'oeuvres, tea sandwiches, cheese, soups, and fruit. On the sideboard sat a five-tiered wedding cake, enrobed in rich frosting.

A string quartet played in the drawing room, which had been cleared out for dancing. Elsie and Charles shared their first dance to the beautiful strains of "The Blue Danube Waltz."

Elsie smiled, hearing the constant chatter of their mothers and the frequent bursts of laughter from her friends. Margaret and Harriet found a quiet corner to sit in while little Brian and baby Pammy slept in cribs that Mr. Anderson had carried down from the nursery. They spoke animatedly about raising their children. Elsie hoped that within a year or two she would be able to share in those talks.

The reception lasted for hours—with so many of the guests staying at Max's, there was no need to end the party. Max kept the champagne flowing and the music playing all through the afternoon and well into the evening.

He pulled Elsie and Charles aside at one point to tell them he was going to California for a few years. He invited them to take over the house while he was away, and to consider it their home even after he returned. Leave it to Max to offer the most ridiculous gift imaginable and the one thing she wanted most: a home to share with Charles.

At last, when the first subtle hues appeared in the evening sky, Charles sought Elsie out among the guests.

"Elsie, it's almost sunset. We don't want to miss it,"

he whispered to her.

They went through the garden and onto the beach, Elsie trying in vain to keep her long white gown out of the sand. The beach was quiet and peaceful after the loud, happy confines of the house. Charles enfolded her in his arms and held her until the pink-and-orange sky had changed to a dusky blue.

Elsie then took his hand and led him back to the house. They quietly made their way inside, while everyone was distracted by the food and music, and crept up the stairs to Elsie's bedroom.

Charles held the door open for her and followed her in.

As soon as he closed it, she turned her back to him. "Help me with my gown?"

He didn't speak but began at once. His hands lingered on her bare shoulders before he moved them down her back. Each freed button was a thrilling brush of his skin against hers. At last he reached the final closure, low on her waist.

She said over her shoulder, "I need a few moments."

"How many is a few?"

She felt his breath in her hair as he lightly massaged her hips and moved his hands slowly up her corseted waist to her bodice. Elsie held her breath as his hands went higher until his thumbs were gently caressing the full curve of her breasts. It seemed he'd stopped breathing, too, for he suddenly inhaled deeply. She leaned her head back. A thrill ran through her as his lips slowly made a trail up the back of her neck and then to her earlobe, which he drew gently into his mouth.

"As few as possible," she said, turning in his arms. She pressed herself against him and gave him a hard, deep kiss before opening the door. He stepped out. As soon as she closed it, she heard him pace up and down the hall.

Once out of her gown, she stripped herself of her undergarments faster than any other day of her life. She then went to her wardrobe and picked out the nightgown she'd bought especially for tonight—almost translucent white satin, embroidered with tiny pink rosebuds, its shoulder straps made of green ribbon. She took the pins out of her hair and let it cascade over her shoulders.

She opened the door, and Charles almost fell into the room. She would have laughed, but the look in his eyes stopped her: a deliciously hungry expression. From far away came the muffled sounds of their wedding guests, but Elsie and Charles were now in a secret world all their own.

The air was heavy with anticipation. Elsie locked the door, then stood with her back against it, gazing at Charles. Within seconds they were in each other's arms, locked in a passionate kiss that sent heat radiating through her body. Every touch of his hands seared through the delicate fabric of her nightgown.

"I love you, Charles," she breathed, sliding the jacket off his broad shoulders.

"Oh, Elsie, I love you."

Their hands upon each other were urgent, reaching into each other's clothes to feel the skin they'd been yearning to touch for months. Elsie had always heard that brides were nervous on their wedding night, but she felt only eagerness pulsing through her as she took Charles's hand and led him to the bed. She stood before him and let her nightgown slip from her shoulders, flowing into a satin pool at her feet.

Charles took a step back to look at her. His eyes roved over her naked body from head to toe. The look on his face turned Elsie's knees to water, and she climbed into bed, covering herself with a thin cotton blanket that did nothing to hide her curves.

Charles couldn't keep his eyes off her as he removed his clothes, his trembling fingers fumbling over the buttons. Elsie waited breathlessly for every last bit of him to be revealed.

Once he was completely undressed, she gasped. She had always found Charles handsome, but he now was a wonder to behold. Even in her dreams she hadn't imagined his legs so powerful, his stomach so toned, his hips so achingly sensual. His smooth, sculpted chest rose and fell rapidly for a man standing still. Every part of him was well formed, solid, and enticing. His shoulders and arms were golden, strong, poised to embrace her.

She held her arms out to him, unable to wait another second to touch him. He slid into bed beside her, and this time he did not stay on top of the blankets.

****

Elsie woke up bathed in sunlight and happiness. She stretched luxuriously in the bed, her body wonderfully supple and warm. Charles lay beside her, naked, still asleep. She pressed herself against him, reveling in the feel of his skin against hers.

Elsie sighed happily, recalling the night before. She had experienced pleasures she hadn't dreamed existed. Becoming one with Charles in all ways had been as easy and natural as breathing. Elsie marveled at how well they fit together, how she had ceased to feel separate from him at all.

She felt a deep sense of unity that she knew would

never go away.

"Good morning," Charles said, looking at her with tender eyes.

Elsie propped herself up on an elbow to look at his sleepy face, his tousled hair. She leaned in to give him a lingering kiss, blushing as she remembered other places his lips had found the night before.

"Good morning," she said through her wide smile.

"Did you sleep well?" He turned sideways to look at her.

"We were up quite late, so not very much sleep. You?"

"I've never slept better than with you at my side." He kissed her softly and lay back against the pillows, his arm behind his head.

"Then you will have a lifetime of good rest, for I intend to spend every night beside you," Elsie said, rubbing her hand across the hard muscles of his stomach.

"You think I will sleep with such temptation within arm's reach?" His lips found hers, while his hands caressed her softest places.

"I said I will spend every night beside you," she said, letting her hands wander where they would. "I did not say I will spend those nights sleeping."

Charles quivered at her touch and gathered her into his arms.

****

A few hours later, they went downstairs to the dining room. The sideboard was set with cold ham, melon, assorted pastries, and a fresh spice cake. After filling their plates, they sat at the table and enjoyed a leisurely breakfast, holding hands under the table.

Afterward Elsie hooked her arm through his and led

him through the house to the back garden path. They meandered along the beach until they reached the driftwood log. They stood before it, arms wrapped around each other.

"It's strange to think that the world hasn't changed when so much has changed for me—for us—since yesterday," Elsie said. "The sun still rises, the waves pound on the shore. Why is the whole world not filled with the same joy that I have in my heart?"

"You have changed my world, and my life. Nothing will ever be the same now that you are my wife," he said, stroking her hair.

"Your wife! How I love to hear you say it. I do so love you, Charles."

"I love you, Elsie." He leaned in to kiss her.

After a few exquisite moments, they broke apart.

"What shall we do on our first married day?" he asked.

"There is one thing I want to do before anything else. It was your idea, in fact. I want to put the sea-glass heart in the garden. The one you made for me."

"I have everything in my room, packed away. You have such a unique collection of glass, and it need not stay in Mason jars. I could add it to the heart."

"My collection can stay there, but the heart will be the beginning of *our* collection, starting today."

"As our life together starts today," he said. "I'll put the glass heart in the garden as soon as we get back to the house. And every day when you see it, remember that my heart is yours."

He leaned in again to give her a long, soft kiss.

Elsie was overwhelmed with love for him and with the promise of the life they would share together. She thought fleetingly of the tumultuous months behind her—enduring the drama and worry, discovering her love for Charles, and finally letting go of the past. She had no idea what the future might hold, but she knew that she and Charles could overcome any challenge as long as they were together.

Elsie smiled at Charles and, his hand in hers, turned toward home. As always, she scanned the sand for the glistening sign that a treasure awaited her. But there was really no need to look anymore. The greatest treasure of her life had been beside her all along.

A word about the author…

Kate Ellington grew up in a small, woodsy town not far from the New England seacoast. She read her first historical romance at age eleven when a teacher challenged her to find a book in the library written by an author she'd never heard of. Thus began a life-long love of love stories.

She currently resides in the Pacific Northwest with her wonderful family and three cats. When not writing she can be found reading, baking, traveling, and spending time outdoors.

Thank you for purchasing
this publication of The Wild Rose Press, Inc.

For questions or more information
contact us at
info@thewildrosepress.com.

The Wild Rose Press, Inc.

www.ingramcontent.com/pod-product-compliance
Lightning Source LLC
Chambersburg PA
CBHW051136030726
47504CB00004B/905